PLASTIC

FRANK STRAUSSER

PLASTIC

A VIREO BOOK | RARE BIRD BOOKS
LOS ANGELES, CALIF.

This is a Genuine Vireo Book

A Vireo Book | Rare Bird Books
453 South Spring Street, Suite 302
Los Angeles, CA 90013
rarebirdbooks.com

FIRST TRADE PAPERBACK ORIGINAL EDITION

For more information, address:
A Vireo Book | Rare Bird Books Subsidiary Rights Department,
453 South Spring Street, Suite 302
Los Angeles, CA 90013

Set in Minion
Printed in the United States

Cover Design by Sean Day Michael

10 9 8 7 6 5 4 3 2 1

Publisher's Cataloging-in-Publication Data

Names: Strausser, Frank, 1960– author.
Title: Plastic / Frank Strausser.
Description: First Trade Paperback Original Edition | A Genuine Vireo Book |
New York, NY; Los Angeles, CA: Rare Bird Books, 2019.
Identifiers: ISBN 9781644280379
Subjects: LCSH Plastic surgeons—Fiction. | Surgery, Plastic—Fiction.
| Celebrities—Fiction. | Hollywood (Los Angeles, Calif.)—Fiction.
| Murder—Fiction. | Suspense fiction. | BISAC FICTION /
General | FICTION / Thrillers / Suspense
Classification: LCC PS3619.T7434 P43 2019 | DDC 813.6—dc23

Plastic: from the Greek word *plasticos*, meaning to shape.

1

"YOU LEFT ME FOR Demi Moore," Helen screamed, throwing a white, ceramic mask, barely missing Dr. Harold Previn's head and smashing the entryway mirror.

"What are you talking about? I don't *do* Demi," Previn said, bracing for another attack.

He'd never wrecked any of Helen's paintings. That his wife would start breaking his sculptures stung.

"What*ever*," she said.

The broken pieces crunched underfoot as he stepped up to her. "It's four a.m., goddamn it!" he said. "You go missing for hours. Hurl my work in my face! This is ridiculous."

"I was driving, something I do when I'm *unhappy*."

Had she been unhappy? "I've got surgery in two hours," he said.

She charged at him again, hitting him with her fists. Her red bangs fell across her face and her blue eyes were bloodshot, which gave her a wild look. He fended off most of her blows.

"Helen!"

"I lost the baby today," she said, crumpling into a nearby armchair. "And you left me for Demi Moore."

He sighed. "I told you, it wasn't Demi. I don't do Demi. I've never done Demi!" Not that he wouldn't. "In any case, I had patients. I couldn't leave…cancel appointments." He bent down to pick up a piece of the mask she'd smashed and held it in his hand as though it were a sick bird.

"Is that all you care about?"

"You told me you'd lost the implantation days ago."

"It wasn't for certain until today. And you weren't there!" She looked at him with red-rimmed eyes. "I called you. Left a dozen messages."

"You know I have consultations all afternoon."

"God forbid you weren't there for them. Demi fuckin' Moore? Come on!"

Although Helen was only thirty-seven years old, they'd nevertheless found themselves making countless visits to a fertility specialist. Helen's idea. She was very sensible about such things. If it'd been left to him, they'd have woken up one day childless and without hope. He didn't like to think about infertility. What man did? It was a source of great stress and inadequacy, and Previn was damned if he was going to let anything make him feel inadequate. Yet it wasn't him having his body biochemically prepped and altered for pregnancy. To assure the implantation took hold, he'd assumed the thankless job of sticking her in the stomach and butt several times a day with syringes flowing with steroids and hormones. So if she seemed a little irrational and hormonal, it was because he'd been injecting her with what amounted to emotional PCP.

But Previn wasn't crazy enough to tell her that.

He'd watched from the sidelines as she'd started taking repeated pregnancy tests days before they could have possibly been effective, observing her obsessive behavior with a professional detachment that made her want to scream, which she often did. Several mornings she'd cried in bed over the results of the pregnancy tests, which were so clearly premature he couldn't begin to match her disappointment. She kept telling him she wasn't pregnant when he knew she still might be. By the time she found out she wasn't, it seemed like settled law. Of course, she wasn't pregnant. Hadn't she told him so days ago? Why wasn't he listening?

He chose to keep his head down. Focus on work. That was something, at least, he could control. This only made her feel like he didn't care. Of course he wanted to have a baby with her. Why couldn't she just relax about it?

They'd get there.

"I can't do this anymore," Previn said. "I haven't slept. Haven't changed my clothes. You run out of here. I don't know where you are. You don't answer your phone. You're making me a wreck. People depend on me. This is big stuff. I've got surgery in—"

"Two hours." In evident discomfort from striking at him, she squeezed her wrist. "I came back to tell you I'm leaving you, Harry. We're done."

He stared at her as he felt the life drain out of him.

◆◆◆

HELEN HEARD HARRY AT the front door letting himself in and braced herself. She tried to imagine telling him she was pregnant. Him turning on his blue high beams and grinning shamelessly as he opened his strong arms so he could pick her up and swirl her round, laughing…giddy.

"I've scheduled the movers," she said as he appeared at the kitchen door.

They hadn't spoken in the two days since their fight largely because she'd avoided him the whole day before. What more was there to say? And it wasn't like he'd actually sought her out. Who knows where he'd been hiding, and it only pissed her off more.

He flushed. "What?"

She thought about the baby…again. She burst into tears, and from some misplaced sense of decorum—call it the last vestige of self-dignity—ran from the room. She couldn't talk to him. There was nothing more to say.

In their ten years together, she'd never so much as raised a hand in anger. Yet having let that violent genie out of the bottle, she knew there was no putting her back. If anything had come of the night of their breakup that felt therapeutic and right, it was taking a swing at Harry. It made her feel like she'd finally come out of herself.

She went into the master bedroom and closed the door behind her. She expected Harry to follow her. To pound on the door. To fall to his knees and beg for forgiveness. She threw herself down on the bed and cried as she waited for the man she'd first fallen in love with so many years ago. He wouldn't have disappointed her like this.

When she'd first met Harry, he was a resident. She wasn't quite sure what that meant because even then Harry didn't look at all like he had anything to do with the medical world. His mandarin-collar, sleeveless wool vest said anything but "The doctor will see you now."

Harry's boss had bought a painting of hers that he'd seen hanging for sale in a restaurant a block from his hospital. He'd invited her to his home the evening he hung it in his foyer. There must have been nine people there and Harry.

As they were leaving, Harry turned to her and said, "Do you think Wallace knows what a good painting he's bought?"

Looking back on their exchange, she must have had trouble taking the compliment because she replied, "I have a distinct feeling his wife doesn't like me."

He stopped and faced her. His hair was very dark and only slightly longer than his designer stubble. He slipped his hands into the two small pockets in his vest, which seemed to say he was feeling very at ease. "But she praised the painting."

"Do you know anything about women?"

He smiled. "Nothing at all. You'll have to teach me."

"I don't think I have the time."

"We all should give back a little. Make the world a better place."

She smiled. "I don't think this has anything to do with the world."

"No. But it could." He touched her elbow. It was the slightest gesture, but it sent a shiver through her.

She deflected. "Wallace said you work for him in his surgery. He also said you're a very talented artist."

"I didn't hear him say that."

She felt herself blush.

"Were you asking Wallace about me?"

He'd caught her. "It's just that I don't think of surgeons as artists. It's like salt and pepper."

"The scalpel is a tool. When I started to sculpt, I realized that its true purpose is not to cut but to shape. I've also held a patient's face in my hand and kneaded it like clay. We're creators, Helen."

He knew her name.

Harry wasn't at all what she'd expected. She'd never had an interest in doctors. Although she was quite happy to sell a painting to one, she'd never imagined herself going out with one, much less going home with one, as she did that night.

She wanted *that* Harry to open their bedroom door, but now some ten years later, he was a no-show. She'd have settled for the newer, shinier version because somewhere underneath it all, there'd always be that man she'd fallen in love with. Or would there?

It'd been a while since she'd taken to their room. He evidently wasn't coming. She opened the door. From somewhere deep within the house, she could hear his voice. He was on the phone. She waited. When the conversation seemed like it was going to continue, she went back into the room and waited some more. After another forty-five minutes, she walked onto the landing again, this time close enough to feel Harry's intensity. The urgency was new…and frightening. He seemed shaken. She tried to make out what he was saying, but couldn't.

Had she done this to him?

2

A RAY OF SUNLIGHT extended its beam through the glass ceiling of
the conservatory, a faint dust making the beam seem stronger
as it passed over one translucent petal. There were other petals, then
folds and a jumble of clear material. The disorder of it was beautiful.
The play of light. The hint of something solid behind it. Yet from
where Previn stood, the bulb-like mass of plastic topping the tall
pedestal in the center of the room quite obviously held a partially
formed clay head. One of his many works of art, still taking shape.
But the plastic that kept the clay from drying out also looked, in that
moment, like a suffocation mask.

Previn ripped the plastic covering from the hunk of clay.
Stepped back from her, he studied her, and then moved closer to
begin. He delicately molded her cheekbones with his bare hands,
but soon delicacy gave way and he began to tear at it with a ferocity
that wasn't him. The replay of Jake Blackburn's desperate 911 call
had played again and again in his head after Previn had read the
phone transcript in an addendum to the autopsy. He could hear that
famous voice. So strong in the movies. So rattled and faltering, "It's
my mother. I can't...she's not. Nothing!"

"Sir. What's happening?" the 911 dispatcher had asked in her
tired voice.

"She's not breathing. Not moving. I can't get anything."

"She's not breathing at all?"

"She had plastic surgery. She was recovering. You've got to get someone over here."

"Do you know how to do CPR?" the dispatcher had asked.

Previn's eyes fluttered as he tried to refocus on what was in front of him. He felt art was very much a part of his profession. On any other day, this'd be an almost spiritual outlet. But today, this female face that had been labored over with care and affection had suffered in his hands. So much so, he wanted to toss her to the floor.

The studio had been like a preserve, but he couldn't overcome his stress even there with the work he most loved. He'd taken over a conservatory on the side of the house and made it his art studio. He liked the light that poured in from the giant windows, although flaming bottlebrush trees afforded a measure of relief from the sun. In an open antique cabinet and on top of it sat body parts in dry clay. A hand. An arm. A foot. Various models for larger works. And many female heads, including a thin one that was just a mask.

As Previn emerged from his studio, still wearing his smock, his hands covered in dried clay, he crossed paths with Helen, who was carrying a large cardboard box. She set it down near some others and with a black marker wrote, "Mine."

He bit his tongue. Plenty had already been said in the twelve days since she'd announced her decision to walk out on their marriage.

"You don't usually go to the studio this time of day," she said.

"It's peaceful."

Helen tried to pin down the box to tape it shut. She looked up at him for help, but he walked off. He didn't like behaving like an ill-tempered brat, but breakups brought out the worst in everyone. He kept thinking she'd change her mind. If he didn't help her pack, if the process was slowed, even a little, things might change. He never knew with Helen.

Surely this wasn't her.

As he passed through the foyer, he caught himself in the mirror. He needed a haircut in the worst way, but then he always did. At forty-six, he still had an athletic build, something achieved with the help of regular yoga classes and a personal trainer. His actor patients had to work at looking attractive. As their surgeon and consultant, he felt he was under no less an obligation to look great. It was part of the job. He might have added that it was his life. All of this was lost on Helen.

She was very much her own person. From the first, she'd always carried a few extra pounds. She wasn't fat. She was healthy. And he loved her for it. She never felt like she had anything to prove. In Previn's world, he was forever being asked to pass women through a cookie cutter, to make them all the same. Not Helen. She wouldn't have wanted her plastic surgeon husband to do a thing for her. And thank God for that. One woman in this town who didn't. Striking and unconventional, she wore a lot of green, which always set off her red hair. Perhaps if she hadn't been the fiery beauty she was, she might have been more sympathetic to the women who sought out his help and had a greater appreciation for his work. There was no figuring it.

He walked out onto the veranda of his white, bold, angular home with a soaring entranceway of glass. He'd just put his hands under the hose when he looked up to see über-agent and Hollywood power broker Richard Barone's black Bentley roll up the drive like a damn hearse. Previn whipped off his smock and braced himself for what promised to be an unpleasant meeting.

Moments later, he ushered Barone into his house. Stacks of boxes were everywhere. The living room was disordered but at least the furniture was still there. Barone didn't seem interested in the chaos around him. Previn knew better than to attempt an explanation. To do so would have felt altogether too flippant given the gravity of the matter that had brought them together.

Barone's fingers tapped on the autopsy report. *Tap. Tap. Tap.* He looked like a lawyer. The overpacked leather briefcase. The gold-rimmed glasses. The starched white cotton shirt. The dark blazer. But this being Hollywood, it also seemed a little affected, as if he wanted everyone to know his bloodlines were pure Clarence Darrow.

Standing beside a large contemporary still life of a bedroom interior, which had already been taken down from the wall, Previn waited impatiently for Barone to speak.

"He wanted to buy his mom plastic surgery for her birthday," Barone said. "To make her feel young again. Ironic, huh? He didn't know where to send her. That's when I said, there's this man..."

"I'm sorry, Richard. I am."

"You know, I never even thought about it till now but you're practically family. Sent you every A-list actor on our roster. We don't even have a contract. You don't pay me. It's just something..."

Barone, who headed up Artists Unlimited, one of Hollywood's powerhouse talent agencies, hadn't overstated their relationship. Were it not for all those starlets he'd sent his way, Previn wouldn't have been on the map. Call it La-La Land. Call it the City of Angels. Call it one big, honking backlot for the dream machine. The Capital of Good Looks. Whatever. Having celebrity clients meant the world. You weren't happening if you weren't doing them. And because of Artists Unlimited, Previn was seemingly doing them all. That was the buzz. He was one happening surgeon.

Helen appeared unexpectedly with a platter full of tea and biscotti.

Barone pointed at the painting. "Harry told me this is your oil. Very atmospheric. And playfully sinister. I had no idea you were *the* Helen Burke. You have to let me come by your studio sometime."

"You collect?"

"Talent. Sometimes on the walls. Mostly on screen." He noted the tumult of their move. "Wish I could see more here, but—"

"The mess."

"If Previn here hadn't offed Jake Blackburn's mom, I'd never have had the pleasure of meeting you." Barone pointed to the coffee table, which was a giant hunk of dark stone. "Petrified wood?"

She frowned and stammered, "Yes. No. Coal."

He put his hand on it. "Coal? No shit? Interesting."

Previn wanted to throttle Barone for dropping this bombshell, but it was already too late. Helen abruptly walked out.

"What are you telling her?" Previn asked.

"You don't talk to your wife?"

"Have you looked around? Not a great time in the marriage."

He had a vague sensation that Helen was still lingering at the door to the study. Just out of his sightline. But he couldn't think about that then. All he could do was flail wildly as he tried to find a credible defense.

"I've hardly been able to eat since I got the call she'd died," Previn said.

"What, I should give a shit you starve to death?"

"That's not what I meant." Previn saw the woman laid out on his operating table eleven days before. All her hair pulled back behind a drape so that it was simply a face. No makeup. No affectation. She was fifty-something with all the attendant signs of age. Bags under the eyes. Sagging cheeks. Pronounced laugh lines.

Further visions of Jake Blackburn's dead mother lying on top of her bed addled his mind. Her face bruised from surgery. Her nightdress open, exposing multiple bandages and AED burn marks where paramedics had tried to zap her back to life. The bedside table filled with painkillers and the like. A man wearing dark Los Angeles County Coroner fatigues maneuvering her into a black body bag while another affixed a label to her big toe reading "BLACKBURN." The body bag being wheeled on a gurney before it was shoved into the back of a van. Although he'd never been to her house, he saw it all vividly, having lived with it from the moment he'd heard about her death.

"Any man who thinks he can heal women with a knife!" Barone tossed the report on the table beside the untouched teacups. "Here. Take the autopsy. I get the picture."

"I've read the thing five times. It's 'inconclusive.'"

"Inconclusive? Don't bullshit me, Harry. You sliced and diced her a million ways till Sunday. Surprised she got home."

Previn was back in the surgery. The blinding white light from the surgical lamp. Loud rock 'n' roll. He could see the drainage tube running into Blackburn's stomach following the liposuction. The heart monitor with a normal heartbeat. Surgical instruments spread out across the table. He could see her like it was yesterday. She was like all the others. Although as a point of fact, he wasn't sure about whether the surgical instruments were on a table or on a tray. But what of it? It was all normal stuff. Stock images. Routine memories.

"Come on. That's not...She...you know, she died more than a day later."

"Really, Harry? You're going to sit there...That can't be normal."

"I advised against home recovery."

"That the best you got? This is my client's mother. Don't fuck with me, Harry!"

Previn saw himself in surgery doing a jig to the music, just a slight pivot really. They were grooving. That he remembered. Were they listening to some old blues tunes? Howling Wolf? There was absolutely that. But he also heard Sinatra sing "Got You Under My Skin" and "Uma Thurman" by Fall Out Boy. Scalpel in hand, he saw himself make the cut into her face along the side of her cheek. The blood running from the wound.

Sara, his thirty-six-year-old nurse, who was a dead ringer for Louise Brooks with black hair in a bob, had turned to him with alarm. "But we were only doing four procedures. It's four, right?"

He laughed. He actually laughed. He must have seemed drunk with power that morning, but it was false bravado. On that very morning, Helen had said she was leaving him. Some people's default mode was to slam their foot on the brakes when in crisis. His had always been to push the accelerator. He looked down at Blackburn, not wanting to believe in the moment that the neck lift would be a problem. She had wanted it done. He'd dabbed at his incision nervously with a sterile pad. "This one's on the house! On the house, baby."

"Do you think I don't feel sick about this?" he said to Barone. "My. Patients. Don't. Die."

Just as he said those words, he saw a shadow move in the hall. Helen was there. He could imagine her shudder at what he'd just said. But there was hardly time to think about that because Barone had him virtually backed to the wall.

"She was practically immortal. She was Jake's mother. My clients don't get much bigger than Jake fuckin' Blackburn."

"I know."

"I could lose Jake Blackburn because of you. I'm juggling here. I'm trying to figure how we can finesse this. And because no good turn goes unpaid, I'm hoping this doesn't blow up in my face."

"He's not going to blame you."

"He might. He just might at that. Doesn't get any more personal than this. We gotta bury her, Harry. I'm talking shovel run. Put the damn body in the trunk of the car and bury her in the desert somewhere."

"What the fuck are you talking about? She was cremated days ago."

"You don't get it. If Jake Blackburn sues for wrongful death, the media will go berserk. You'll be known as the surgeon who killed the mother of a beloved movie star!"

Previn looked at Barone, alarmed. He had hoped somehow that he'd never have to have this conversation. He thought when he'd read the autopsy that she was as good as buried already.

"Seen it before," Barone continued. "They'll all but lynch you. Call you, 'Dr. Mom Killer'!"

"But that's so not true!"

"Don't start that again."

"I've never lost a patient."

"I came here 'cause Jake asked me to get to the bottom of this. I gotta talk him down. Bury this storyline before it takes on a life of its own."

"You'd do that for me?"

"A lawsuit gets me nothing. Besides, you can give my actors another ten years. Not six. Ten, Harry."

Barone stood up, ready to leave.

Previn took Barone's hand. "You're a good guy."

Helen stood with Previn on the veranda like a happy couple as they watched Barone climb into his car. Helen actually raised her hand to say goodbye. So adept and convincing was she in this role of first lady.

"I want to love you. I just can't. I can't love this man."

"Hellie. Not now."

"You *were* an artist. But this. What is this?"

He inhaled to steady himself.

"You like playing God," she continued. "It was amusing at first. Giving women back a few years. But now they're dying."

"You've been waiting for something like this to happen. Finally gives you a rationale for leaving. You can tell your friends."

She whipped around to stare at him. "I won't be talking about this. You think I'd talk about this?"

He stared into her blue eyes that were so sharply defined by black eyeliner that they were both severe and beautiful. One bang of her red hair dropped along the right of her face. The rest of it was tied up in a playful knot on top of her head.

He turned from her. Watched Barone's car drive away.

"This is a long way from that crazy medical mission/honeymoon in Mozambique where I thought, my humanitarian hubby is going to change the world…and make a lot of money. But it was just money, Harry. I hardly noticed. It's easy not to."

At that, the battle was joined. "You hardly noticed, as you stand here in *this* house!"

She let out a sardonic laugh. "Jake Blackburn's mom have a name?"

"Is that important? She's Jake. Blackburn's. Mother. Think if she were Tom Cruise's mother. Same thing."

"Listen to yourself," she said. "You've become such the Hollywood star fucker. Something compels you to be around celebrities. And when you're not doing them, you're doing their mothers. Their mothers!"

"You want this life, it comes with a price," he replied.

Her intense blue eyes suddenly became very large. "Do you really think you can bury this?"

"There's nothing to bury."

"You killed this woman!"

"That's…How could you say…I didn't kill her. You know that. You know that!"

She looked away.

There was his answer. And it hurt. With that one turn, she'd driven the shiv right into his heart. "Maybe you don't."

3

As Helen stared at the crimson circle, it began to bleed into its yellow background much as color did in a Rothko.

The painting caught her eye from the moment she walked into the gallery. It wasn't her thing at all. But for those buyers who were taken with the colors and couldn't afford a Rothko—*And who could anymore?*—it had its appeal. All this color theory in art annoyed her because it often felt like it was more design than art, which needed to come from a more unexpected place.

"Helen!"

Guy Hennessy's deep baritone voice gave her a start. She swung round. There he was, a forty-two-year-old art wheeler-dealer prodigy who looked like he'd stepped right out of a Prada catalogue. Though he was dressed down, everything from his shirt to his shoes said moneyed style. That he greeted her with a million-dollar grin made what she had to say positively awful.

"I can't do the show." There. She'd said it. Her mouth went dry as she awaited the inevitable rebuke.

"What?"

She'd walked into the Hennessy looking for Guy Hennessy, her art dealer. The man who'd virtually discovered her. Made her collectable. Put her work into the Frieze London and the main floor at Art Basel Miami while finding opportunities to include her in group shows in London, Paris, Milan, and Toronto. Who had long ceased taking on unestablished painters when he'd picked her out of oblivion and placed her on his much-looked-to list, Artists You Must Own. She hadn't made an appointment because how do you schedule such a bombshell? Up until that moment, she'd been perfectly happy to stand in the main gallery floor critiquing other artists' work, knowing all the while she was just trying to put off this very conversation.

"I only have seven paintings," she confessed.

"What's going on?"

"I thought it'd come."

"You had a year. You had a goddamn year, for Christ's sake. See the walls. They were yours. I play this game with you where you show me as little work as you can because I believe that you'll come through. You don't walk in here to tell me this. You don't do that!"

She couldn't face him. She looked away.

It wasn't even seven paintings. Seeing as she wasn't happy with four of them, that left three. The Hennessy had asked for twenty-three seven-by-nine-foot paintings for her show. They had a huge gallery and their walls certainly required a lot of art. Her shortfall was nothing less than staggering. She deserved all the bile Guy wanted to throw at her.

"I called," he continued, turning away from her, stroking his blond hair at the back of his head as though it could calm him. "Did you call me back? No. I chalk it up to an artist thing. Helen's working. Helen doesn't want to break the flow. Helen must be onto something big. I had you so wrong."

Of course, he had. He'd called her many times. She'd put off calling him back because she hadn't known how to tell him her life had swallowed her creativity. That she was trying to have a baby. Again. And that she wasn't feeling supported in her marriage. That she wasn't herself. How could she begin to tell Guy these things by way of saying that she was going to drop the ball?

The Hennessy was such a prestigious gallery. When he'd told her she'd be having her own show more than a year ago, it had meant the world to her. She hadn't showed in LA in ages. Over the years, Guy had placed her work with some of the leading galleries in the world. The White Cube in London. Thaddaeus Ropac in Salzburg. Among others. But those had always been group shows. This would've been her show.

"This isn't the Helen Burke I know!"

She hadn't even noticed her tears until he pushed one off her cheek with his thumb as though she were a four-year-old girl.

"Let's get out of here," he said.

◆◆◆

"I'VE SPENT THE MORNING dealing with a leaky roof," Guy said, as he tossed his menu on the table after they'd sat down in the courtyard at Gracias Madre. "People think the art business is glamorous, but then there's all this *stuff*." Helen was certain he was referring to the problems she'd created.

Guy had represented her for almost six years. In all that while, she hadn't discussed her marriage. But who does? She prided herself on being a private person. There were artists that were *the* story. She'd never wanted to be that talked-about artist. Her work was the story.

As she sat in the sun-drenched white courtyard in the shadow of an olive tree, she resented Guy for bringing her there to wring the juice out of her about her personal life. She knew the game.

However, something had changed. Steady Helen. Hardworking Helen. Overachieving Helen. That woman didn't have personal crises. After all, she'd married well. Artists always had problems. And drama. Not her. She was built differently. Simply put, she felt inordinately uncomfortable playing a loser.

How could she explain it?

Guy dipped into the salsa with a tortilla chip, and then popped it in his mouth. "We'll fill your spot. That's simple enough."

Just like that, her solo show had come and gone. Poof! She started to cry again. It was so unlike her to feel this vulnerable.

Hearing him say that…he'd given her no fight. He didn't even suggest a postponement.

"I've left Harry."

"What? No! You didn't. He's great. He was like…big-time. He had good buzz."

"You don't live with him."

He wiped his hand with his napkin distractedly. "When did this happen?"

"I've boxed up everything. That's the easy part. Packing up a life. You know, it's a job. And he let me take pretty much everything."

"Wait. Wait. Time out." He made a T with his hands. "I had no idea, Helen. You've got to back up. You're saying this is happening right now? Like today?"

The boxes piling up were sheer melodrama. But a woman had to stand up for herself. She'd known women who had to deal with men who asked for a hall pass so they could have affairs. She wasn't one of those women. If Harry was forever choosing to be with flashy celebrities rather than his own wife who was trying to have his baby, then theirs wasn't a marriage. If he'd taken one moment to show her she counted more than his patients. To offer a few words of support. To show a little sensitivity when it counted. Was that too much to ask? As the boxes had piled up, she thought she could always unpack them, that perhaps it had all been a crazy overreaction.

Then that woman died…

"When I look back it seems like it's been happening for some time," she said. "I'm out tomorrow."

"Tomorrow?" Guy lowered his voice and leaned toward her. "Does he hit you? What did he do?" He rose up. "I can't believe this. If he's hurt you. If that son of bitch, if he—"

She grabbed at his arm to calm him, though she desperately needed to hear someone come out swinging in support of her. It was so unexpected, particularly after she'd let him down, but so welcome. "No, Guy. It's nothing like that. He's a good man. He provided for me. Got me the studio. You know this. I can't say bad things about

Harry because if I do, I'm going to wish to God I hadn't. Don't make me do that."

She choked up. The last thing she wanted to do was get emotional with this man yet again.

He studied her with his big brown eyes. They were dog's eyes. Sympathetic. Loving. "Where are you moving to?"

"I haven't been able to look for a place yet. I'm thinking I can camp out at the studio until something comes up. I'm putting all my paraphernalia into storage."

The whole thing was so ill-thought through. But who plans for such a scenario in anything approaching a thoughtful way?

"What about the house?" he asked.

"What about it?"

"Who's staying there?"

"Harry."

"You're new at this whole bust-up thing, Helen. I've done it twice, darling. Ask me, I know how it's done. You could have stayed. You should have asked him to move out. Put him out on his ass."

"No, I couldn't! It's his house. And anyway, it's so big."

"So he's staying there?"

"I guess."

The conversation had taken a surreal turn. She didn't deserve his graciousness.

Of course, had Guy attacked her, she would have had to mount some pathetic defense, but she was ill prepared for his kindness. She found it disarming and actually quite confusing.

"You can stay at my place," he said.

She smiled uneasily. "I'm not staying with you, Guy."

"I leave tonight for a whole month. Who's gonna water my plants, goddamn it?" He pointed his finger at her. "If my plants die because you had too much pride…"

"Are you sure?"

While she hadn't meant to question his generosity, it was about as close as she could bring herself to saying thank you.

4

P OST-OP PATIENT ROSIE BOTTOMS, a fading thirty-five-year-old film star, walked out from behind a folding Japanese wood and rice paper screen butt naked. Her body was golden from her toes up, helped by spray tan and highlights. Her breasts were ramrod erect. Sara shot Previn a bemused look.

"Oh. Rosie," Previn said, barely disguising his surprise. "I only need to see your top. The smock. Why don't you put it on?"

Rosie walked past a wall-sized Helmut Newton print of a gaggle of four nudes in spiked black heels before disappearing again behind the partition. He noted that Rosie had also come out wearing heels. Newton was evidently on to something.

Wearing lime-green scrubs, Sara leaned against the uncut slab of black marble he used as a desk, nudging aside the framed photo of Chumma, a six-year-old-African boy, a treasured keepsake from the aid work he'd done years before in Mozambique. "Rosie always got naked in her films," she said.

"Some actresses are very free."

"Except she was always flat as a sheet of drywall."

"Sara?" He shook his head.

There was no editing her. That was one of the things he loved about her, though. She was definitely one of the boys when it came to making light of it all. She'd been his right hand almost from the start of his practice. He liked to think he was intensely loyal, but why would anyone dispense with someone like Sara? She was also a very beautiful woman. He fancied himself a lover of beautiful women. He was an artist. The one thing Helen and Sara had in common was they were utterly natural. He'd never thought to change them. It wasn't necessary. The idea was almost unthinkable. Sara's skin was near perfect. Almost as fair as a Caravaggio. Her black bob accentuated the contrast.

Rosie returned. Her breasts had a blue cast to them from the bruising, and thin bands of white tape were visible near her armpits, at the base of her breasts, and along the base of her nipples in the shape of a smile. She looked down at them forlornly.

"Is it bad?" she asked.

"Do we live in the Capital of Good Looks or what? They look terrific. Right, Sara?"

"Bikini time!" Sara never ceased to say the right thing. Didn't seem to matter how many breast augmentations she'd seen.

Previn felt the breasts for lumps or rigidity. "There's still swelling. But they've got form."

"My nipples sting."

"You've added a great deal of bulk. The body responds with inflammation. Nothing unusual. And the stinging, typical. May go on for another week, ten days. It'll stop when the bruising's gone."

Like many people in the business, Rosie had already been divorced three times and had confided in him during their first consultation that she was now very much in love. But ten days out from surgery, his patients were usually more upbeat.

"How are you doing otherwise?" he probed.

"Fine."

"And the boyfriend's loving life?"

She toyed with a strand of her blond hair while gazing at the ceiling impatiently. "Dumped me."

"He what? Not after the surgery?"

"Yes."

Sara put her hand on Rosie's shoulder. "Oh, honey."

"Sorry to hear that. But these puppies will put some *vavoom* back into your career so…"

Rosie looked at him sharply. "They're not me."

"Not you? Who are you? Who am I? We're what we become." Previn pointed at her breasts. "This *is* you. The new Rosie Bottoms."

"You don't know me. It's horrible. What have I done?"

Sara stepped up. "Rosie, Dr. Harold Previn is no ordinary surgeon. He's an artist. A sculptor. Look!" Sara pointed to a white bronze of Helen that still remarkably sat on Previn's desk. Not only was he proud of that statue—he simply wasn't ready to remove it from his life. No more than he was Helen herself.

"There were no surprises here," Previn said. "I gave you the breasts you wanted. Even drew them for you to see. Remember these?"

He frantically rifled through her file and pulled hand drawings of Rosie with her breasts augmented just as he'd intended. He tossed them across his desk. They were surprisingly artsy. But that's how Previn was. This was more than an affectation. Other surgeons were using computer-generated mapping to plot their augmentations. He preferred a charcoal pencil because it made him feel like he was molding the breast as if it were clay. Doing it with his hands.

"This is about your ex, isn't it?" he said.

"They're fake," she said.

"Well, of course."

"They're plastic."

"Silicone. May I?" he asked as he reached for the lapels of her smock to look again at her new breasts. "They're beautiful. There's nothing wrong with them. If your ex wants to characterize them as 'plastic,' he's a damn idiot." He tightened his grip on her smock as he spoke. "It's just like our so-called partners to speak their minds when they don't have any idea what they're talking about."

Sara stepped forward. "Harry!"

He released the smock.

"Why are you saying he said this?" Rosie asked.

"Because he did. Didn't he?"

Rosie covered herself timidly. "No. He didn't say anything."

"That's just my point. Why the hell didn't he?" Previn demanded.

Sara stepped between them. "Rosie, Harry's wife has left him. This isn't about your breasts. Or about the augmentation. It's about Harry."

"What?"

Sara and Previn locked eyes.

"I'll put my clothes back on," Rosie said as she walked behind the partition.

"Sorry, Rosie," Previn said at last. "Why don't you come back in a week? We'll take another look. Figure it out."

After Rosie had left, Sara faced off with Previn in the hallway in front of, as it turned out, one of his Helen Burke oils, of which there were several. This one was of a giant blue door, part of her door series. The color seemed so alive it vibrated. "You want to get sued?" Sara asked.

"Well, what does it take to make people happy?"

"That's not how you please an aging actress like her. It's delicate, or so you're always telling me."

Such were the truisms of Hollywood. She was an actress in her twilight. Soon her agent would be releasing her. So too would her manager, if he hadn't already. While there were different rules for stars, Rosie hadn't scored anything substantial in several years. "She's thirty-five. Not much we can do about that."

"Show some sensitivity. You just had to bring your own shit into this, didn't you? It's not right. You've got to stop it!"

"You're way out of line bringing my personal life—"

"This is not you, Harry. I know it's been tough lately, but—"

"Rosie has unrealistic expectations."

"They're all chasing perfect."

"What's perfect?" Previn asked.

◆◆◆

THAT NIGHT, PREVIN RETURNED to an empty house. A place alive with his dead marriage. Helen had cleaned him out, taking virtually all the furniture. Other than a few boxes they were coming for in the morning, the only thing that remained in the living room was the white grand piano, which only served to make the spacious room seem even more vacant. Worse still, he didn't even know how to play piano.

It'd never been the plan for Helen to leave him with the house. It's not that he wouldn't have gladly left; it's that he had hoped she was so much invested in it she'd never leave. How wrong he'd been.

The enormous business of moving house had only invested her more in their separation. Had he played it differently, were he to do it again, he'd have left her in the house because he had so little it'd be so much easier for them to put their own lives back together again. But as he encountered her absence, he began to realize that after her move, it'd be a radical reversal for her to bring all her stuff back.

Of course, people don't stay together because it's too much trouble to move. There was much more to it than that. At some point as he was soaring professionally, Helen was suffering a crisis of confidence in him. She simply hadn't signed up for the same ride. There had been signs like her disinterest in doing the scene. He hadn't clued in to it until then because a crisis is never a crisis until it's a crisis.

He walked up to the piano. Pushed down on one key. He felt forlorn. Lost.

He went over to his studio where a block of clay lay waiting on the round pedestal. The director of aesthetic surgery at Cornell had first introduced him to sculpture. Previn saw the connection between plastic surgery and the craft of shaping heads immediately. Something elegant about the idea of becoming a true artist really grabbed him. He started taking sculpture classes in tandem with his medical studies. What he saw was a lineage that went back to Leonardo Da Vinci. The stories of this great Renaissance artist cutting into dozens of stinking cadavers in an effort to unlock the secrets of anatomy were the stuff of legend. It spoke to the very logical connection between anatomical science and sculpture. Hard to imagine Da Vinci creating his *David* had he not unlocked the secret of human anatomy. The first time Previn was asked to cut into a cadaver, even though it stunk of formaldehyde, he'd believed it was nothing less than his Da Vinci moment.

Previn made a few tentative gestures to manipulate the clay, but stopped. The feel of the cold, white clay in his hands was a salve. It was organic. It brought him closer to the earth. But there was so much more to it than pushing the clay around. Normally, he made exploratory sketches. He came to it with ideas. A creative vision. The seeds of something. Anything. But today he had nothing. He'd come there out of a need to feel it in his hands. That was all. He put the plastic back around the clay so that it wouldn't dry out and left the room.

5

HELEN WATCHED THE MOVERS put the last boxes into their truck. She signed the papers and then turned back to the house, which was mostly empty but for the two suitcases that she'd positioned near the door. Just as the truck turned onto the street, Harry's silver Jag appeared. He pulled it up to the front of the house and climbed out.

"What are you doing here?" Helen said.

"I had to come."

"What about your work?" She sighed. "I'm sorry. It's your house."

"I'm not the villain here."

She could feel the blood rush to her head. "And I am?"

"I didn't say that. You're way too defensive."

She crossed her arms and looked away. He wasn't supposed to see her off. She didn't want to see him. Didn't he know that his being there wasn't helpful? What was he thinking?

"It's hard," she conceded at last.

He looked at her. "I know."

At least they'd found that much to agree about.

He followed her into the house. "Wow. They've really cleaned this place out."

"What are you going to do?" she said.

He grinned. "Get new furniture. Buy new art."

"It's so easy for you."

"I didn't say that," he replied.

"I didn't ask for you to see me off."

"I know."

She grabbed the suitcases.

"Let me." He took them from her hands and carried them toward her car. "Where are you off to anyway?"

She didn't want to get into how unsettled she was. She didn't feel like she owed him an accounting. "Somewhere."

He nodded. "I've been there. You won't like it."

She studied him. He'd brushed his dark hair over his forehead as he always did, but it'd gotten longer than any conventional doctor would call appropriate. Some of his had fallen forward, giving him a manic look. He was really quite handsome. They're always great when you're leaving them.

"You can reach me at the studio."

He kissed her. She didn't resist. She should have. Probably. It really didn't make much sense to her, all this. How does one end a marriage? She'd felt the kiss was dignified. Hadn't meant a thing.

◆◆◆

GUY HENNESSY LIVED IN Brentwood on a lush acre not far from where OJ lived at the time he was accused of murdering his ex.

A small woman wearing faded jeans stood at the big door to Guy's home as Helen carried her two large suitcases into the foyer. Helen looked back at her Saab parked in the middle of the palm-lined motor court. "You must be Maria." The woman nodded. "Is it all right to leave my car there?" Helen continued.

"Mr. Guy say, *mi casa es tu casa*."

"Did he really say that in Spanish?"

Maria smiled. "No, Mr. Guy no speak Spanish. But I do. Come. I show you your room."

The two-story house was Hollywood Regency. It had round windows in the front, black-and-white stone floors inside, and wrought-iron railing going up the staircase. A quaintness that Helen felt might just help to heal her broken heart.

Maria stopped to show her the code for the front door. How to activate the alarm. She picked up one of Helen's suitcases and led her to the guest room across from the study. They stood around for what seemed like more than a few awkward moments before Helen realized she was waiting for a tip. She rounded up a few crumpled dollar bills and pressed them into to her hand. Anything for peace and privacy. Helen was very relieved to hear Maria's car drive off, at which point she opened her luggage and began to unpack. Several of her dresses were already on hangers. She merely transferred them to the closet. That done, she left the two cases open as they were on the floor and walked over to the window where she watched the gate open for Maria, who departed in an old, smoke-belching American car.

Helen turned and unfastened her dress so that it fell to the floor. She thought she'd feel relieved to be there. Not two days after her lunch with Guy, she'd left her home and was now in the far corner of a foreign place, but somehow had not emotionally left the home she'd shared with Harry. She spread herself out on the bed and looked up at the white ceiling. Would she ever have a family?

The question unleashed a torrent of emotion. Her body shook as she sobbed. She buried her head in the pillow, which stifled the sound and absorbed her tears but did nothing to console her. A well-honed sense of dignity and poise had helped her hold it together until that moment.

What was she going to do? Was this it? What had she done?

When Helen got up from the bed, she caught a glimpse of herself in the mirror. Was that her? She could hardly believe how much weight she'd put on. She'd always been shapely, but not fat. Previn had done that to her. That was his final gift, to leave her looking fat and unattractive. That was the irony. He'd looked so fit when she'd seen him a few hours before.

The fertility treatments had always had this effect. It had been the same each time she'd done them. It was as if she'd had a baby but without the baby.

No baby to show for all her flub.

In a daze, wearing nothing but pink thong underwear, she walked through the house to the kitchen. Opened the fridge. Helped herself to a bottle of rosé. Walked back to the room, dragging the drama of her infertility and the collapse of her marriage with her like a corpse. She wanted to cry, but hadn't she already done that?

She made several more trips to the kitchen to refill her glass, oblivious to everything around her. Despairing her predicament. By the time it occurred to her to bring the bottle back to the room, she was pouring the last of it into her glass. She looked around the kitchen. One thing about Guy—he had wine everywhere.

She was making her way back to the room, down what had become a dark hallway, when she stopped to stare at a giant Alex Katz, which seemingly would not allow itself to go unnoticed one more time. The painting featured the same couple slow-dancing as seen from two angles. The man was looking at her with love and devotion, but the woman seemed to be somewhere far away. Lost in thought. Helen flicked on the light to see it better. The light lit the yellow painting with a gallery quality, which was not surprising given that this was gallerist Guy Hennessy's home. The couple came alive. Katz painted in a flat style that was influential. She suspected that this was one of his very high-value early works. Possibly from the seventies.

She was suddenly aware that she'd been in Guy's home for hours and hadn't even taken note that his home was filled with art. Absolutely chock-full of masterful paintings. It was so unlike her not to have noticed. Usually it was the very first thing she looked for when she walked into anyone's home, their art. Much in the same way some people like to look through bookshelves.

Across the room was a Daniel Richter. It was loud. Aggressive. He could be quite painterly but then there was a graffiti aspect added. It contained several menacing figures carrying M-16s.

She continued to wander, switching on lights in the various rooms as she went. Allowing the art to light up. Guy had a great collection. He even had one of her paintings hanging in the hall. It wasn't exactly a prime location. But then she hardly felt her work held its own beside Katz, Richter, and Gilbert & George. It was a gift that he'd let her stay in his home. A reminder that there was more than Harry Previn.

These paintings were her touchstones.

She arrived at the master bedroom and flicked on the light. He had a Sophie Von Hellermann hanging there. Kind of whimsical. She painted fast. You could feel her energy. The way the brush strokes conveyed feeling. The painting was of a couple having a duel. Their pistols pointed skyward moments before that fateful turn.

Guy had left the room in some disorder. The inevitable chaos of packing for a trip. Try packing a life, Guy. Her eyes wandered across the very rumpled bed to the nightstand. He had several books there. A thriller. And a biography of Coco Chanel.

On the coffee table were several books about contemporary LA architecture. And on the chair lay a section from *The Wall Street Journal* called "Mansions." Guy was evidently quite interested in homes.

The door to his walk-in closet was ajar. She didn't know what possessed her to look inside, but she did. She opened the door and flicked on the light. What she saw made her gasp.

On the wall of his closet hung a watercolor of her. A nude.

She was lifting herself up from the sheets. Looking forward, her red hair all mashed. At the time, it had seemed like a serious life study, but seeing it now, it looked more like porn. That's what happens when you pose for your boyfriend.

They'd just had sex when he decided that he wanted to capture the moment and she didn't mind because she never did mind being painted. Jonathan Gold. God! It had been years. She looked so young there. And her body was so firm. She inadvertently covered her bare breasts with her arms as she looked at the painting. She didn't like the comparison. That wasn't her. That was another woman from another time. A happy girl. That's what she was. Happy.

She'd gotten entangled with Jonathan Gold for a few months. He had a beach house in Malibu. In those pre-Google days, before you could just look someone up and find out exactly who they were and what they'd done, she thought he must be an accomplished artist, but all he was was much older. The son of some famous Hollywood director. It was probably his father's house. Jonathan. Jonathan. Jonathan. How naïve she'd been to think she was going out with a modern-day Egon Schiele. He was simply a dirty old man with a trust fund and a yen for bedding and painting young girls.

So how did his work end up with Guy Hennessy? And in his bedroom closet?

She stepped back until she found Guy's bed and sat down on the edge of it still staring in stunned awe at the painting. What was going on?

6

Helen was all wavy red hair and big eyes.

Previn wanted romantic. He'd picked the garden restaurant of the Chateau Marmont Hotel, a Gothic candlelit courtyard. A milieu of wine and conversation on a warm night—there were few places like it in LA.

He'd picked out an oversized artsy, handmade black coat, an immaculate tapered white shirt, and black jeans for the occasion, although given his hip clientele and his own temperament, this was more or less everyday attire.

The pretty hostess, whom he knew from countless visits, threw her arms around him. They shared a laugh before she led him to his table. Under the vaulted archway, Helen was seated. Alone. Thoughtful.

She stood up and he embraced her. In that eternal moment, he felt his grandiosity to her smallness. He hugged her like she needed it. And she did, didn't she? He finally stepped back from her, his hands steadfastly clutching her shoulders.

He noticed one button on her green silk shirt seemed particularly stressed, as though it were almost too much to hold her breasts. The thought crossed his mind that they should get out of there and go back to his place. Something about that. His. Only ten days before it had been *theirs*. Now there was "his." And presumably "hers." Suddenly their getting together didn't seem so simple.

"Let me look at you," he said.

She smiled. "Still the girl who fell off the turnip truck."

"I loved that girl. Still do."

After they'd sat down at the table, the waiter came over. Previn didn't bother to glance at the wine list; he knew exactly where he was going with this. "We'll do a bottle of Bollinger."

Helen gasped.

Previn laughed and reached for her hand as the waiter walked off. "We're celebrating!"

"Harry—"

"I'm so pleased to see you. I'm rattling around in that damn empty house for ten days and…Oh, God, Hellie. I can't do this. We can't. It's so great we're sitting here. Finally! Let's forget about everything. Forget all the bullshit. I'm getting hard just being close enough to touch you."

She pulled her hand away from his. "Sorry if I gave you the wrong impression." She slid an envelope across the table. "I could have had it served. That's just not me."

He felt all the color drain from his face. "What?"

"I'm an all-or-nothing kind of girl. You've changed, Harry. I wouldn't have…I wanted to give it more time…"

He didn't know how to respond. He'd embarrassed himself. He felt a mix of disappointment tinged with anger. How could she allow him to bring her to this picturesque garden and order champagne if she'd intended to nuke their marriage?

"I'm sorry," she said, her eyes downcast.

Previn looked away impatiently, absently watching a platinum blonde as she walked her catwalk across the courtyard, her nubile body all but spilling out of what looked like about eighteen inches of aluminum foil. He was sure she was someone.

◆◆◆

IN THE DARK, THE statues and the furniture seemed mysterious and haunting. Faint sounds unsettled Helen. Got on her nerves. Though she was loath to turn on the lights. She felt more like hiding.

She'd been sitting on the floor in the middle of Guy's living room since returning from the Chateau. She hadn't wanted to come back here. The only other alternative she could think of was to go to her studio. Yet how could she look at her work at a time like this?

She remembered pulling the divorce papers out from her handbag. The rest was kind of a muddle. Had she really gotten up to leave moments later?

Harry had caught the first words on the front page of the legal document. "Why are you doing this? What the hell is the matter with you? You drop something like this on me here?"

She was stunned at the intensity of his confusion. How could he not know this was coming? She'd left the house. Spent days packing. Brought in movers. There was no confusing her intentions. When she'd told him this, Harry had countered that she only had one gear, which seemed to suggest she didn't know what she was doing. And in any case, she wasn't a car.

Her attorney had asked her repeatedly why she wanted the divorce. Men always seemed to need to know why. Harry and the lawyer shared this need to know the fine points, but only so they could argue them. There was nothing to debate. She didn't want to be with Harry. The lawyer had actually asked her if Harry beat her. Or if he'd been unfaithful. Didn't feelings matter? Of course, if she hadn't lost the baby, it might have been different. She'd have fought to hold it together for the baby's sake. But now, there was nothing holding her...

"Is it because of what happened with Blackburn?" Harry had asked as she'd stood up to leave. He'd grabbed her arm. "Sit down. Won't you?"

She'd gripped her handbag and turned to walk away. She hated to make a scene. That was so not what this had been about. She'd actually thought she was being very civilized about this unpleasantness, though her lawyer had cautioned her against doing the service personally.

What was she to do? Wait for Harry to file? She'd said from the start she wanted out of their marriage. That meant lawyers. Until someone figured out how to do it some other way, they were a necessity. Someone had to draw up the paperwork. Delivering them herself just seemed like an important, original shift from the usual banality of these things.

She may have been wrong about that.

Her iPhone sounded off with a ringtone like a field of crickets. Guy. She'd been avoiding him for days. However, if she could serve Harry divorce papers without a qualm, she could certainly handle speaking to her art dealer on the phone. She returned his call.

"Helen. Are you okay?"

When the sound of his voice caused her to break down, she realized this wasn't such a great idea. At least he couldn't see the tears streaming down her face.

He was a talker. He seemed to be reading off a prepared script. "I called you a few days ago. I was tempted to send Maria over there to make sure you hadn't run off with my Anselm Kiefer."

"It's too big to steal."

He laughed. The painting was literally twelve feet wide. "Point taken. Though I would have thought Holocaust art might be a problem, but not so much. People love Kiefer."

She sniffled and it sounded like a laugh. She still couldn't help wondering about that painting of her hanging in his closet. He must have looked at it every morning when he got up and every night before he went to bed. That was more than a little creepy.

"You know, most of my paintings I don't even own, but while I wait to find a buyer for them, I figure I might as well enjoy them. I've got the wall space, all right. Truth be told, the house is an extension of my gallery. I write it off. So I figure I might as well live with the art until I can find someone who will ante up."

"I'm happy to be here, Guy. It's been…" She couldn't go on.

"I know."

"No. You don't."

"Have you been painting?" he asked.

"I can't paint."

"You can always go back to Harry. You need to get your footing. A marriage is incredibly grounding."

Her heart started to race with what she thought was fear. "I'm not going back there. Why are you saying I should go back to him?"

"I didn't say you should. I said it's an option."

She lost it. "It's not an option. Not for me."

She couldn't believe the same man who had her naked in his closet could suggest her going back to her marriage. After the day she'd had, she found his championing a reconciliation maddening. While she felt very ill at ease about whatever fantasies he must have about her, as evidenced by his having that nude, it annoyed her even more that he obviously didn't want her anymore. Just like that. This man didn't know his own mind. It was just like her art opening. He'd canceled it without batting an eye.

"I've had more breakups than you could know, Helen. I've gotten to this place where I'm asking myself if the issues driving the madness mattered. In the moment, everything seems like such a big, big deal. I'm alone. I don't want to be alone. But here I am. Maybe I was always too quick to run."

"We're different people, Guy."

"I can't say I know what it'd be like to be married to a plastic surgeon, but most artists need someone financially substantial to anchor them."

"That's not why I married Harry. I married him because I thought we were kindred spirits."

"Previn? You're talking about Previn? He does facelifts and boob jobs!"

Was she supposed to defend Harry? One moment he was proposing she go back to him, next he was belittling her husband.

They were such different men. Guy was younger. Competitive. She got that. Some men just have that territorial thing going. He did. Maybe that had something to do with him bringing her into his house. In art school, she'd been trained to strip things down to their essence. Helen looked at the two. On the face, Previn was an artist, Guy a dealer. But when she really tried to find an appropriate association, she saw Previn as a lion. Regal and commanding. Guy was a tiger. Agile and cunning. He was capable of surprise. Previn had long ceased being capable of that.

"I'm sorry," Guy said at last. "That didn't come out right."

"You don't understand Harry."

"That I don't! How he could let you go?"

"Don't."

"I can feel your anguish, Helen. Have you weighed all your options? Couples counseling? Of course, sometimes a little time apart is a good thing."

She found herself crying again. She'd been crying so much lately. Surely, she wasn't the first woman to suffer a broken heart.

"I'm worried about you," he said. "My home is a happy house; I can't have a woman getting all emotional there. It'll mess with the karma of the place."

She sighed. "I want everything to be perfect, but nothing's perfect."

She recalled the sickly look that had come over Harry's face as he'd read the cover page of the divorce filing. She'd had so much on her mind. She hadn't been able to think clearly. How could she have hid behind some stranger appearing at his office with that envelope? It may have been as awkward as hell, but at least she'd had the nerve to show her face to him. To stand with her convictions.

"You need to get back into the studio," Guy said.

"I can't."

"Trust me on this. It'll be good for your soul to throw some paint on a canvas. I'm not saying this as your dealer, I'm saying it as your therapist."

"You're not my therapist."

"Do you even have a therapist?"

"No."

"Okay then. Helen, meet Guy Hennessy, therapist."

Helen turned on the light over the Alex Katz. She looked at the two images of the same couple dancing in the painting. So at odds. That woman just didn't seem to be into the man at all. Yet he was looking at her like she were the only woman in the world.

She couldn't very well tell Guy about all the fertility treatments she'd had, how she felt unattractive, and how the estrogen and prednisone had flattened her imagination to the extent that all she'd been able to think about was the loss of that baby. She'd tried to tell Harry that. Men didn't get it. They couldn't know. She'd really tried to be creative. To conceive the most amazing art any woman could possibly hope for.

It was going to be a girl.

She lay down on the floor again. Guy was saying something about her work—how amazing he thought it was—when she fell asleep.

◆◆◆

PREVIN PULLED HIS CAR into his driveway. The top was down, but he didn't get out of his liquid-silver XK Jag. He simply stayed put. The spotlights in the trees cast a golden glow. The buzz of the crickets was the only sound and it soothed.

The car was new. His second Jag. He loved it for its style and elegance. The only thing was, he'd had to settle for liquid silver, a non-color. But then, it had become a monochromatic world when it came to cars. They were all seemingly some shade of black. As if life in the Capital of Good Looks were itself a black-and-white movie. The cars in sepia tone. At least liquid silver popped.

The moment was broken by his cell phone's ringtone, the opening chords to David Bowie's "1984." He hesitated. The caller ID indicated it was a private caller. It could be anyone, but in that moment, it could only be Helen.

"All right. Here's the deal," said a man's voice.

"Brick."

If there was ever a time Previn didn't want to talk to anyone, it was then. And his anesthesiologist and friend was no exception. But cutting him off would beg an explanation. He didn't want to go there.

"The deal." Brick was way too animated to be sober. "You ready? I'm sitting here with two lovely actresses. Told 'em about you and they want to meet you. Now."

Previn didn't respond.

"We're at Cecconi's. The patio. You know, by candlelight."

"Got it."

"You've got to get out. Get on with your life!"

"Actually—"

"Don't actually me. You don't have surgery tomorrow and I would know because I'm the gas, remember? You're living in an emotional sewer right now. Helen. Helen. Helen. Hey, I've been there. Life's too short, Harry."

There were no secrets. Everyone at work had lived through the disintegration of Previn's marriage. They knew him almost too well. They knew Helen. He didn't have to get into specifics.

They could see he hadn't been the same over the last few months, not knowing about the stress he'd endured going through the fertility treatments with Helen, and then coming up empty. The last ten days with Helen moving out had been particularly bad.

Then of course, there'd been Blackburn dying.

Brick and Sara were two of his closest friends. They'd been working together since he first put out his shingle. That meant daily surgeries and consultations. It also meant drinks after work more than a few nights a week. When his marriage went south, that changed. While a drink or two might have soothed him some, he hadn't had the heart to sit with his friends. He didn't want to talk about it. Didn't they know that? That he just wanted to be left alone?

"Where are you?" Brick asked.

"I was just pulling onto my street—"

"Okay. That's fifteen minutes."

"Twenty."

"All right then, I'll spot you another five. Get here."

◆◆◆

PREVIN WAS STILL SITTING in his car after Brick's phone call. He'd put his head back and closed his eyes. He could have stayed there the whole evening, as he felt no desire for laughter nor the company of Brick and his women friends. But the ringing phone seemed to challenge that.

"Where are you, man?" Brick bellowed.

"I'm coming! The traffic's fuckin' intense."

Previn put the phone down on his lap. The damnedest bit was he thought Helen had never looked better than she had that night. How terrible her idea had been. Did she really think there was some civilized way to divorce him? She knew how invested he was in their marriage. He couldn't fathom how they could have possibly enjoyed dinner together with her divorce papers sitting beside the breadbasket. The phone suddenly rang again. Why couldn't Brick leave him alone?

"No. Brick. I can't!" he barked. "I'm not in the right headspace, okay?"

"It's Barone."

"Richard?"

"We've got a woman in need," Barone announced with an offhandedness that didn't pass muster. What was the head of Artists Unlimited, one of the largest talent agencies in America, doing calling a plastic surgeon after 11:00 p.m.?

"What? Now?" When Barone didn't reply, Previn asked uneasily, "What kind of need?"

"I'd like you to handle this."

◆◆◆

AFTER BARONE'S CALL, PREVIN battled the typical nighttime congestion along the Sunset Strip and retraced his steps to the Chateau. After leaving almost a full bottle of Bollinger sitting in ice when he'd left dinner with Helen, it was surely the last place on earth he wanted to go. The waiter had actually asked him if he'd like to take it home.

Previn's car whizzed along through a blur of taillights. A building-sized ad loomed out of a bloodred background, *How to Get Away With MURDER*. Billboards were everywhere. The new Angelina Jolie. Calvin Klein underwear. A huge bottle of Absolut. Megan Fox lying in a bikini. The image of Nick Valentine dropping from the sky.

He pulled into the parking garage at the Chateau Marmont, where he handed the car to the same valet as earlier. He lingered with his medical bag in hand and wondered if he'd have to call Barone for more instructions as to where he had to go when a youngish woman with an edgy, intense red dye job approached. "You wouldn't happen to be Dr. Previn, would you?"

"Yeah."

"I'm Rox. Johnny Tout is over here," she said, carrying her iPhone in one hand and walking with authority. Previn guessed she was Tout's personal assistant. It seemed like everyone in Hollywood had at least one. Previn assumed that Tout worked with or was associated in some way with Barone. But now that he was there, he wished he had asked Barone about Johnny Tout.

To his surprise, she didn't lead him into the hotel, but deeper into the garage. Jammed with parked cars, it wasn't a rectangular space, but an L-shaped one. Previn followed his guide to a black limo parked around the bend. The woman knocked on the dark window and the door opened.

A man with sun-damaged, leathery skin emerged, introducing himself as Johnny Tout. He appeared to be fifty, if a day, with a lot of Peter Pan about him. The bright green paisley shirt with its ultra-high collar beneath a rumpled gray sports coat, skintight black slacks, and pointed boots said, "Look at me!" He was a look-at-me kind of guy.

Clearly, Tout worked out with a personal trainer. But for all that, he wore all his years and then some. Smoking may have contributed. Drink. Stress. Most notable were the bags under his eyes. Previn could not look at his face without wanting to reach for his scalpel.

"I won't bother you with small talk," he said very quietly in a guttural Australian twang. "She's in there." He pointed to the car.

Previn found a young blonde woman sprawled out on the back seat. Bloodied paper towels were scattered everywhere. Her hair and what was a scant silver skirt, her sole attire, were covered in dried blood. He couldn't tell if she was conscious or not as her head was turned away from him.

With the greatest gentleness, he reached down and with one hand guided her face round, so he could see it better in the poor light. He still couldn't. The problem was there were wads of paper towels clinging to the wounds on her face. To touch them would only cause her pain. Askew, her nose was probably broken, but checking it was a low priority.

His attention was drawn to the aluminum foil-like wrap that so inadequately covered her when he suddenly recalled seeing her walk past him only a few hours before as Helen was asking for the divorce. He'd been unable to take his eyes off her. And now here she was.

She let out a faint moan and waved him off, and then became still again. He released her chin and moved to get up, only to notice her dress was torn. Difficult not to think assault and battery.

When Previn got out of the limo, Tout motioned for him to wait, finished his telephone conversation, then handed the phone to his assistant who continued talking into it.

"Well?" Tout asked in a near whisper.

"We better call an ambulance."

"That bad?"

"You understand, I'm sure, it's hard to give her a really proper examination…in a parked car," Previn said, affecting a tone of this-is-my-considered-opinion. He thought it important to establish up front that for him, the wily veteran, this was business as usual. And it was, up to a point. But the truth was, while he'd viewed many horrible wounds, he rarely went out into the field like this. "I recommend Cedars."

"No way."

"It's a great hospital," Previn replied.

"I said, no!" Tout continued in an undertone.

"You don't think…?" Previn stopped himself. There was no point in pressing until he understood Tout's objection. "When did this happen?" Previn continued, trying a different tact.

"Thirty-seven minutes ago." Tout hesitated. "Look, I don't want to keep you in the dark. Barone said you're one of us. Artists Unlimited, they dig you, mate."

"I know."

He looked around and lowered his voice. "She went through a window. Messy business. Drunk. Walked right into it." He smacked his hands together like a thunderclap.

"That it?" Previn asked, raising his eyebrow.

"May have done some coke, y' know."

"She's pretty out of it."

"Oh, I gave her Valium."

Previn couldn't contain his annoyance. "You *gave* her Valium?"

Tout motioned for him to keep his voice down. "I didn't know what to do."

"Get her to a hospital," Previn announced.

Rox closed the case around her iPhone, then came over and stood beside Tout. He looked at her impatiently then turned back to Previn. "I don't understand. You're a surgeon."

Previn stared at Tout for a long time. He wasn't entirely disagreeable. The kind of man who would go down well with a few drinks at the bar, one place where his apparent lack of candor would hardly be a shortcoming. No doubt, he had many entertaining stories to tell. And Previn loved a good story.

Rox's phone broke the impasse. She stepped only a few feet from them and began to engage in an intense conversation. Previn looked away but caught most of it.

"Stay away from Johnny, Sid!" Rox said. "He doesn't want to hear from you. You'll set him off again. Yeah, we're talking to him now."

Previn turned back to Tout. "The girl…she's in a bad way. We'd have to do lab work. I don't even know her blood type."

"You're fucking with me!" Tout barked suddenly at full volume. "They said…Barone, he…I know you're good. You can handle this."

Rox joined them again.

"I gotta call Barone," Previn said.

Tout grabbed Previn's hand before he could get his phone. "Don't complicate this. He asked you here."

"It's after midnight. You got a drugged-up woman lying in the back of a car with facial lacerations."

"Okay. Okay. We're tits up. I get it."

"You get it? You get it? You don't—"

Tout put his hand on Previn's shoulder and dropped his voice. "We're on the same side here."

Previn stared at Tout and Rox.

"This is my cock-up," Tout said at last. "I should have leveled with you right away."

Previn nodded.

Tout looked around, as if to be absolutely certain they were alone, and lowered his voice. "That woman in there…is Fay Wray."

"She's a singer, right?"

"A singer?"

"She's the shit," Rox replied. "They call her 'The Face.' She's that beautiful."

Previn was still trying to stomach the idea that Tout had given her a Valium after her injury. Who did that? It was just this sort of enabling, irresponsible behavior that led to Whitney Houston dying in a hotel bathtub.

"It's like this," Previn said. "I'm not a paramedic. There's malpractice."

Tout was in a sudden rage. "What kind of doctor are you? She's about to bleed to death!"

Previn wasn't used to having to contend with bombastic people like Tout. What's more, he didn't like it. A surgeon is the boss, indeed the benevolent dictator, and his celebrity patients usually didn't bring intermediaries.

Previn could only think that Barone didn't know the extent of this woman's plight. What began as a favor...It seemed like this was asking so much more of him. He walked back to the car again and looked in. She wasn't about to bleed to death. The bleeding had mostly stopped, which is not to say that to the unpracticed eye she didn't look half-dead. She definitely needed medical attention.

"Okay. Follow me."

Tout walked with Rox back to the limo. Previn got into his car, but as he passed the limo, Tout appeared at the passenger window. He reluctantly opened the door and Tout climbed in, leaving Rox to ride with Fay. The acrid stench of Tout's cologne announced itself so forcefully, Previn was quick to put down the top again.

The last thing Previn could have imagined at the start of the evening was that he'd be driving back to his surgical facility with someone like Tout. He watched with annoyance as Tout adjusted the charcoal leather seat so that it was in a sharp recline. Previn liked both seats upright.

"What a night!" Tout said.

Indeed! Previn was having one of those *Sunset Boulevard* moments. The William Holden character is lying facedown in the pool, dead, and asks in the voiceover, "You're probably wondering how I got here."

He didn't do things like take some injured pop diva to his surgery in the dead of night because he'd been asked to by a Hollywood big shot. But this was exactly what he was doing. He wanted to blame it on Helen. She'd put him on his back foot in asking for the divorce two hours before surgery. However, he knew that'd be a cheap cop-out. On any given night, he might have felt compelled to do what he was doing. Rather, it went back to a whole series of choices he'd made that had to do with his embracing a world that was all about money and beautiful people. Opening a surgery center in Beverly Hills factored into it. The rent. It was about the rent. In the early years, he could barely make the rent, and then he bought a luxurious house because he could. But it wasn't paid for. Nothing was paid for, and people like Richard Barone were like his creditors. So if he felt like the character at the beginning of *Sunset Boulevard* just then, it was because he felt virtually as helpless as that character did floating face down in the pool.

Previn needed to look no further than his own hard-driving father, who had struggled with innumerable business ventures before finding modest success later in life doing mergers and acquisitions. Previn knew that success wasn't such an easy thing to come by. He'd ridden that harrowing roller coaster all through his youth, watching his family file for bankruptcy protection twice. If he was driven to cash in, it was because of that.

Somehow, it had led to Tout sitting there beside him in his car, a gnawing reminder of his bad decision to consent to take Fay to his surgery.

"This brings me back to my first wife," Tout mused. "She was a handful. Pretty as sin, made for sex, but barking mad."

Previn looked over at Tout. He wasn't actually going to start sharing stories about his former wives? All this was hitting way too close to home. But there was no stopping him.

"The first time out of the box, we like 'em that way, don't we, mate? I remember this one night like...like it was yesterday, we were in the penthouse suite at the Chateau, and she was standing on the windowsill saying she'd jump. I don't know what I'd done to make her want to jump out the window, but probably something with one of the girls. She was a jealous bird. Rightfully so. I can admit it now." He chuckled as though the memory of one of the birds had just come to mind. "I climbed up there to reason with her. When you're up there, don't look down. I looked and it was almost me who went out the window. She caught me. Learned something that night. That woman was always going to come out okay no matter what drugs she'd taken. Me, I had to watch out for myself. Kurt told me. Kurt…had some very sage advice and he was up to his gills in the same rock 'n' roll insanity then. His bloody wife was jumping off stages every night. Doing coke. Heroin. Kurt knew, and I'll never forget what he said. We there yet?"

"Less than ten minutes."

"Wise advice, that." Tout nodded thoughtfully.

"Well, what was it?" Previn asked impatiently.

"I don't know why I'm talking about my first wife on a night like this. It's disrespectful, mate. I need to forget about her. I do."

Previn felt cheated. He wondered about what sage advice Kurt Cobain could have possibly offered Tout. He thought he'd shift gears. See what else he might learn. "Tell me, how did you come to be involved in all this?"

"Spotted Fay in some poor excuse for a club about two years ago," Tout replied, easing into what sounded like a well-rehearsed story. "Gave her a name. Yeah, the blonde hair made me think Fay Wray. You know, that siren King Kong had a yin for. Why not?" He laughed. "I have an eye for talent. Or should I say, an ear."

"That's very interesting, but what I meant was, how did you hear about her accident? I mean it's not like she called you, is it?"

"Let me explain something, mate. You're not the bloody *National Enquirer*. You're just the fix-it guy."

Tout lifted himself in his chair and set his jaw, staring fiercely at Previn. Up until then, he'd been, at worst, an unpleasant distraction, but Previn was getting the idea that this man was some kind of thug. That a respected, big-league Hollywood player like Richard Barone had brought him in on this was baffling.

Previn couldn't remember ever being part of anything remotely like this. There had been patients he'd seen late at night. Car accident victims, mostly. A few injuries on movie sets. Even a tennis racket into the face early one Sunday morning. But he'd always treated them in a hospital.

Tout evidently decided this hard-edged approach might be counterproductive. As though what had just transpired was but a hiccup, he smiled radiantly and said with simple finality, "Sorry. The answer is, I just happened to stop by."

That was a thoroughly inadequate answer. An evasion. One of many thus far. Previn really had to get another look at Fay, but even after his most cursory inspection, he didn't buy the window story. He could continue to play dumb. That was what everyone wanted. Maybe Barone didn't know the extent of all this. Previn wondered if he should sneak a call to him.

"How long is it before we get there?" Tout asked, staring out the window.

Previn had stopped listening to Tout. He was looking through the rearview mirror again at the limo. "They've stopped."

Previn put the car into reverse, backing it almost one block along the dead-of-night stillness of Wilshire Boulevard. He brought the car to a stop in front of the limo as Rox and the driver both jumped out.

Rox screamed, "I can't deal with this. I won't. I just won't."

The driver was equally hysterical. "Get her out! Get her out! She's gonna wreck my seats. This is my car, man. I own this—"

A bus violently raced past them. The film poster titled *Falling* was stuck to its side. Nick Valentine cascading down from the sky.

Tout ran toward them. "Rox, what? What is it?"

Rox, who had been such a model of composure until then, pointed aggressively at the limo. "Her!"

Keeping his cool, Previn paused beside Tout long enough to notice Rox had blood smeared across her cheek and silk blouse. He opened the passenger door to find Fay on the floor moaning. When he went to her, she shrieked, "Don't touch me, you shit!"

"I'm a doctor. I'm here to—"

As Fay turned to look at him, he saw the paper towels had come off. Her face was ripped up pretty bad and bleeding. There was blood everywhere.

"Fuck you!" she shouted.

The incongruity between this woman's silky, luxurious blonde locks and the savage gashes running across an angelic face was difficult for Previn to absorb. She'd become almost rabid.

"It hurts…I know," Previn said as sympathetically as he could. "Hang in there—"

"Get…get away from—"

"I'm here to help." Previn reached toward her.

"Don't touch me!"

"Shhhh—"

"Where are you taking me?"

Previn saw terror in her eyes. He touched her tenderly. "It's okay." He stepped out and shouted, "I'll ride with her. She's going to Cedars. Now!"

A black Bentley hurtled to a stop not three feet from where Previn stood, scaring him for a moment. While its engine idled like a beast, its headlights blinding him, the driver-side door swung open.

"Richard?" Previn gasped.

Barone didn't bother surveying the situation. He seemed to know. He got right in Previn's face. So close Previn could smell scotch on his breath.

"What's the holdup?"

"We've got to get this girl to a hospital," Previn replied, stepping back, trying to find space to breathe. Where did this man come from? Did he ever sleep? He must have followed them. People like him didn't just materialize in the middle of the night.

"One of the biggest movie stars in the world thinks you killed his mother," Barone said, his voice low without a trace of emotion.

"I thought that was over."

"Over? He wants to sue your ass. Go public. But I keep talking him down. 'Let it go, Jake. Jake, let it…forget that goddamned son-of-a-bitch, Harold Previn!' If you don't wise up Harry, you won't go near another celebrity with a heartbeat ever again."

"You'd play that card?"

"Did you kill her? Did you kill that poor woman? I'm not so sure you didn't. Not sure!" Barone glared at Previn for a long moment before walking back to his car. In stunned disbelief, Previn watched him drive off.

Barone knew he had Previn where he wanted him. If people started whispering he was a mom killer, that they thought he'd killed Jake Blackburn's mom, no matter the merits of the charge, it'd be poison to his standing as a surgeon. Poison to everything he had. If Barone had wanted to remind him of this point, he'd done a pretty damn good job. He'd shaken Previn right to the core.

He'd forgotten Tout and Rox were still standing beside him. Tout broke the silence. "So?"

Previn threw his car keys at him. "Drive the Jag, I'm going with Fay. If we get her to my OR and I don't feel like I can handle it, I'm calling nine-one-one."

If this one night was the price he had to pay for Jake Blackburn's mom, penance to get Barone off his back, so be it. Previn climbed back into the limo and shut off the light switch after sitting down. Maybe in the darkness Fay might fall back to sleep.

He could handle Fay. He knew that. One might say that the best surgeons didn't take reckless chances, but the truth was they did. They were that confident of their abilities. They were like fighter pilots who got an adrenaline rush whenever they tested the limit. So it was with Previn. Although taking some pop star back to his OR at this ungodly hour with massive facial lacerations of dubious origin was not something even he had ever imagined doing. The only part of this he really felt confident about was the medical side of it. He'd get her through. If he could just stick to doctoring, maybe the rest would sort itself. After all, it wasn't ethical to refuse treatment to someone truly in need. A surefire rationalization, but true enough.

Previn looked closely at her, reaching in to feel her neck. Her eyes fluttered open. She was inches from his face as he tried to ascertain her condition.

"You're here," she whispered. "I knew you'd come."

She tried to kiss him. He pulled away, shocked as she slipped into further delirium.

"Sid. Sid. Are you taking my...don't! I don't want." She snapped as if she saw something coming at her, "No!"

Previn took her small hand in his. "Shhh. It's okay."

There had always been something odd about Barone, coming down from his place in the heavens to pull his nuts out of the fire. Up until that fateful afternoon when Barone had driven his black Bentley up Previn's driveway to discuss the autopsy report, Previn had only met him a few times at AU. Barone would drop in on a meeting and even thank him for taking care of their talent. It just had to be Previn's bum luck that the one patient he'd ever lost just happened to be the mother of one of the biggest stars in Hollywood. Barone could not have known that he'd want to call on Previn a mere two weeks later, but in the lexicon of how business is done in Hollywood, he must have thought he was collecting some kind of chit. No good turn goes unpaid. Previn knew this.

Jake Blackburn's mother had been dead and buried for less than a month but the statute of limitations meant he'd have to wait at least a year to be clear of it. Maybe more. He wasn't really sure. At what point, Previn wondered, would he ever be done with her? Done with the whole sorry chapter?

As he held Fay's hand in the darkened cab of the limo, he tried to fathom how he could contain the damage from the death. If Barone, with all the machinery of Hollywood behind him, wanted to destroy his credibility, he certainly could. A scary development. Given Helen's repulsion over what had happened, he knew all too well that this thing had the power to unsettle people deeply. If even his own wife wouldn't stand with him.

The limo finally came to a stop at the rear of Previn's building, a well-lit prewar red brick building with bougainvillea running up its walls. He directed the driver to park. He helped Fay out of the door and onto a gurney he wheeled up beside the limo.

"Need me to do anything?" Tout asked as Previn paused at the door to find his key.

"Stay out of the way. Can you do that?"

Tout raised his arms in the air, as though he were surrendering. "Okay, chief!"

Previn maneuvered the gurney into an annex cramped with medical file cabinets next door to his operating room. Had he been able to take her to an ER, the doctors would've given her a CAT scan right off. This was the one glaring difference between what he had to offer in his operating facility and what most major hospitals had available. He would have liked the medical backup as well. Although in many small towns, doctors treat injured patients without these benefits. Previn kept reminding himself of that.

His first concern was that Fay may have suffered more than the superficial injuries already evident. Another concern was when someone has been hit once, it's not unlikely they've been hit twice, and not always near the other injury. He'd observed Fay, for all her agony, move her neck pain free. While she lay on her back, he probed for fractures. He opened her bloodstained dress to look for any other wounds or bruising. Satisfied that other than a probable broken nose, she didn't appear to have any other fractures, he sought to determine if she'd suffered a brain injury.

With Tout lingering in the background, Previn tried to make light conversation as he worked. "Let me know if anything I do hurts," he said to Fay.

"It all hurts."

"I know. I know. We're going to do something about that but first..." He shined a light in her eyes to assure her pupils reacted and had her follow his finger as he moved it across her line of vision. "Look into the light. That's good. You're a very good patient. Sooner we do this, the sooner we—"

"Don't hurt me."

Previn shot Tout a questioning look. "We're going to put you back together. Get you on your way with a little help from Mother Nature."

"Oh, God."

He palpated her neck, cheeks, and the bones around her eyes, jaw, head, and ribs as he talked.

"Do you think if I asked you a few questions...?"

Fay's body stiffened as he held her head in his hands with what he took to be alarm. The overhead light shined brightly in her eyes, which she could barely open.

"Relax your head. That's it. That's right. What's your real name?"

"Sue."

Shock was his friend. She'd become suddenly lucid. Adrenaline seemed to be carrying her, though it was different for everyone. As her body settled down, the pain from her injuries might overcome her. He had to hurry. It'd be useless trying to talk to her later because an anesthetic would numb the pain and her mind. She was as alert and present as she'd ever be in the next forty-eight hours.

He continued, "The whole name?"

"Plouse."

"How do you spell that?"

"Why are you asking?"

"Standard stuff. I don't know who you are. I mean, I don't even know if you're allergic to anything."

"Give me drugs."

He looked up from the form he'd been filling out. She couldn't have been more than five foot three, much shorter than the women he typically found attractive. But as with many short people, he could tell she had an oversized personality.

"What's your social security number?" he asked.

"I'm dying."

"I need your social security number. And who your usual doctor is."

She didn't have one. But she remembered her social security number.

"You're how old?" Previn asked.

"Nineteen."

"Where are you from?"

"Iowa."

"Nearest relative?"

"My mother. I don't know where my dad is. Why do you—"

"Because we may have to contact her in the event you were to become incapacitated." Previn collected her mother's telephone number then proceeded with his questioning, "You allergic to anything?"

"No. I told you I'm perfectly healthy."

"Any major illnesses?"

"No."

"Bone fractures?"

"Never."

"Have you taken any medication tonight that I should be aware of? That includes narcotics. Coke. Booze. Pot. Anything?"

"All that."

He opened a drawer and pulled out a handful of bandages wet with antiseptic. "This will feel good. The more I dab your face with these—"

"I don't want to feel."

"I know." Previn began by wiping along the edges of her wounds, removing the clotted blood and soothing her pain. "That's better."

Fay shrieked with agony and shoved his hand away violently. "Oh, God. Aaaah—"

She needed heavy anesthesia—no question about it—which he wasn't qualified to administer himself. If they'd been at Cedars, he'd have used an emergency room anesthesiologist, but that wasn't available to him. He looked at his watch. It was almost 2:00 a.m. He hated to call in his staff at that hour. But waiting wasn't an option.

◆◆◆

PREVIN HAD JUST PUT down the phone when Tout and Rox walked into his office.

"I've called in my team," Previn announced. He'd phoned his normal crew. Sara, Brick, and a scrub tech named Raj, who'd all agreed to arrive within the hour. "You never finished telling me, what did Kurt say to you?"

"Kurt? Oh, Kurt. Yeah. He said, stay away from guns."

Previn's jaw dropped. "He said that?"

"Prescient."

They both took a moment. The man only blew his brains out with a shotgun. Previn didn't want to ask how long after he'd said it that the singer had actually killed himself. It seemed indelicate. Wrong. Of course, Tout had dropped his name. He'd done it casually, and Previn wondered if he'd worked with him. He'd heard the same spontaneous, first-name-basis name-dropping round people who'd worked with other stars. Celebrity had become such, everyone felt like they were on a first-name basis with stars, even if they hadn't met them. Though Previn knew stars often went by other names to the people who really knew them. There might even come a time when Fay Wray would become known simply as Susan to her friends.

"How is she?" Tout asked.

For the first time that night, Previn felt a tinge of sensitivity toward Tout. He was sad for the man, but he didn't know quite why. Previn put his hand on Tout's arm. "Her nose is broken."

Tout turned away. His jaw set. Barely able to conceal his annoyance.

"The good news is we can fix that."

Tout raised his voice. "So what's the bad news? Come on. Give it to me."

Previn grabbed the white bronze sculpture of Helen that sat prominently on his black marble desk and handed it to Rox. He'd worked very hard to capture her—call it sentimentality but also artist's pride. He was damned if he was going to remove her from his desk. He still loved Helen, even if she had passed divorce papers across the table that very night like she were passing the butter.

"Hold this, Rox," Previn said.

Rox took the sculpture in her hands. "Who's this?"

"My wife. Look here." Previn gestured to one side of the sculpture's face. "The direction of the lacerations along her left cheek run both with and counter to her lines of tension which—"

"Dot. Dot. Dot. Medical speak."

Previn took Helen's head back from Rox. He set it back down on his desk with a care that seemed misplaced.

"I'm not a miracle worker."

"You've got to make her right, mate. You got that? I don't care what it costs."

◆◆◆

FAY WAS STILL LYING on an examination table wearing the surgical gown Previn had given her. The bloodstained dress he'd tossed into a clear plastic bag and put to one side. Previn checked her pulse as Rox hovered at the door.

Fay sat up. "I don't want my mother to know."

He gently pushed her back down. "Please. Lie down."

"I should call her."

Fay's pain level had skyrocketed. She was clearly on edge. She needed to conserve her strength. "You need to be quiet."

"The police? They called them. They did, didn't they? Are they here?"

Although Previn didn't know where this was all going, it was more than evident that he was up to his ears in something bad. That bloodstained dress of Fay's was evidence and he knew it might be valuable. While talking with Fay, he managed to sneak the bag with her dress off the table into a drawer. When he turned, he met Rox's eyes. He didn't think she'd seen him hide Fay's dress.

Fay sat up again. "Nobody's asked me about—"

He pushed her back down. "Shhh."

Alarmed. "They're not going to do anything!"

"I don't know."

She burst into tears. "I'm scared. You can make it all go away, right? There won't be scars. Tell me my face won't be scarred."

Previn stroked her hair. "Now, now. Let me do my work. Close your eyes."

◆◆◆

THE FIELD OF PLASTIC surgery had its origins in the treatment of battlefield casualties during World War I. The new ability to do facial and body reconstruction was one of the more positive things to come out of a very ugly war. In the years that followed, surgeons found civil applications. Even after suffering burns and lacerations, patients no longer had to look like monsters. However, the science had its limits. Rarely did people suffer grievous injury and not come out of it altered. One of Previn's greatest struggles was getting patients and their partners to accept sometimes dramatic, but not always disagreeable, changes in appearance.

Fay's lacerations were in all the wrong places and at the wrong angles. Indeed, they were brutal. He couldn't imagine how a window could have torn Fay Wray up to this extent. And what hotel window could it have been? She wouldn't have asked about the police if it had been a mere accident.

Previn had been lied to. Yet there was something electrifying about being called out so late at night to tend to some beautiful victim. Fascinated and compelled, good sense no longer ruled. Though he wasn't a fool. He knew the Hippocratic Oath afforded him a good deal of cover. And if he had to, he'd play that card.

♦♦♦

BRICK RIPPED OFF HIS motorcycle helmet as he rounded the corner in the hallway outside Previn's office, flipping through the patient clipboard. Walking and talking his way to Previn. He'd been drinking.

"Midnight office party! Love it. About time. Gives a whole new meaning to last call." Brick seemed pretty engrossed in the history and physical Previn had prepared because he suddenly blurted, "What the fuck is this?"

Previn knew there would be trouble. He'd known this man for far too long and Brick was never one to pull a punch. In that light, the scar on Brick's forehead from a childhood toboggan accident in Maine seemed particularly pronounced. They'd talked about it. Brick didn't want Previn to correct it. Brick was the rugged type and he was right to leave it as it was. It gave him a look.

"It's cool," Previn said, trying to be offhand.

"What? Who is this?"

"Susan Plouse."

"I can read. Who is she?"

"Fay Wray."

"*My baby loves me and he shows me how,*" Brick sang, delivering a lively rendition of Fay's hit song as he continued reading. "*My baby—*" He dramatically let the clipboard fall to the floor. "Drugs?"

Previn knelt down to pick up the clipboard. "It'll be okay."

"Okay? Fay Wray? You fuckin' kidding me? This is celebrity shit. It's never, ever going to be okay. Fay Wray? Please!"

"Brick."

"She has a seizure and dies. That okay? I'm to put her under. I don't know what the fuck's in her? All she's good for is a lawsuit.

Ever hear of Dr. Conrad Murray? You get taken down for shit like this. This is Hollywood Michael Jackson shit. Drugs. Drugs. Drugs!"

"You're going to give yourself an aneurysm."

"Drugs, Harry?"

"It won't—"

"They'll sue our asses. Sue me. Take my house. My sports car. The Ninja. My Ninja!"

As if Previn didn't know this. Hadn't he tried to make this very point with Tout an hour before? Previn could feel the color drain from his face as the gravity of it all, the whole misbegotten evening, caught up with him. He felt a shortness of breath. Was he about to have a heart attack? He turned to face the wall, bracing himself against it.

"You okay? What's up?" Brick asked.

When Previn turned back to Brick, the strain of the night must have registered on his face.

"You need a vacation," Brick said.

"I'm okay."

"No. You're not! Get on a freakin' plane for Cabo. Now. We'll send that pop tart to a hospital and you to LAX."

"I can't."

"Get on a plane, dude. You're done here."

"Brick, you know I may have killed Blackburn's mother."

"Blackburn is Helen's fault! You weren't of sound mind."

He had come to the surgery an emotional wreck. Brick was right. He remembered how he'd decided in the moment to add stomach lipo to the procedure. He was angry, not thinking. He'd had such a damn, wretched night with Helen.

He remembered tearing up during the surgery as he contemplated his plight. He was angry with Helen. He had looked down at Blackburn's inert body through his tears. He couldn't even cut straight. He made more of a show of it by actually doing a jig to the music that was playing, trying to cover for himself. It may have been that spit-in-the-face-of-misfortune bravado that prompted him to add the extra procedure. He'd never know if that was what had pushed her over the edge. Brick seemed to think it had.

Previn brought his hands to his face. The memory of it all was too distressing. "Oh God."

"It's done."

"It wasn't Helen. It was me. I added that procedure. Thought… I don't know what I thought. And now I have to live with it. I *live* with it."

"It's okay."

"It's not okay! They know I killed her. Jake Blackburn thinks it. And Fay's people are…Blackburn's people."

"Blackmail? Motherfucking blackmail. Do you know what you're saying? One bad turn doesn't have to lead to another. This is insane."

"It *was* a bad turn."

"You're fuckin' tellin' me? I was there. I held your hand when the call came that they'd found her dead in her house. I've lived this. That's what I'm telling you. Let's call an ambulance. Get this pop tart out of here."

"We've got to attend to this woman."

"Like hell I do!"

Brick started to walk off.

"Brick. Don't do this."

"This is crazy on so many levels. Don't get me started."

"I need you."

◆◆◆

MINUTES LATER, BRICK ADMINISTERED the general anesthetic.

Dreadlocks pushed up in a hairnet, Raj turned on the stereo. A frustrated musician, Raj was always synching the tunes from his iPad into the surgery. Any other time Previn might have relished the snide humor of Raj starting them off with "Touch Me in the Morning" as Previn readied to cut into the patient, but the only thing cutting was Roberta Flack emoting about loss. Why were love songs always sad?

The next track brought them back to Raj's regular playlist, the latest in British synch pop. The others seemed to welcome the lift the music gave them at that early hour of the morning.

Previn, Brick, Raj, and Sara, all in green surgical garb, put their latex gloves on and prepared the theater for the operation. Fay was out cold on the table. Her shoulders, bare. A white drape covered her chest area. There were four jagged cuts running roughly parallel along her right cheek. Also a pronounced hole where the impact had occurred.

Sara took five digital pictures of the injury, each punctuated with a *click* and a flash.

Raj began the work of cleaning her wounds. He washed her face, then took a brush to it and scrubbed the wound until it was almost raw. They cleaned it up, and then Sara took several more digital pictures of the injury.

"One thing about this gig," Raj said, as he irrigated her wounds. "I've met more pop stars than if I'd worked at the Forum. Her stuff though, soft porn."

"You can dance to it," Sara said. "I like it."

"Too Hello Kitty for my blood."

Previn saw Tout and Rox in the hall through the window of the door to the surgery. Tout was pacing about as Rox watched him uneasily. Previn was stunned to see him suddenly grab her and kiss her desperately. He let Rox go and walked from view.

Sara turned to Previn. "Thought you had a date tonight, Harry. Not burning the midnight oil with us all."

"Dude! You had a date?" Brick said.

"Dinner with Hell," Sara blurted. "Sorry. Helen."

"But that's over," Raj said.

"It was," Sara replied.

"Then why?" Raj asked.

Sara couldn't help herself. "Because it's never over till it's over. Don't you know that, dummy?"

"People. We've got a patient on the table," Previn said as he stared down at Fay.

"Oh, dear. That bad?" Sara asked.

"Can we…?"

"I'm sorry," Sara said.

They were all friends. They all knew about each other's lives. And they all knew about Helen. But this didn't mean he was in the mood to share his disappointment.

"I can't talk about that. Do her. Think. I can't think!" He continued to study Fay as she lay on the operating table, a breathing tube jammed in her mouth, her body rising and falling with her breath. "Kill the music!"

"No soundtrack!" Raj shrieked. "Come on, Harry. It's after one a.m."

"Helen will come round, Harry. She's a good girl," Sara said.

"I don't want to talk about it, okay? Now let's focus, people. People, focus."

The music was off. Raj placed a plastic zip bag containing two shards of green glass on a metal tray. Previn considered them for a moment. As he'd suspected all along, these fragments were not from a window, not at all. He pocketed the bag, an action that didn't go unnoticed by Sara. But what else could he do? He knew those fragments could be important.

His thoughts went to Barone. That man must have known. He'd gone nuclear, bringing up Jake Blackburn's mother. It was nothing short of extortion. Previn had thought Barone had done him a favor, but now he knew better. Nothing in life is free. Everything has its price.

The slow up-and-down rhythm of Fay's chest filling with oxygen was a reminder he was about to operate on a living being. Since his early training, he'd become increasingly removed from that fact. He'd long since forgotten the apprehension he'd felt making his first incision, when he couldn't help but fear he might hurt the patient. Then it'd taken three strokes to do what should have taken one.

An image he carried with him into surgery was that of the Teatro Anatomico in Bologna, the oldest operating theater in the world. Forget the Old Globe. The Teatro Anatomico was alive with true drama. Everything seemed to radiate from the dissection table around which were rows of wooden benches and statuary of the greats, including Hippocrates. As he stood in that gallery, he realized there is always an audience. Surgery *is* theater. It was an idea that appealed to him. In that moment, as he looked down at Fay's face, the audience didn't seem to be there anymore. He felt very alone.

Sara passed him a pair of scissors, and he cut away some loose tissue, as dead tissue could never heal.

"I could give a shit about the marriage," Previn said finally. "It's over."

The surgery stopped. The others stared at Previn.

"Harry, shut up!" Sara said.

He stared down at Fay's facial wounds. She'd been lucky. No nerves had been cut, as that might have made her face droop. Nor had any major arteries been severed, though there was plenty of bleeding to minimize. There was also one rather pronounced hole where the impact must have occurred. Her being struck more than once could not be ruled out.

They put a drape over her face to restore it to its natural position, and then began the work of sewing the wound back together. Previn sewed underneath first, to anchor the laceration, then sewed the skin shut. They washed it again and applied Polysporin vasotrate ointment.

◆◆◆

STILL WEARING HIS SURGICAL garb, Previn found Tout and Rox both asleep in the waiting room, her head against his shoulder. With the lights off, the reflections in the windows made it a virtual house of mirrors.

Previn flicked on a lamp. They woke.

"She'll need further reconstructive work."

"Bottom line, mate."

Sleeping in the waiting room had left Tout and Rox looking disheveled. Tout had a very grim five-o'clock shadow coming on. He'd gone from suave to just plain mean looking.

"Bottom line? This stinks of assault and battery." Rox and Tout looked at each other. "We found glass in her face. As in wine bottle."

"An accident," Tout replied. "All you need to know."

"Bullshit! You're asking me to commit a felony. I have a legal responsibility here."

"To do what?"

"To report this to the police."

"Where's your integrity?"

Previn did a double take. "What?"

"I'm going to call Barone. Why should I waste my time with—?"

"Call him!"

"No!" Rox crossed in front of Tout to address Previn. "We're all wiped. We know you're stressed."

"You people lied to me and were trying to involve me in a crime. I'm not a mob doc," Previn insisted, as much because he needed to hear himself say it. As he did, the reality of it all became that much more apparent. What respected surgeon would go along with this? Hadn't he become a mob doc already?

"We know that," Rox said, addressing Previn's reflection in the window.

"Of course we do," Tout conceded to Previn's image. "Try to understand our position."

If it was a felony not to report a crime, what was it to cover one up? To surgically make it go away to protect the assailan? Had that ever been done?

It was late. Previn felt he must be tripping. This couldn't be what had been asked of him. It certainly wasn't what they were telling him, but not much of what they'd told him to that point had been the truth. In any case, minimum, it was a felony not to report treating someone brought to him with a wound from what had to have been a violent assault.

Previn stared back at their reflection. "I'm thinking about Fay."

Tout turned away from Previn's reflection. Got right in his face. "And we're not? What are you saying about us? I've been here all night. Shielded her from a PR nightmare. Brought in the best surgeon I could find. You think you're here to help her. That woman in there is Cinderella."

Tout grabbed a copy of *Harper's Bazaar* from the coffee table. Fay Wray owned the cover. The cover lines read, "Fay Wray. The Face of Spring."

"See this? Cinderella. And you're killing her. Killing the dream."

"I'm telling you about my legal and ethical responsibilities."

"Legal? Bugger that! What's legal? To splash her face, that bloodied face, all over *Gawker* and *TMZ* and *The Smoking Gun…*" Tout threw the magazine at Previn. "And *Harper's Bazaar*, for fuck's sake!"

Previn thought about Fay lying there in the recovery room, still semiconscious, and bandaged with an IV in her arm.

"You have any idea how this is going to impact? Do you?" Tout barked.

Previn didn't respond.

"They're going to present this as some seedy tale of degeneracy, violence, and drugs. People won't forgive that. It'll destroy her. And why? Because you feel a responsibility to take this to the cops."

"I know you're a good man," Rox said, addressing his reflection.

"I'm not a good man. And I certainly don't feel like one."

"You don't want to hurt this girl. She's got a pretty good thing going and she didn't harm anyone."

Previn exhaled heavily. The cuts to Fay's face were difficult to pass off as anything but a vicious assault. He didn't like it. Didn't like having to have this conversation. At this hour. With this man. About this situation. And of course, Barone hovered.

He was damned no matter what he decided.

"I don't have to file immediately," Previn said at last.

♦♦♦

THE NIGHT WAS NOT over. Heavily sedated, Fay was loaded back into the limo and taken to Tout's home. Previn followed it as it wielded its way along Wilshire Boulevard and up Vermont through the still-sleeping city to Los Feliz. A leafy enclave with palatial old homes from the twenties and thirties.

They stopped in front of an old wrought-iron gate. Tout got out of the limo to open it. They drove into a pitch-dark motor court. A shadowy home loomed in front of the car. Tout directed the limo to a service entrance at the side of the house. The kitchen light lit up the black car as Previn and Rox helped Fay inside, leading her through the kitchen and down a hallway into the maid's room. Still in her surgical gown, Fay was placed on a single bed that seemed almost too small.

After Previn instructed Rox in how to care for Fay while she recovered, he placed another blanket over Fay. She looked up at him and in a weak voice asked, "Am I okay? Am I gonna be okay?"

"You need to rest."

"My face. You repaired my face, right?"

She seemed rightfully agitated about her looks. It was normal. But in this case he really felt constrained from saying too much. She was the patient. However, stress was not good for healing. And there was something else: Tout was running the show, not him. While Previn felt for Fay as he would any patient in her predicament, he was keenly aware of a hierarchy.

"Shhh. You're good. It's all good." He turned to Tout. "I've told Rox how to tend to her. I'll have my nurse check in on her tomorrow."

"Let me explain something, mate," Tout said. "I only deal with the top people. I don't do subordinates, you understand?"

The room was so oppressively small, Previn found himself having to engage Tout over Fay, who was listening. He looked back at her twice as he replied, his voice but a whisper. "My RN is not a subordinate. She's the ideal person to care for a post-op like Fay. This is what nurses do."

"You're not pawning her off on a nurse."

"Pawning her?"

"Yeah. Pawning."

Previn looked down at Fay who seemed aware of their conversation. There was something unseemly about virtually every aspect of what had transpired that night. But to accuse him of "pawning her off" on someone else right in front of Fay was beyond the pale. "Can we discuss this outside?"

"No. It's settled."

Previn took a moment to gather himself. "Ever hear of someone named Florence Nightingale?"

"Good try, mate, but I'm not having it. Another thing. I won't have your associates trouncing through here, spouting off about all this."

Previn got the distinct feeling that this had nothing to do with the level of care and everything to do with keeping Fay's condition secret. He wanted to limit the people who were exposed to her, but the fact was, and Previn didn't quite want to admit it, there was a reason why nurses attended to patients and not doctors. He hadn't ever had to give this level of bedside care. It wasn't done. It was like recruiting a general to storm a machine gun emplacement.

The best tact seemed to be his dealing with the privacy issue rather than raise alarms that somehow he wasn't up to caring for Fay.

"Nurses always respect their client's privacy, it's what they do. You think Fay is the first celebrity client to need private care?"

"I don't think you understand. You're the only person who I will allow to go near Fay."

"That's crazy! I don't do post-op at home—"

"You do now!"

Tout left him standing there. Rox shrugged.

Previn hadn't had such a long day since he did his residency at Cedars. At one point, he had to put in a thirty-six-hour shift. He could handle it. Maybe that's why they put doctors through those marathons. But he hadn't been trained to handle divorce. He was still gutted about Helen. It was such a temptation to wallow in it and Fay had prevented him from doing so. As if fate had intervened to deny Helen from hurting him further.

Rox went down the hall and when she returned, she handed him a CD. "If you'd like to get to know her."

He took it. "Fay Wray?"

"She has her fans."

◆◆◆

PREVIN ARRIVED HOME AS the sun was coming up.

There was no one to greet him. At one end of the living room sat the lonely white grand piano. He walked on to the family room. The bar was a built in. No taking that away. He poured himself a glass of cabernet. Coffee seemed wrong, given all that had passed. He put the CD in the stereo. Pressed play.

Fay's strong vocals came forth though a sugar rush of teenage nonsense. Still, there was something about her powerful voice that grabbed him, wouldn't let him go.

He emptied his pockets onto the counter. The contents included the divorce papers and the bag containing the bits of broken glass.

His eyes went to the freeze frame of her CD cover on his flat screen. He studied Fay's face, her unbroken beauty. Though no more risqué than a shot of Fay baring her shoulders, the CD cover was cropped to suggest she was nude. Set against a sky-blue field, her face had an immediacy and warmth he hadn't seen till then. She looked so buoyant, idealistic, and young. The central focus of the photo was her big green eyes, which were full of wonderment. He couldn't help but juxtapose them with the look she'd given him in the recovery room through the opening in her bandage. The same eyes, but bloodshot and barely open.

The title of the CD took its title from her hit song, "Not Now, Later."

Previn held his thumb out so that it covered the part of her face that had been ravaged. Took it away. Then put it back. If only it were as simple to erase an injury as it was for him to place his thumb over the damage. If only it were so easy to hide a crime from view.

7

HELEN WOKE ON THE floor of Guy's living room in the wee hours of the night with the phone still in her hand.

An intense pang of hunger prompted her to recall that she'd walked out on Harry before they'd even ordered dinner. Next time she'd hold off on passing the divorce envelope until at least dessert. After throwing some grilled veggies onto a bed of quinoa, she felt a sudden impulse to flee Guy's house.

Her car pulled up to the dark alley behind her art studio in Venice Beach. She walked up five iron steps and opened the heavy industrial grade door. Through the skylight, the moon cast a glow. She walked in without turning on the powerful overheads. She stopped in the middle of the room and took it all in as if for the first time. Since she'd started the latest round of fertility treatments, she'd been unable to endure even paint fumes. Her reaction had been so bad, the last time she'd ventured in, she'd run onto the steps to wretch. As she inhaled, she was surprised to find that the smell that had made her so ill and put her off her art seemed almost fragrant now.

She opened a can of paint. It smelled like paint.

The months of non-creativity had left her feeling moribund. What was life if she had nothing to express?

She opened the skylight and all the windows then spread a six-foot-by-eight-foot piece of canvas on the paint-splattered concrete floor. Painting took her out of the present and to a calm place where all her troubles fell away. Doing art was akin to meditation.

She put four large brushes into her hand, dipping them in different colors, and began the process of discovering her subject. She was an intuitive artist who worked in euphoric waves of inspiration. She began with a chair. Not her best effort, but actually intriguing in its lack of symmetry. That gave her a benchmark that she decided to follow. Everything would be off-kilter just like she felt. If it seemed as if her whole world had tipped on its side so she might slide right off, she'd paint that. The colors she chose were hothouse. Lurid pinks and greens and blues. No black. She wanted to avoid that starkest of colors.

For the first time in months, she was free. She painted through the night and into the day without eating anything but some coconut milk ice cream she found in the fridge. Her head felt light and airy. The sensation of finally creating was such that she was reluctant to stop for a moment because maybe she'd lose it again.

Though she was always described as a still-life painter, she had never seen it that way. She saw people in her interiors even though they weren't literally present. It was the difference between inanimate and animate objects. Her paintings throbbed with life. There had come a point in art school when she'd started to feel it was too easy to put people in her interiors, that it was much more interesting to find ways to reveal them without actually showing them. The furthest she'd ever gone in placing someone in her work was a woman's reflection in a window. A woman who she felt at the time was going after Harry.

The popular wisdom was that she was supposed to pick up the brush after she left Harry. Even Harry had the nerve to suggest as much at their dinner. "Have you been painting?" he'd asked.

"Do you know anything about me?" she'd shrieked at him. "Anything that's been going on with me? How could you be so…?"

Up until then, she had actually wondered if she had it in her to hand him the divorce papers. Harry was being Harry. It felt almost like they were off the clock. No pressure. She was just getting comfortable. Enjoying the romantic charm of the Chateau. He'd ordered Bollinger.

But Harry might just as well have asked how she was liking her vacation. Of course, she couldn't paint. It felt as though he were so self-absorbed he didn't have the faintest idea who she was. What she'd just been through in losing the baby and what seemed to be any chance of one, ever. With that one question, he'd brought back her anger and disconnection. She had all but tossed the divorce papers at him.

She so wished she'd found some other moment than the one in which he'd gotten her dander up. If she was going to go out, she wanted to be the classy one. But that was not to be. He'd denied her that, too.

As she swept her paintbrush across the canvas so that the blue and the red became purple, she realized painting was all she had left. She didn't have children. She didn't have a husband anymore. She didn't even have a house. No. Her paintings were her children.

The thought made her smile.

8

"THAT THING CALLED THE court of public opinion," Ty Fanning, Previn's attorney, continued. "You can't discount it."

"Yeah. Yeah. Yeah."

"The minute you start talking about the death of the mother of someone famous, you're fucked. It's not about the law, it's about people. People think things. You hope they understand the facts, but that's not your problem."

Previn had called Fanning hours after operating on Fay Wray. He didn't like the way Barone had suggested that somehow he had Blackburn's death hanging over him, not the least of which because he now felt he had Fay Wray hanging over him, too.

Ty Fanning had been his attorney for years, which meant they'd known each other socially because Previn kept Ty's wife looking like the day Ty met her. Margaret Fanning had invited Previn and Helen to their house in Malibu many times. Ty was known for easing countless celebrities through the legal system. He was often associated with Charlie Sheen, though he'd never actually represented him. Previn thought he'd represented the TV network, but it may have been one of his TV producers. Fanning had confided in Previn that his work really was simple family law, but somehow he'd "fallen for the whore I call Hollywood."

His office was in a Santa Monica high-rise overlooking the ocean. His hair was bleach blond. He was trim and ruddy looking.

Pictures of him surfing some of the most exotic beaches filled his office. Everywhere from Costa Rica to Australia.

Seated beside Previn on his leather sofa, Fanning said, "If a Hollywood player like Richard Barone offered to finesse things with his client—"

"It's blackmail."

Fanning nodded thoughtfully. "Such a big word."

"Ty, you weren't there. You should have heard him. And now I feel like I've dug myself a deeper hole, having done Fay all night."

Fanning tapped Previn on the thigh. "That's another matter, Harry."

"It's the only matter. I got to go over there in a few. They want me to keep attending to her."

"Wouldn't you want to, as her doctor?"

Fanning made it all seem so reasonable, but he hadn't had to talk to Johnny Tout at 6:00 a.m. about his trying to pawn Fay off on a nurse.

"Not if a crime was committed."

Ty grabbed Previn's arm to silence him. "As your attorney I have to advise you, you don't know anything about that."

"If this isn't a questionable situation, then what is? And Barone knows what's going on. I'm not an idiot. It stinks!"

"You were asking me if Jake Blackburn has a case."

"I was."

Fanning stood up and walked over to the window, where he looked out for a long moment. With his chest busting out of his blue cotton shirt and the ocean set behind him, he looked like he could star in the surf film *The Endless Summer*. Hard to imagine this man could trade the beach for the courtroom, but his practice earned him his freedom.

Fanning turned back to Previn. "The answer is, yes and no. What Barone has given you is a pretty good reading of your predicament. This is not a legal case. It's a PR disaster. If this gentleman is offering to keep it from—"

"It was more than an offer."

"You remember Kanye West's mom?"

"That was a while ago."

"That situation was not unlike your own."

"Oh, come on."

"You don't think so? That plastic surgeon operated on Kanye West's mother and a few days later, she died. I wouldn't say it's at all clear that…the inquest absolved him, sure. But the publicity killed his practice, and ultimately the publicity was irreparably damaging to his reputation."

"Dr. Jan Adams. I remember him. Was like one of the most educated surgeons you'll ever meet, and a character!"

"Dude, he used to be on *Oprah*. He was a big deal."

"Don't think there wasn't a lot of jealousy because of that, but what surgeon walks off the set of *Larry King Live*? I remember it like it was yesterday. It's industry lore. He wasn't on for more than a minute. Unclips his mike. Walks off. Larry's left there with an empty chair. Never seen anything like it."

"And you don't want that to be you." Fanning clutched the back of his black leather chair and leaned in toward Previn like he were pressing his case at trial. "Great to have celebrity clients because you bask in their reflected glory, but it's Icarus, baby. You fly too close to the sun, you get burned. Remember that."

The longest eighteen inches are between the heart and the mind. That's what Previn had been told in med school. Didn't matter about the medical basis for anything, feelings were often in conflict with wisdom. His patients felt they needed the surgery even when they knew it was too much. He always had to pull patients back from the brink.

But with Blackburn, he'd gone the other way. He'd risked one more procedure. He'd told her that they could come back later for that. Case closed. Then he'd gone and done it anyway.

Morbidity was always a possibility whenever he operated. Previn knew that there was that risk factor. And yet it was never really discussed. Not properly. It was buried in the fine print, of course. There were papers he had patients sign in which death was mentioned. Yet he never told patients they may not actually survive or that they could even die thirty days after surgery. He spoke about what miracles he could work on their looks. He gave hope. Like almost any surgeon out there, he wasn't one to bring talk of death into it.

He typically prescribed anticoagulants after surgery because blood clots were one of the most common risk factors. And sometimes the body didn't react well to the drugs. Cutting into the body, and then attempting to medicate for pain and for varying complications from the stress of it, were all variables. The anesthesia was also one. Sometimes patients reacted badly to it, though such a reaction seemed improbable since Blackburn had regained her composure prior to her discharge.

Blackburn's body was compromised only to the extent she was unable to endure the surgical load. That seemed to be the only answer. The autopsy hadn't shown a pulmonary condition. Hadn't found cancer. Or disease. She didn't have any of the variety of risk factors that he'd have looked for in the history and physical. Nothing. And the autopsy hadn't found anything either. But there was that one, the one that was the most insidious and unpredictable of them all. Age. It was the one thing that made patients need surgery, and yet it was also the one factor that argued against it. Better to operate less as one got older. Yet as his patients aged, they wanted more work done. Of course they did. At some point, one of them wasn't going to come through alive. It was simply the law of numbers. Yet he knew damn well he hadn't helped her prognosis by adding a procedure he'd counseled against including. What had he been thinking? What had possessed him that morning to go for it?

All he could say in his defense was that he hadn't advised that she go home within twenty-four hours of surgery, though it was not unusual among celebrity clients. They could afford at-home care.

However, if Blackburn had gone to a recovery center, she'd be alive. That he knew as sure as day. But who wanted to hear that?

"What's your personal situation?" Fanning asked.

"I'm getting a divorce."

"Jesus, Harry! Helen? No. I'm sorry."

"It's the shits."

Fanning took a seat beside Previn again. "What I was getting at is how are you set financially?"

"The house is mortgaged up to the…everything's mortgaged. But Helen's not looking for much, I don't think."

"That's the least of it, Harry. If it gets out that some questionable choices led to Simone Blackburn's death, day one, you lose fifty percent of your client base."

Previn didn't need Fanning to do the math. He didn't have a rainy-day fund. He was hocked to the hilt and even a 30-percent falloff in his business would cause his practice and his home to come tumbling down like a house of cards. It wasn't supposed to happen. He was supposed to keep building his practice and his home was supposed to appreciate, but that assumed he'd bought well. He'd bought at the top of the market and the house was only now hitting an appraisal that was even close to what he'd paid for it.

What Fanning didn't seem to get, though, was that no one would benefit from filing a wrongful death suit. Why would Jake Blackburn expose the memory of his dead mother to all that?

"But if you say the case against me isn't so strong…"

"You keep coming back to that. I keep telling you, Harry, the court of public opinion is cruel. By the time the inquest came back, that surgeon who operated on Kanye West's mother was cooked. He was already so associated with her death, he might as well have strangled the woman."

"Christ!"

"The good news is you have Richard Barone in your corner."

"That's what worries me."

9

PREVIN WALKED UP THE stairs and through an open door into an industrial space with a high-vaulted wooden ceiling and bare concrete floors and walls. It had been used to store drilling equipment back when Venice Beach was an oil field. Now the building was Helen's art studio. Other than a workbench and a ratty sofa, the space was stark. She'd stacked several dozen completed paintings against the far wall. In the middle of the paint-splattered floor lay one large outstretched canvas. As was her way, she was literally on her hands and knees with her paint can and brush on top of the canvas itself. She'd taken to laying her work on the floor and getting into it, as it were, like the great German postwar painter Georg Baselitz, though he'd been inspired in turn by Jackson Pollack who painted the same way.

Helen was lost in her painting. Her bare arms and trousers were both smeared with paint and seemed to make her blend into the canvas. Her red flaming hair made her look wild.

After taking a truckload of fertility drugs and hormones, Helen had become blocked creatively. It would have done in anyone. The galleries didn't understand, and she didn't explain. What surprised Previn today was to find her up to her elbows in paint having only asked him for a divorce the day before, as though it had finally gotten her over the miscarriage. Did she feel that liberated?

They'd wanted kids. Though wanting and having were two different things. It'd gotten harder heading into their last disappointment. Thing was, being a surgeon didn't make him a fertility specialist. And it didn't improve his sperm. He could study the medical books as much as he wanted. Hadn't helped.

The one pregnancy that really took, they'd miscarried after five months. A girl.

Only as he stood there watching her paint did he realize that in the eighteen months following that loss, he'd never come down to visit her at the studio. Could that really be true? He tried to recall the last time he'd been there and it must have been several years at least. He reckoned that Venice Beach was simply too much out of his way. After all, it wasn't like he didn't have his own art to labor over. And of course, there was his medical practice, something that was all consuming. He'd actually become busier and seemingly more productive since the miscarriage. Funny how they differed in that. He wondered if perhaps she'd come to think his interest in her had dwindled.

On the other hand, she was the star artist. He had no problem with that. He'd even encouraged her to hang her work around the house, which she had extensively. Not surprisingly, after she took her paintings down when she moved out, he felt her absence that much more.

When she finally looked up, Helen seemed startled to see Previn by the door holding a bouquet. He walked up to her and put it in her hand.

"What are these?" she asked.

"Roses."

"I ask for a divorce, you bring red roses?"

"It's counterintuitive."

"Very!"

Up until that moment, he couldn't see the painting. He was surprised she'd chosen their house as the subject. It'd been his fear that she'd already moved on. But evidently, not so much. "Huh. The way it was. It's as if we're still living together."

She'd heard him. She knew that she'd been caught. He saw it in her eyes. She stepped off the canvas with the bouquet in hand. "What am I going to do with these?"

The still life was classic Helen Burke. She'd captured the living room down to the slightest detail but had given it a chill air. It was a curious bit of nostalgia, which gave him hope. He pointed at the painting. "Put them in a vase on the white piano."

He watched her look down at the piano she'd painted, which seemed to vibrate like a Van Gogh, and then smelled the bouquet. Seeing her inhale gave him hope.

He waited.

"Oh, I'm sorry. My vase is too small."

She was playing with him. The fun he treasured in Helen was still there, flickering like a dim light. It's why he'd come. He smiled. "You could paint a larger one."

"You and me, Harry, not going to happen."

He studied her face, trying to understand. "Then why are you making paintings of our house like it was before you moved out?"

"Because I'm living in the past, okay? But it's still the past."

He'd never believed that she could actually leave him. That was why he'd come with the roses. He wasn't a masochist. Or so he had to remind himself. "If we were done, you wouldn't be recreating our house."

She shook her head as she fought back a smile. "Paint what you know."

"At least you've gotten past calling me a killer."

"A woman died."

He felt the blood rush to his head. "After I spent the whole night tangling with you, yeah! Is there a surgeon in America who could have held it together after the grief you put me through?"

She walked around in a circle, shaking her head.

"Forget I said that." Even to his own ear, his accusation sounded discordant and wrong. Blame it on his having not slept the night before. "I didn't come here to argue with you. I don't know what happened to Simone Blackburn. She died. And I'm really upset about it, not least of which because my wife who I love more than anything called me a murderer the other day and now she wants a divorce."

"Wait. You're saying you operated on her the morning of our fight?"

He waved it off. "The beginning of a long string of bad shit."

"So her dying's my fault?" she said.

He looked over at the bouquet regretfully.

Somehow, it had been easier to accuse her of murder than it was to admit that she'd broken his heart. "Forget it."

10

THE NEXT DAY, A Saturday, Helen found herself seated on a park bench staring at her friend's three-year-old twin girls, who were going up and down on a seesaw. She was enjoying them almost as much as they were enjoying the playground.

"What are you thinking?" Larisa asked.

"How to steal your children."

Larisa laughed.

"I'm not kidding."

"Wait till they wake you in the middle of the most wonderful dream so you can help them crap. That's what I did last night. And hello, when it's two, it's double the trouble."

"I think you should go freshen yourself up so I can pack 'em both into my car and head for the border. I love your kids. Just love them to bits."

Helen had known Larisa since studying art at UC Santa Barbara. It had always seemed like Larisa would be the one who succeeded at it, but after struggling for a while, she shocked the world and gave it up to teach art to second graders at a fancy private school. Some people just seem like they're on a path to motherhood. Taking the job at the school was a sure sign. It hit Helen that she couldn't be further from such a path. That perhaps she'd never convincingly been on it.

"Are you okay?" Larisa asked.

"I'm getting a divorce."

Larisa's jaw dropped. "Did Harry leave you?"

"No."

"What's going on, Helen? You guys were such a cute couple." They both stared at the kids. "Don't tell me he was cheating on you!"

Helen turned to Larisa who looked every bit like a Cabbage Patch doll with her golden hair in pigtails and rosy complexion. Larisa had cultivated this look in art school as though she were herself some kind of pop art project, though pregnancy and motherhood had definitely aged her.

It suddenly occurred to Helen that Larisa had introduced her to Jonathan Gold. She probably wouldn't have remembered were it not for her having just discovered his painting in Guy's closet. She knew Larisa had had an affair with Jonathan, too. In those days, everyone was sleeping with everyone else. It seemed absolutely normal. Maybe in someone else's closet somewhere there was a Jonathan Gold of Larisa. Seemed like that was the way of things.

"He doesn't know me, which is to say I don't know him," Helen said. "And we were married for years!"

"How is that possible?"

"The fertility process failed. Again."

Larisa grabbed Helen's hand. "Oh, I'm sorry. I was afraid to ask."

As if they were waiting for their cue, the two girls ran over to keep their mother from getting too focused on her friend's difficulties.

"Mommy! Mommy!"

"Yes."

"Can we do the swing?"

"I need a moment with—"

"Now!" one of them wailed.

Larisa turned to Helen. She looked genuinely annoyed at the interruption only seconds after Helen had dropped the D word.

"I'll push them," Helen said.

They walked over to the swings and pushed the girls as they continued to talk. Helen brought her up to speed.

"Well, how are you going to start a family if you and Harry—?"

"Do I know?"

"But—"

"It wasn't happening. That's a sign. I'm exhausted, Larisa. I can't keep going back to the well with this man. His head isn't in it."

Larisa dug through her bag and gave her girls juices and a small box of cookies. While the girls went running over to the sandbox, Helen and Larisa resumed their seats on the park bench.

"I haven't had such an easy time," Larisa conceded, raising her voice to compete with a motorcycle speeding along Beverly Glenn. "It's hard having kids and being romantic. I feel old. I know Danny thinks I look like a hag. Can't imagine fertility treatments could have been easy on your marriage either."

Helen sighed. Larisa would never admit she'd done IVF herself. But having become something of an expert herself, Helen knew she had. She remembered Larisa gaining weight and behaving erratically, and then suddenly she was telling everyone, miracle of miracles, she was pregnant with twins. The probability of twins was very low, but not with IVF.

"Do you remember Jonathan Gold?"

Larisa stared at her sardonically.

"Well, of course you do."

"Those were the days," Larisa said with a naughty laugh. "Why are you bringing him up? He finally get arrested for statutory rape?"

"Guy Hennessy put me up at his place, and he has the painting Jonathan made of me in his closet."

"In his where?"

"Closet. His bedroom closet!"

Larisa's jaw dropped and she dramatically grabbed Helen's shoulder. "Girl, you have a much more interesting life than I ever could have imagined. How did it get there?"

"Just what I was wondering."

She dropped her jaw a second time as if with a shocking epiphany. "Are you fucking Guy? Is that why you left Harry?"

"No!"

Larisa jumped up and down in her seat. "You are! You so are."

"He isn't even in town. You think I'd be staying at his place if he were?"

"I wish someone had a nude of me hanging in their closet. Hanging anywhere. Aren't you flattered?"

"Are you for real? My whole life has come apart."

Larisa turned away as if to collect her thoughts. "I wanted to ask. You being around it and all. Do you think my eyes are okay?"

She had bags under her eyes, which were all the more pronounced because her blue eyes were so striking. "They're bloodshot."

"Don't make me have to spell this out. Do I need surgery?"

"Larisa!"

"I know. I know. I'm like Mrs. Whole Foods Market, but I don't remember the last time I had a good night's sleep and I feel like a dishrag. No. My face looks like one. I'm thinking about going full pup. Why not?"

Helen stared at Larisa's face in semi disbelief. Her friend had been in for Botox. And she'd had filler around her lips. Badly done. But Helen wasn't going to debunk her speech about her being all-natural any more than her insistence she'd never done IVF. Harry didn't talk about women going "full pup," but she knew it meant Larisa wanted to go back to her puppy years. Larisa wanted to look like a little girl again. Helen had never seen it done well because it always cried out plastic surgery. She hadn't gotten together with Larisa to talk about her face. Helen wanted to scream. Her friends were always coming to her to discuss aesthetics because of Harry. But she wasn't him.

"Why don't you ask Harry?" Helen said.

"You're kidding, right?"

"He's the best."

"You're getting a divorce!"

Helen looked at her friend like she was telling her something she hadn't heard. This was such a new situation. She hadn't told anyone except her parents who had been knocked over by it, but she was surprised that she might be expected to cordon Harry off from friends who genuinely could benefit from his skill.

"Helen! I'm not going to him if you're not together."

"Am I to keep you from getting what you want just because we're over?"

"Yes!"

"Then what, are you asking because you don't actually think I'd refer you to another surgeon? Harry's the best there is!"

"Honey, if you're getting a divorce, you sure aren't talking like it."

◆◆◆

THE FIRST THING PREVIN saw as he turned into Johnny Tout's driveway was Tout standing in the center of the grassy median like some emphatic sentinel. His hands were on his hips. "Where have you been?" he asked.

Tout didn't want an explanation, because no sooner had Previn started to offer one up, he cut him off. "Do you have any idea how bad this is?"

Previn shut off the engine and climbed out of his car. "Figured it being Saturday and it being your home, you wouldn't—"

"I don't even want to look at her face. Actually worse since you touched it."

"Excuse me?"

Tout started walking toward his house, hardly looking at Previn as he spoke. "I don't need to repeat myself."

This might have been a good moment to tell Tout he had to give it time, but he didn't seem to want to hear it. The minute people heard he was a plastic surgeon, they usually conferred qualities upon him that were impossible to live up to. However, it seemed arrogant to have to remind Tout he wasn't a magician, particularly when he wasn't up to date on her status.

Hours after leaving her at Tout's home the first time, Previn returned to check her vitals and see how she was holding up. As might be expected given the pain and anti-inflammatory medication he'd prescribed, he found her groggy but comfortable. After losing Blackburn, he knew better than to leave this patient at arm's length, although he'd deliberately chosen to come a half hour before Tout said he'd be there so as to avoid him. This did mean he'd hardly had a chance to look around.

Now with more time and in the broad light of day, Previn could finally take a proper look at Tout's house, which was a two-story Mediterranean. It was classic 1920s Los Feliz: oversized, with beautiful Catalina tile on the steps, iron gates and grillwork, and a large portico leading to a grand spiral staircase, which could have doubled for the stately one in *Gone with the Wind*.

It occurred to him he knew very little about this man. He recalled seeing through the window in the surgery Tout kissing Rox. Until that moment, he'd thought she was merely his PA. Evidently, she was more than that. Did she live with him? How many times had he been married? The house was quite formidable from the outside. Seemed too big for one man to live in alone, although the same might have been said about Previn's home.

In the large framed mirror near the foot of the stairs, Previn caught a glimpse of himself, wearing his white tennis shorts and shirt, and hardly looking like a doctor at all but for his medical bag.

"You coming?" Tout asked after Previn had again paused, this time to see what he could of the downstairs. Tout stopped at the top of the staircase, and then pointed to a door at the end of the long hallway. "She's in there. In that room. I'll wait for you downstairs."

They'd moved her. He was hopeful that this was an upgrade from the closet-like maid's room near the service entrance. Previn knocked gently on the door. When there was no reply, he went in. Fay was asleep. He walked over to her bed and looked down at her. While a big bandage obscured her wounds, he could see that there was a great deal of swelling on her face, leaving it red and puffy even in the areas that weren't affected. He pushed some hair away from her face then gave her a little stroke across the top of her head.

He found it hard to reconcile the sight of her, lying there sleeping, and the rebellious teenager described online. She'd left home at fifteen and apparently never looked back, notwithstanding whatever she'd muttered about her mom the night she was injured. She was presented as someone who had materialized out of the cornfields of Iowa to spark a bidding war between several record labels all on the basis of a demo she'd cut using the money scraped together from waitressing at the House of Blues on Sunset. How she managed to get hired at a bar when she was herself underage was never explained, but then it wouldn't be a fairytale if it resembled reality.

This was a different story than the one Tout had offered up, which was that he'd essentially found her in a "poor excuse for a club," and named and all but birthed her. If a star could be packaged, her look and sound, then surely her backstory could be dressed up to be something it wasn't. Previn surfed through the articles about her and found himself none the wiser. The problem was he didn't know what to believe. All he could really trust were his own lying eyes.

She struck him as young and delicate. Probably not much more rebellious than any nineteen-year-old who'd come blasting into La La Land on a hit song. It could be such a reality distortion field. How could someone like her look in the mirror in the morning and still see Susan Plouse?

Previn heard footsteps and turned. Rox stood inside the doorframe, dressed in faded jeans and braless in a red T-shirt, which matched her hair. "I've been washing her face three times a day like you told me," she announced.

Fay woke.

The swelling was such that Previn was surprised she could make him out. Her voice was very weak. "You're here. They won't let me see it. I wanna see my face!"

"You look great!" Rox said.

Fay turned away.

Previn felt put upon to say something. "Some good work was done."

To be honest, her bloated face was completely unrecognizable from the girl on the CD cover, much less the one he'd operated on less than twenty-four hours ago. This was not abnormal. Some people suffered swelling more than others did. This was nature's way of healing. He prepared an ice pack to help bring the swelling down.

"Why can't I see?" she asked as he gently applied an icy plastic bag across her cheeks.

"We'll sit down, discuss all that when—"

Rox snapped at him like a frisky dog. "No."

"What?" Previn asked.

"Johnny does that."

"Yeah. Right. I'll talk to Johnny."

"It's my face!" Fay pleaded as she winced in pain.

Previn felt answerable to Tout, as though Fay weren't the patient. This was an awkward and unusual predicament, one he'd never been in before. He waved her off. "Everything in its time. You're still healing, Fay. Got to go."

She grabbed his hand. "Don't leave me."

He didn't want this to get too personal. He'd certainly befriended his share of patients. Yet this one he really wanted to keep at arm's length. No good could come out of him getting involved. He had to say something. He gave her a half-hearted, "I'm around, Fay. I'll be around."

All plastic surgery patients had to recover somewhere. Home recovery was often preferential precisely because many patients didn't want anyone to know they'd had anything done. Many surgeons placed their patients in a suite at the Montage Hotel in Beverly Hills since it was close to their practices and it offered the kind of luxurious surroundings such clientele expected. Usually a nurse was assigned to help them through their recovery, administering painkillers and sedatives. Room service could bring in food and the nurse could receive it in the suite, and then bring it to the patient in the bedroom. Complete privacy. When the recovery was complete, the patient could leave the hotel without anyone knowing they'd had work done.

The closeting of Fay in Tout's Los Feliz estate was not so far afield from how other patients were handled. The big difference was Tout had asked Previn to keep her sedated, as only a licensed doctor could administer aggressive drugs. Rox was not a nurse. Not even close. In the two days following surgery, Tout had her stay with Fay round the clock, but more as her minder than nurse. And that's where it got weird. What seemed like an otherwise regular recovery regime started to feel more and more like she was being held captive.

Before he went downstairs, Previn opened the door to the adjoining bathroom and paused. In the lime-green room, the area above the sink and behind the door displayed white rectangles where the mirrors had been.

◆◆◆

"So?" Tout asked when Previn arrived downstairs.

Previn stopped at the edge of the living room. Looked around. The house was appointed in a style that was truly old Hollywood. There was not a trace of modernity anywhere. He wondered what Helen would say. She was one of the great readers of rooms as an artist who used them as her subject. Some of the furnishings were deco. There were also some older antiques. Tout was hard to fathom. This was, after all, a guy in rock 'n' roll, but there wasn't a trace of pop about the place. Previn found it an adventurous choice.

"I didn't invite you here to admire my house," Tout barked. "I know I have a great home. I don't settle for second rate, you understand?"

Previn decided to cut right to the question that had been on his mind almost from the first. "Is Fay safe here?"

Tout poured himself a cup of tea from a pot that was sitting on a tray by the wet bar. He seemed distracted. He didn't offer any to Previn.

"Are you going to answer my question?" Previn said.

"Of course she's safe."

"I'm worried about her. This is weird. The whole setup."

"Nobody's more on edge about this than me, mate. That's why you're here," Tout countered.

"To surgically erase all traces of a crime." There. He'd finally said it. Finally gotten what he thought off his chest. "This is not me. This is not what I do."

"Spare me."

"I didn't see it at first. But this is what it's all about, isn't it? It's like restore the crockery and put it back on the shelf, pretend nothing happened."

"If you ask me, the crockery don't look so good. Just saying."

"Somebody struck her with a bottle multiple times. Is nobody going to do anything about this? Who are you protecting? You've got something going on."

"You think I did it?"

Previn didn't reply. Of course, he'd wondered. The whole business stunk. He couldn't figure what Tout was doing there that night. And why he didn't seem to have any curiosity or interest in pursuing whomever had struck Fay. Previn thought he'd asked an entirely reasonable question and Tout had suddenly made it personal. He hadn't wanted to go there. But if there were a list of suspects Previn might put together, certainly Tout would be on it. And why not?

Tout finally spoke. "Well, thanks for the vote of confidence, mate! Her sunglasses broke. There's your bottle theory shot to shit."

"Except the cuts are inconsistent with an object like that."

"Then you tell me what happened, Sherlock. If you don't know, shut the fuck up!"

"Who's Sid?" Previn asked, remembering Fay's mutterings in the limo.

"My business partner? What about him?" Tout treated this like a non sequitur. He stopped and thought. "For fuck's sake, you don't mean to say he did it?" He laughed. He actually burst out laughing. The first time Previn'd seen him show a little joy.

Previn didn't know what to say. It wasn't a laughing matter.

Tout became deadly serious. "I called you because I was told you were the best. Then I go up to see her and…" He shook his head sadly. "It ain't good, mate. Looked in on her, I wanted to retch."

"I made the scars as favorable as I could."

"Favorable? Who do you think you're talking about? This is Fay Wray." He put great emphasis on her name, as if it had an almost mythic quality.

"Her cells don't know that. I told you about the lines of tension. The lacerations run counter to—"

"Doctor speak! She looked pretty good after you operated on her but now she looks like shite."

Previn smiled. Of course, he'd see it that way. Previn had failed to recognize that Tout was the equivalent of a rattled husband after his wife's facelift. They were usually horrified. As well they should be because the swelling and bruising was awful. They didn't always believe it got better. It always looked worse before it got better.

"Recovery is always this way."

Tout softened. "If you knew how she was."

11

FAY WAS RUNNING FROM a psychopath with a chainsaw. Previn watched her music video on YouTube before his next consultation. In front of him was a form that his next patient, the wife of Sam May, the famous director, had filled out. Some prospective patients could be very coy when it came to describing what they wanted done. This one had written the all-encompassing word, "Facelift."

He paused his computer and buzzed Sara. "Send her in."

Sara came to the door and politely introduced a woman, Jean May, who by her own account was sixty-three years old. She wore a shin-length Donna Karan dress, and her wavy, dirty-blonde hair cascaded over her shoulders. She had a generous smile and was quite tan, as though she had just dusted the sand off.

"You didn't get that tan here," Previn began, taking her hand and giving it a squeeze. He motioned to a chair in front of his desk, and then took the seat beside it to help in breaking the ice.

"I've been away." She looked down at her hands, which she'd folded in her lap. Her fingers were long and fine and her nails had been painted red.

"Somewhere wonderful?" He tried to appear interested.

"Cape Town."

"Oh. The people. Rich culture. What a place!"

"You've been?"

He looked over at the framed photo of the little black boy knowingly. He'd flown with Helen through Johannesburg on his way to Mozambique. "I did medical relief work in the region, but that was a long time ago."

Helen had been with him. Getting on that subject wasn't going to help anything. Wasn't going to get this woman the face she wanted. Though the memory of better times was still with him. Would always be with him, even if his marriage to Helen was at an end. He'd just have to keep it stashed away in a box somewhere in his mind like an old photo album.

It was a Monday. A new week. New life. Sigh.

"You're a beautiful woman," he said, turning to Jean May and looking straight into her blue eyes. "I don't know what you're doing here."

She grinned. "You can't look at me with those dark, sultry eyes of yours and say that." She shook her head. "Oh, well, I suppose I've aged gracefully."

"So what are you doing here?" She was pretty, but her face had begun to sag in ways that decidedly went against the conventional notions of beauty. He'd never volunteer that. She already knew. Better that she came forward and said what she thought the problem was.

"I went to visit my husband in Nigeria where he's shooting a picture."

"I've seen all his films."

"I was on the set for one week before they broke for ten days. When I first arrived, Sam says to me I'm going to like the female lead, Aura McAdams."

"Oh, yes." He smiled appreciatively. She was definitely the *it* girl at that moment, having had large parts in two of the bigger films of the year.

"And that he's told her all about me. He gets very enthused with his stars and likes to talk to them about all sorts of things, you see. But he adds, 'Of course, I didn't tell Aura how old you are.'"

Previn sighed. He'd heard this story before, but it never lost its power to bring out the vulnerabilities in a woman. That fear about becoming old. Too old.

"The whole time we were there, I just wanted to leave. Come home," she continued. "I told Sam I can't come back to Nigeria. Doctor, I need a facelift."

"You're a pretty woman, Jean. Don't sell yourself short."

"I'm tired, Doctor."

All too often plastic surgery was about something larger. In this case, a marital crisis. Previn couldn't talk to her without thinking about his own. He regretted having dropped by Helen's studio. He'd been such a fool. Whatever he thought he was selling, she wasn't buying. Why hadn't he figured that out at the dinner when she'd ambushed him with the divorce papers?

He wasn't thinking straight. The best thing he could do was forget Helen, though it was hard when patients like this came to him. His work seemed hardly much different from that of a therapist. How did they turn it off? How could they sit there, talk about people's troubles, and not think about their own?

Instead of saying, "I need a facelift," Jean May might just as well have said, "I need help with my marriage." Working on so many actresses, he felt he was taking a professional interest in his patients because their work was all about being presentable to the camera, but even the actresses were often driven to come to him out of personal desperation. Not getting sufficient male attention whether you were married or single went right to self-esteem. What he was offering these women was renewed confidence. He couldn't save their marriages any more than he could his own, but he could make them feel better about themselves. That was the secret. He just wished there was something he could do for himself.

He stood up and motioned for her to follow him. "Let me look at you."

She stopped in front of a large mirror. He didn't need to look at her there. He knew exactly what she needed done. His eyes had been all over her already. What they were doing now by looking into the mirror was for Jean May. He wanted to bring her in on it as though they were discovering her needs together. As though they weren't evident to Previn's practiced eye.

"I'm a sculptor, you know. I work with clay. It's not so different from working with the human form. The face is a thing of beauty, Jean. But it's always about accentuating. Balance. Emphasis."

He flicked on a powerful light. "You have fine bone structure and your face is symmetrical. What I would suggest is…I'll put this in layman's terms. Tighten it all round. Eyes. And above the throat, too. I wouldn't overdo it. We make an incision just above the hairline, and then do the lift." He looked with her into the mirror while running his finger above the hairline at the temples and downward following the natural line in front of the ear. "As for the neck, we make a small incision below the chin. You have to decide how far you wish us to go. Do you have a daughter?"

"I have two of them, but they're away in college."

"You want to refresh your face, but you don't want to appear to be competing with them."

She sighed. "Sometimes I wish I'd had sons. Daughters can be so…They're always after me about the clothes I choose to wear and… They're terrors, really. And I can't imagine what they'll say when they see I've had a facelift."

"You said they're away."

"Thankfully."

"With time, your face will settle in. They may never know."

"Oh, they'll know."

Jean May belonged to a group of patients, probably still the majority, who didn't want people to know they'd had work done. These more discreet patients wanted to be snuck out the back door after their operations lest anyone should find out. They told friends they were going off on a vacation when in fact they were having the bags removed from under their eyes or having their cheeks enhanced.

Previn had colleagues who had actually hosted coming-out parties for their patients. Galas in which friends and family were invited to toast the difference. This other, growing school felt plastic surgery was a rite of passage to be celebrated. For many of these patients, it was a social statement. The equivalent of arriving home with a luxury car. They wanted the whole neighborhood to see. To know. To eat their hearts out because, damn it, they were back on top.

He pulled a camera off the shelf and asked her to stand against the white wall space next to the mirror. He took several digital pictures of her, checked her blood pressure, and then asked that she return in another week for a follow-up consultation.

"But what about surgery?" she asked.

"You have to be sure you want it."

"I couldn't be more. I have to do this before he gets back from location."

"I don't usually like to rush."

"But Doctor." She looked at him with the most pleading eyes.

She was desperate. Her marriage was at stake. At that moment, he knew exactly how she felt. "Okay, let's take a closer look and we'll check with Sara about scheduling you in."

She clasped his hands. "Thank you! You don't know how much this means."

He smiled. "Oh, I think I do."

◆◆◆

"If someone put a gun to my head," explained actress Gina Fallon, "and it was a choice, a choice I had to make, I'd definitely go bottomless before I'd take my top off."

"But you don't have a gun to your head," Previn countered.

"I've been offered a part, a really delicious role. I just see myself chewing up the scenery with this one, but there's a hitch."

"What's that?"

"Nude scene."

Previn nodded. Gina was known as a comedian. A cut up. She'd had the lead on a sitcom about a beauty parlor called *Salon*. In this female domain, the women dished and dished, mostly about men. And Gina dished with the best of them.

"And?" Previn said.

"That's it. Nude scene. The whole deal. The contract doesn't allow for a body double. This is like giving the whole world bedroom privileges. That's what putting this on film is."

"Relax. You're a very pretty woman."

"You don't understand! I've got to become a male fuck fantasy."

Previn shook his head and smiled. He'd listened to enough patients to know how she felt. For most everyone it all came down to the same thing—that great sex scene in the sky. That's why they came to him. That's why they kept coming.

But Gina was forgetting her star power. She had an audience that had watched her on television for years, and some of them would certainly have had a prurient interest in seeing her do it. The star factor canceled out virtually all else. In the final analysis, it almost didn't matter what she was like physically. Stardom was blinding. People would see what they wanted to see and little else.

Looking at her just then, at her long bare legs and sleeveless shirt with perhaps one button too many open, he recognized there was certainly a difference between dressing sexy and being sexy. But there was something perhaps innate about this that really wasn't something a plastic surgeon could ever give her.

"This is a sex scene. If they're keying in on body blemishes—"

She sighed. "Blemishes."

"Enough!" Previn replied, standing up. "Let's take a look." He buzzed for Sara and tossed Gina's file onto his desk, which landed on his keyboard, setting off Fay's music video again. Fay was running through a bloodbath wearing next to nothing while some man

pursued her with a chainsaw. She was actually singing, "My baby
loves me and he shows me how…"

"Fay Wray!" Gina charged round to his side of the desk to look
at Fay sing, "Not Now, Later" in close up. "Is this what doctors do in
their down time, listen to Fay Wray?"

Previn blushed. He couldn't believe he'd been so careless. To
think he was trying to keep his connection to Fay secret.

"Someone must have been using my computer," he replied rather
lamely as he tried to stop it.

Gina twisted her hips to Fay. Sara was quick to get down with
her. "Don't turn it off. The party's just getting started."

Watching Fay's music video had begun innocently enough, but
in that computer was a blonde angel who almost from the first time
he went onto YouTube had come to haunt him. Raj was right. It was
soft porn. But porn was infectious. He was embarrassed with himself.

He clicked it off. "Sorry," he said.

"Jeez, Harry," Gina said. "I thought you were a fun guy."

He asked Gina to remove her clothes so he might examine her.
Gina disrobed down to her bra.

"Step over to the mirror," he instructed, very pleased to be
getting back to business. "And lose the bra."

"Oh," she stammered, unfastening her bra also.

Her cellulite was modest, mostly around the thighs. Not terribly
noticeable and difficult to treat. Her skin was coppery and her body
in fine condition. From the standpoint of the nude scene, her major
problem was not cellulite, but her breasts. They were large and they
sagged. But putting her through a mastopexy, or breast lift, was
problematic because it was a substantial operation and would leave
scarring. He wondered what her breasts might look like if she were
lying down.

As he stared at her, he caught sight of himself in the mirror. His
eyes were dark and intense. A clump of black hair had fallen over his
forehead as it did again and again, and he pushed it back affectedly.

"You have mild fat buildup in your lower stomach area," he said at last. "We can do some lipo down there and you'll be good to go."

"What about the cellulite?"

"You know, that won't show up on camera." He smiled at her, all the while wondering if she hadn't really come to him about her breasts. No director would shoot them in a way that was unattractive. A good director would do more for her breasts than he ever could. Previn imagined a scene shot with a man's hands on them throughout. That'd fix everything.

His eyes traveled back to some small Asian lettering tattooed onto the area just above her right thigh. "Incidentally, what does that mean?" He asked.

"Come up and see me sometime." She chuckled. "You know, Mae West."

◆◆◆

"THAT WAS HILARIOUS," SARA said when Gina Fallen had left. "I've hardly ever seen the great surgeon so rattled."

"It's stupid. I must have—"

"You like her music, don't you?"

"She's talented."

"Poor dear."

His thoughts went back to Fay recovering in that tiny room they'd brought her to that first night.

Sara continued. "Why do you think they insist on you going over there instead of me? You're useless outside the OR. I wouldn't even put you with kids."

"I think I'd make a great dad."

"You do have the odd bit of bedside manner."

"Thanks, Sara. I'll take that."

"Doesn't mean day-to-day handholding and pain relief management is your forte. You have to be able to read a patient. They say one thing, but you just know they mean another. Nurses bring a warmth surgeons simply don't have. I'm sorry, Harry. You're dreadful in this department."

"I feel this is a good experience for me. It's refreshing to get out of the surgery and see how patients cope."

"She's not an experiment. She needs to be tended to."

"You know, I may be a better nurse than you realize."

She dismissed his statement with an elaborate wave of her hand. "My job is more than secure. Maybe more so, now."

He smiled. He'd made the same case with Tout. But having watched Fay's music videos, he'd begun to feel a personal connection. It wasn't like he hadn't seen his patients on film. Which of them wasn't a star? Actually, it had nothing to do with Fay's music or her celebrity or how she looked. Truth was the music was rather insipid. Not his thing at all. It was just that he empathized with her relative isolation. She'd seemed so helpless shut away in that little room. Since he'd lost Helen, he'd felt so self-involved. He felt it'd do him a world of good to look in on Fay precisely because it wasn't something he did.

"Oh, my God!" Sara jumped up from the chair beside his desk. "Your next appointment is still sitting in the waiting room."

Sara soon returned with post-op, Darlene Fallows. She'd had a rhinoplasty and a lower bleph two weeks before. She still showed some modest inflammation in the area beneath her eyes where he'd removed the bags, and her nose was fuller than it would be when the swelling went down, but overall he was pleased with the result.

"Darlene! I'm sorry. I just heard you were waiting out here."

Sara rolled her eyes, and then turned heel as Previn led Fallows into his office.

"It's been insane around here. Got backed up with surgery this morning, and then...but hey!" He put his hands on her shoulders and steered her into the light. "Looking good. Terrific! Yeah. You look terrific. How do you feel?"

"I'm happy."

He smiled. "Good."

A second post-op was usually not a long meeting. He'd take a look at her, ask if she felt any major discomfort, and usually stop her anti-inflammatory medication and the painkillers, which were clearly in this instance no longer necessary.

He motioned for her to sit, but she looked back at the door.

"If we're done then I can get back to my boy," she said.

"Oh, you brought your son?" he asked, though he already knew this.

"I'd arranged to pick him up early, but then I realized—"

"The post-op?"

"Yes."

Had Sara not said he was bad with kids, this might have ended here, but her comment gnawed at him. He wasn't bad with kids. How did Sara know that? "How old is he?" he asked.

"Six. But he's a little man." She shook her head. "He's not at all pleased his mom had some changes done."

"He only has one mom."

"Yes."

New face, same mother. It must be a difficult adjustment for some children. It would be a great subject for a magazine article or a radio chat show.

From time to time, he felt like his work was an out-of-body experience. He was an objective observer. One step removed. It didn't matter that he'd performed the surgery. It wasn't his face. Had his training left him so emotionally detached? He didn't want to become so bloodless. He wasn't a machine.

"Harry," Fallows said, breaking into his reverie. "If we're done—"

"Yes." He had an idea. "Maybe…maybe I could have a word with your boy. Sound him out about this, you know." Then he added reassuringly, "I won't be too heavy."

"Would you? Since his father and I separated—"

"I understand. We'll talk man to man. What's his name?"

"Matt."

Previn walked out into the waiting room where he immediately spotted the boy wearing red corduroys and a blue-and-gold San Diego Chargers sweatshirt. But first he whispered to Sara that she should go in and entertain Fallows in his office.

When they were alone, Previn turned to the boy, who was studiously paging through a copy of *Hot Rod Magazine*, pausing at the pictures.

"You must be Matt!" Previn began.

The boy looked up. He had his mother's old nose, her hazel eyes, and curly brown hair. In operating on the mother, Previn had also done something to the son. He'd taken away some of their resemblance.

"I'm Dr. Previn. Your mother's surgeon."

The boy looked at his magazine again. Was he giving Previn the silent treatment?

Previn sat down next to Matt, where he could look over his shoulder at the cars. "You know I drive an XK. Even been in a—"

As he reached for the copy of *Hot Rod*, the boy bit Previn on the hand, then scurried away from him.

"Ouch!" he shrieked. "You little—"

Fallows raced into the reception area followed by Sara.

He was holding his hand. "Your son just bit me!"

The mother scolded her son in the most loving tone of voice. "Matt. That's not very nice. Say you're sorry, Matt."

The boy frowned but didn't apologize.

"It's okay," Previn said.

Matt ran over to her, clutching her skirt.

Fallows ran her hand through his hair affectionately. "We'd better go, Harry. Sorry for this. He's sensitive."

Previn nodded as he watched them leave. Children had an innate understanding of life.

"You all right?" Sara asked.

"Now I've got kids biting me!"

"Teething."

"He can teethe on somebody else's hand, thank you very much. I knew he was upset. Poor kid. That's his mother. And he..." Previn did a double take as he noted the empty reception room. "We're done!"

"One more."

"Who's that?"

"Rosie Bottoms."

"The one who wants to exchange her implants for another set?"

"Can't tell you how insistent she's been about seeing you. Calls several times a day."

He shook his head. "It's great to be wanted!"

They left the office about twenty minutes later. Rosie Bottoms had failed to show...and hadn't called.

◆◆◆

"THINKING ABOUT MY LODGER."

Helen could have guessed the conversation would start out with a grand expression of concern from the moment she saw Guy's name come up on her caller ID. He was trying to be helpful, but she found his calls intrusive and confusing. Something about accepting an invitation to stay at a man's house who had a nude of her hanging in his bedroom closet was hard to let go of.

"How are things in Helen world? Painting yet?"

"No," she lied.

"I'd order you to get to it, but I know you wouldn't listen."

"I'll get back to it."

"Good to hear!"

"You still in London?"

"The best laid plans of mice and impresarios!"

She laughed. "You're an impresario now?"

"Sounds good, doesn't it? I'm always looking for a grander stage, which has something to do with my ending up at a party in Hamburg. And now I'm at the airport on the way to San Sebastian because someone told me the food there is to die for. Did you know they have more Michelin chefs there than just about anywhere short of Paris? Bilbao is not far. Have to go there. I don't know what I'm doing. Helen. I started out looking at art and I got distracted. I'm so easily pulled away."

Helen never understood where Guy's money came from. It didn't quite seem like art could sustain such a life and at his relatively young age, but then she kept reading, like everyone else, about the huge art sales. It was evidently a racket. People were parking money in art and Guy had tapped into that. How, she didn't know. Although these trips were to hobnob with buyers and that was just about it. He made it sound so grand and it was, but they were glorified sales trips. His clients were living large and collecting art and moving money around the globe in LLCs and it was another way to launder money. That was the only way she could figure how Guy did it. Though she was hardly in a position to complain. She had become a modest beneficiary of whatever it was he was really doing.

Helen turned the page of the coffee table book she'd been browsing through about Georgian architecture. "I've been reading some of the books in your study."

"Which ones?"

"Only the racy ones."

"I thought I'd put those under lock and key."

Helen took a deep breath. "What are you doing with a painting of me in your bedroom closet?"

"What?"

"You heard me."

"The redhead?"

She had to get it out. Sitting on this for weeks wasn't her. Wasn't healthy. Yet the conflict she'd felt in raising this issue with him had been eating her alive. She shouldn't have been nosing around in his closet and he had every right to tell her to get out of his house. But what was he thinking? She was his charge and now his ward and it called into question his motivations. She'd actually thought he believed in her. Not that she was just someone he fancied in that way.

She heard him either laughing uneasily or trying to catch his breath.

"Well?" she pressed.

"The Jonathan Gold? What? That's you, Helen? I would never have thought that was you. That girl is so young."

"I was young. Once."

"Sorry. I didn't mean it that way. It's just that I didn't see the resemblance at all. It's really not such a good painting but it does have something." He started to laugh again. "It was certainly good enough for my closet." He continued to prattle on nervously, which only made it worse. "I would never have thought it was you, though, honestly. I'm really going to have to take another look at it when I get home."

"Go fuck yourself, Guy!" She ended the call.

He called back instantly. She turned off the phone. She had no patience for this. Of course the painting was her. She found herself gushing tears and she didn't quite know why. She never expected to feel so wounded. Had she become that unrecognizable? Odd as it was, she'd actually taken some satisfaction in being reunited with what had seemed like her carefree self.

She ran back to his bedroom and turned on the light in the closet. Of course, Jonathan had his conceit. He painted fast. He would only paint her after they'd had sex, which meant that he had to get her back to that sated moment before he could paint her. The idea of his so-called process amused her at that time because it was so baldly self-serving. But she was young, and he had that great beach house in Malibu.

How could Jonathan have sold her? He'd never wanted for money. Maybe he'd married and his gallery of sexual conquests no longer meant what they had. She still remembered the other nudes in his studio and the obvious implication that he'd fucked each and every one of them. He called them his life's work.

That was part of the allure. Part of the romance. What was she thinking?

It was always going to be awkward, bringing up the painting to Guy. She had expected him to come back at her, rightfully demanding to know what she was doing in his closet. She would have respected him more if he'd copped to it and laughed the whole thing off, saying he'd never thought she'd see it. He might have called it a gift that he didn't know what to do with. He might have said so many things, but to claim he didn't know the painting was of her...

She stripped off her clothes into a pile at her feet so that she stood before Guy's bathroom mirror naked. Her body wasn't near as taut as it was when she was nineteen. Her hair was about the same. Her eyes seemed to sit deeper in her face currently, though they were just as blue. One difference was she couldn't find the expression she had in that painting for the life of her.

The fertility treatments had changed her. She wasn't as sexy. She certainly didn't feel sexy.

She hated Guy just then. He'd turned her into an insecure woman. Pretty soon she'd be back at Harry's door, not because she missed him, but because she needed him to restore her. Botox. And fillers. A stomach tuck. Maybe lift her breasts. Hell, he could give her new ones.

Their relationship had never been about that. He'd never worked on her. He'd never asked. He'd actually loved her for who she was. Whatever his crimes, and there were many, Harry had never, ever rejected her physically.

She set herself down naked on the edge of Guy's bed and stared vacantly at the image of herself visible through the door of his closet.

Simpler times, they were.

12

THE CRYSTAL CHANDELIER IN the entrance way was on.
Although Rox had opened the door for Previn, Tout stepped forward. When Previn started to speak, Tout pointed upstairs. "Not here," he whispered.

If it had been anyone other than Tout, Previn would have thought the concern was rooted in Fay's well-being, but he sensed it was more that Tout didn't want her to hear what they were saying.

He led Previn into his study. The lights were off. Doris Day and Rock Hudson were mixing it up on a giant screen in one of their cheery romantic classics. Not quite what Previn expected to find Tout watching. Above the sofa hung posters for *Chinatown* and *Some Like It Hot*. Classic film posters were a very LA thing to have. The room was so dim, he thought that whatever it was Tout wanted to say, it'd be quick.

"How you been keeping?" Tout asked.

Previn shrugged as he waited for the other shoe to fall.

"I'm sorry if I was a little rough with you the other day. That's not me. Problem is, I care way too much about Fay." He held his smile until Previn started to feel uncomfortable. "Damnedest thing, this. I've had artists where there's just nothing to work with, if you know what I mean. I've had to have their pictures on their CD covers doctored. No pun intended." He chuckled as he motioned for Previn to sit on the black leather sofa across from his chair. "Fay has such heart."

"That'll help her through."

He paused the film. "You think? All they see is the star. I see beyond that. I see her as she was when I first met her. Young girl sitting in my office with Midwestern innocence written all over her."

It was not lost on Previn that this account was different than the original one Tout had given him in the car about how he'd discovered Fay performing in a club. Perhaps he'd only heard her at the club before meeting at his office.

"I'm sorry," Previn said.

"What do you have to be sorry about?" Tout snapped.

"That I can't do more."

He burst out laughing. "Richard said you were a nice guy."

"What's that supposed to mean?"

"She was not so innocent, Fay. Trusting is a better word for her. She's very trusting. Doesn't know how to say no to...*anybody*! She's got this man, if you can call him that. The most loathsome, sodding, moneygrubber. A friend of her mother's. Lay you odds he molested her as a child. She pays his rent. Can you believe that? Of course, I see all the charges because I see everything. I've tried to reason with her about it, but there's no reasoning with Fay. No reasoning at all. Some sixty-year-old wreck of a man and she pays his rent!"

"He did this to her?"

"No! I'm trying to explain Fay and all you want to do is find your villain. There are no victimless crimes, mate. None. That's what I'm saying."

"I don't know what you're saying. You tell me you care about her, well, cool—then who did this to her?"

"There are people out there who, if they knew what happened to her, would sell the story to *TMZ*. They'd do that to her. And those are her friends."

Previn had been around celebrity culture long enough to know this was true.

"I need time, Harry. I need time to help her help herself."

Previn stood up. "Bullshit!"

"I try to have a heart-to-heart with you."

"And?"

Tout turned away for a long moment and when he looked back at Previn, he had tears in his eyes. "I go up there to look in on her. See those bandages. Makes me physically ill thinking she has to suffer. If you only knew what it feels like to walk in my shoes. You think this is some sort of game I'm playing. Is that what you think?" he asked. "I'm responsible for her, okay? I see her suffering and…" He looked down at his shoes. "I got to thinking though, she doesn't have to suffer. You could take her to a happy place. You can give her meds that will make it all… copacetic." He managed a smile. "Dose her, mate. Put her in a place where she'll hear the birds chirping and everything will feel all soft and warm."

He really wanted to hate Tout. It'd be so much easier.

◆◆◆

HER FACE WAS STILL bandaged so that only her big sad eyes were revealed. Fay jumped up onto her knees when she saw Previn at the door. Sitting on the windowsill, Rox looked up from her iPhone.

"You're here!" Fay whispered.

Through the opening in the bandage, her eyes peered out into his. He had only seen her eyes in her photo and on the video. He was captivated. Only a few days before, her eyelids were virtually glued shut. She didn't seem to blink as she stared at him.

Suddenly Fay started to fall backward but managed to regain her balance.

"We've been having such a day!" Rox mumbled.

"Are you feeling bored being cooped up in this room?" he asked Fay. "If you are, nothing unusual in that."

Fay started to fall backward again, but Rox caught her.

"Why don't you lie down, Fay?" Previn said.

"I want to call my mom," Fay said.

"That isn't a good idea," Rox replied. "You know that."

"Why?"

"Because you ran away from home to follow your dreams. Yada, yada, yada…"

"Don't make fun of me."

"She was only a kid when she left home, and she's guilt-tripping over it. Fay, you've had years to fret about your mom."

Fay put her hand gently on her bandage. She started to tear up.

"You're giving me a migraine," Rox said.

Fay stood up on her knees again. "She told me, God has a plan for you. She said that. Now look at me!"

Previn's heart went out to her. "It's okay, Fay."

"I've got to call her," she whispered.

Rox swung round. "First, you're gonna call her, then you're not. Make up your fuckin' mind already!"

"I'll call her."

"No. You won't."

"Why are you saying that?"

Rox threw up her hands. "I can't deal with this."

"You've got to call her, Fay," he insisted.

He looked over to Rox, who simply rolled her eyes.

"What?" Previn asked.

"Not my life!" Rox replied.

Previn couldn't believe how callous Rox was, but then this was one rock 'n' roll gig she hadn't signed up for. She was merely there because Tout wanted her to be.

It was not uncommon for a patient like Fay to become anxious, confused, or both. It could be a side effect of the medication he'd been giving her, not to mention her predicament. "Here, take these. They'll help."

He watched her down the pills that were double the count from the day before and immediately regretted what he'd done.

Fay set down the water glass. "We have the same name. My mom, I mean."

"Susan Plouse?" He had sudden visions of a meddling stage mother. Among his clients, he'd seen countless. Which of them didn't have a son or daughter they wanted to put in the movies or start a modeling career? "Did your mother make you a star?"

"My mom? God no! She's a bookkeeper for a grain company. I was too much for her. The only thing she ever did to help my career was get me into the church choir. She thought she'd save my soul. I think she fucked up. Don't you?" She laughed for the first time, which turned into a grimace. It evidently hurt to work her face like that. The smile went away. She gently touched her face. "I did learn how to project my voice and play the organ."

She continued to tell her story while he waited for her eyes to become heavy as the pills took hold.

13

F AY WAS STARING AT her reflection in the face of a serrated steak
knife.

Previn walked in, and she jerked her head up and dropped the
blade. He hesitated at the door long enough to prevent Rox from entering the room before Fay could hide the knife beneath her pillow. All the
while, Fay stared back at him, pleading with him not to reveal her secret.
The sight of her with a knife didn't sit well with him, but he understood
her need to see herself. The process of her coming to terms with her
injury had to begin sometime and six days after her injury was as good
a time as any. Although a proper mirror would have been preferable.

Previn went about his business. Rox stood a few steps away as he
removed Fay's stitches. Her cuts had healed reasonably well, though
this did not reduce the overall prominence of the scarring that had
already begun to occur. Rox continued to hover, something he found
to be more than a little annoying. There was a fine line between
dedicated watchfulness and confinement, even house arrest. He
believed it had been crossed, wherever it was.

"I listened to your record *Not Now, Later*," he said at last to Fay.
"I expected...well, I don't know what I expected."

He chuckled. He wasn't really some adoring fan, although he
must have sounded like one.

Her gaze stayed on him as it had the time before. He found
himself drawn in. Hypnotized. If there were such a thing as eyes

that were windows into the soul, this was that portal. There was no sparkle in them, but depths of emotion. The moment became increasingly awkward. His gaze fled from hers. When he looked back at her, she was still staring at him and he felt himself blush. What did she expect of him?

Rox coughed loudly, as if to call attention to the fact they weren't alone.

Previn turned to Rox. "Could I have a moment with Fay?"

"I can get you both a hotel room if you want," Rox replied.

"I'm her doctor. I'd like to have a few words…"

Rox planted herself between Previn and Fay. "Nothing you can't say to me too."

Previn shifted his position so that he was able to at least include Fay in the conversation. "This is crazy. She's not in witness protection."

"You want to ask her about what went down that night."

"What if I—"

"Off-limits!"

Previn handed Fay a glass of water and three pills, which would certainly knock her out. "I have a right to know. I'm her doctor."

"You're not my doctor. You're their doc," Fay said faintly, but with conviction.

He didn't like her calling him out on this. He was *their* doc. It didn't sit well with him. It never had. But her articulating it made him want to prove her wrong. "Who hurt you? Was it Sid? Was it your mom's friend?"

Fay began to cry.

"You don't remember?" he said.

"What about me?" Fay whispered. "What about my face? What are you doing for me?"

Rox put an arm on Fay as she confronted Previn. "She's scared. She needs you to do your job."

At that moment, he hit a wall. He felt helpless. Surgically, there was only so much he could do. She seemed to be asking him for help, but what could he do beyond change her bandages and prescribe medication she really didn't need? Surgeons rarely had to attend patients like this. Normally, he'd see them after a few days and then again after a few weeks. Not day after day. He looked over at Fay with what were probably sad eyes.

"Back the fuck off!" Rox screamed.

◆◆◆

PREVIN WAS ON HIS way home, following the exchange with Rox and Fay, when he brought his car to a sudden halt. He muttered Rox's words, "Off-limits!" This would not do. He turned his car around.

Previn went back to where it all started. He stood in the rear of the parking garage where the limo had been parked. He spotted a door labeled "EXIT." He opened it and walked up the stairwell. From the parking garage, he took the staircase up to the lobby of the Chateau Marmont. On the steps, he found what looked like dried drops of blood.

When he got to the lobby, he took the elevator one flight down to the parking garage. He tried to imagine Tout and Rox leading an injured Fay Wray into the garage and over to the waiting limousine. Since the Chateau was relatively small and consequently private, they very easily may have made the journey without anyone noticing them. But it seemed more likely that they'd taken the back staircase, although without testing the blood, how could he be sure it was hers? A larger question was that over the last week, the scene had been contaminated. And what if, after it'd been tested, it wasn't her blood?

Previn walked back up the staircase and into the hotel lobby. There were times when the Chateau seemed like a monastery. And this was one of them. There was that musty quality about the air; the walls were thick and heavy, and the light, dim. Even the floor tile was a dour chestnut color.

Though its wooden furniture felt positively medieval and even its wall candelabras evoked a world gone by, Previn found his thoughts wandering to Helen. He'd brought her to the hotel that fateful night because she simply adored the place. While it couldn't have been further from Helen's modern design ethos, it was just the sort of fanciful, old Hollywood pile, so very unlike their own home, where an artist could find inspiration. The Chateau very much wanted to be a Chateau. Invariably they wouldn't ever mix old with new. Though one of her paintings would not have looked out of place.

As Previn took it all in, he pondered how the incident with Fay couldn't have possibly occurred in one of those soulless, prefabricated hotels of more recent construction. If it were to have happened anywhere at all, it just had to have happened in this neo-gothic landmark, a place notorious for celebrity scandal and death. John Belushi overdosed there. Jim Morison almost jumped off the roof during one of his binges. Helmut Newton died after his car sped out of control in its driveway.

If the hotel was old world, the selection of magazines spread out on the table in front of the reception desk made a statement that the reading tastes they catered to were decidedly up to the moment. Everything from glitzy fashion magazines to trade publications like *The Hollywood Reporter*.

Previn turned to the man at the reception counter, which was built into the wall, and said, "I have a friend who was staying here. Could you see if they've checked out?"

"Sir?"

"Name's John Tout. That's T-O-U-T."

He entered the name into the computer. "Sorry. No one by that name here."

"I know he was here on Wednesday."

"It'd show if he had."

"That's strange...hmm...try his girlfriend...Susan Plouse."

He tried again. "Sorry."

"Not even last—"

The youngish receptionist was already too officious for even an exclusive hotel. "Sir, if she'd been here at all—"

"I know they were here. Try—"

"I can't go through my register with you."

Invariably, Fay had been assaulted in someone else's room and that could have been virtually anyone on the register. And to further confound his ability to get at the truth, it occurred to him she may not have even been assaulted in the hotel at all. Perhaps they'd driven the limo into the garage as a good a place as any to park it while waiting for Previn to arrive. Though if that were the case, wouldn't a side street in the hills above the Chateau have served the situation better?

Previn hardly knew why he'd bothered trying to figure all this out. He wasn't Philip Marlowe. He even knew better than to think he could find the smoking gun at the reception desk, though it hadn't stopped him from trying.

This wasn't a happy place. Too dark for that. Too old. Previn looked over at the reception area with its comfortable couches and the overlarge lampshades adorning several standard lamps. This was old Hollywood chic. The one painting, a nude with a black face veil, was deliciously decadent.

Previn heard a woman laugh, and then turned to watch a couple disappear behind a heavy wooden door that led into the garden. The woman was blonde. She could have been Fay. And for a moment, she was.

14

"I THINK YOU AND your husband should try again."

Dr. Perez, her fertility specialist, had already become tire-omely predictable. Now several weeks after her loss, she'd rallied herself enough to meet with him alone. Several photos of newborns were on the wall. A photo of his blond wife and two three-year-olds on the shelf behind him.

"I've asked Harry for a divorce."

Perez swallowed. "I see."

They both sat there for what seemed like a long time without speaking. Helen didn't feel like she needed to say more. Though Perez might have wondered, if she wasn't going to continue with the marriage, then what did she want with him, her fertility doctor? It was too early to consider trying for a baby on her own.

"When did this happen?" he asked.

"Recently."

He bit his lip stubbornly. "I see," he said yet again.

"What do you see, doctor? My whole life has collapsed around me. I thought I was going to be a mother. I thought I was well married. I had an art show that I don't have…There's nothing to exhibit. Nothing. I'm dry. Dry like I am as a mother. Prospective mother."

"Did he ask you for the—"

"No. I asked him. Of course, I asked him. What was I to do? He's not there for me. He's a disappointment. That's all I'll say." But then she went on to say more. "I don't know him. They say you know who your friends are when the chips are down. Well, where was he? What was my husband doing while I was losing out on motherhood? I'm not important enough. But his patients, they're important. They're so much more—"

"Oh, boy."

"What?"

"You cannot make this decision now. In your state."

She felt her blood rise. "Excuse me?"

"This is the hormones talking."

"I can make decisions for myself. Thank you very much!"

"No, you can't!"

She jumped up. "You're a sexist ass!"

"Helen. Please."

She opened his office door and was already exited to the hall when he came running up behind her and grabbed her arm.

"Please give this time. Things will look different. They do. The hormones you've taken are enough to drive anyone mad. My wife. I wanted to end it with her when we did this and I know this stuff. It's a moment of madness. It'll pass. It will. Trust me on this."

She looked down at his hand, which was still tightly clutching her arm. He looked down at it too, which was when he relaxed his grip and she took back her arm and walked away.

◆◆◆

AMBIEN. THE ANSWER TO Dr. Perez. He'd left Helen feeling despondent. She hoped that on the other side of a nap, the world might seem different somehow.

As she stirred from what had been a deep sleep, she licked her lips and stared up at the white ceiling. Her eyes wandered around until they happened on a loose thread coming from the "Dr. Harold Previn" inscribed on the blue medical scrubs she slept in every night. She pulled at it, but she couldn't break it off. She fancied a glass of

water. With her head still gummed up with sleep, she walked into the
hall and crashed smack into Jake Blackburn.

Jake Blackburn!

An imaginary shell had been fired. She could hear it whistle
through the air. In that moment before impact, she saw a man she'd
seen in countless movies, billboards, and on supermarket tabloids,
but she wasn't some impressionable, starstruck girl. His stardom
wasn't what came to mind. The shell became an ear-piercing scream.

Helen's fist caught his right cheek with enough conviction and
force to make any of her kickboxing instructors proud. The one thing
she'd remember, as though it were in freeze frame, were Jake's eyes
crossing as the blow registered.

Jake grabbed her hair and tugged it hard, which made her shriek.
She tried to kick him in the balls when, of all people, Richard Barone
threw his surprisingly muscular arms around her and dragged her
forcefully down the hall, careening into this and that before arriving
in the kitchen.

"Leave her to me, God damn it!" Richard hollered to Jake and a
middle-aged woman with a Cleopatra cut and duck lips from bad
dermal fillers, something Helen noted immediately (thank you, Harry).

Richard pushed Helen through a side door that led into the
garden.

"What the fuck!" he said as he set her loose.

At that moment, all Helen saw was red. She charged forward
again as if to have another go at Jake. Richard clamped her shoulders
with an iron grip and looked her in the eyes to steady her.

She stopped.

What about her karma had brought Jake Blackburn to her home?
Or, for that matter, Richard Barone? This was a side of Harry's life she'd
run away from and here they were. If the ghost of Jake Blackburn's mom
herself had come to her door, it couldn't have been more terrifying. All
she could think was that they'd come for payback.

"What are you doing here?" she said.

"Calm down and I'll explain."

"This is the man who's threatening Harry," she said. "That wants to bring him down."

Richard smiled wryly. "It's not what he's most known for."

She attempted to break free of him again. "How dare he!"

"He lost his mother."

"What's that got to do with me?"

She glared at Richard. They'd broken into the house to avenge Jake's mother. That Richard was an unlikely candidate for breaking and entering, let alone a revenge killing, didn't occur to her in that desperate hour. If she had a gun, she'd have blasted them and asked questions later.

She looked to her right and saw her path to freedom.

As she attempted to flee, Richard grabbed her arm.

"I had nothing to do with it!" she pleaded.

He let go his grip. "Who said you did?"

"Even if I walked out on Harry just before the operation, that couldn't have had anything to do with what happened. He could have done her with his eyes closed. He's that good!"

Jake suddenly appeared at the door, rubbing his very reddened cheekbone. "I've been in a lot of action pictures and I've never been belted with a roundhouse like that."

Richard took a protective step between his star and Helen.

She was surprised to see how short Jake was beside Richard. She found his face surprisingly soft and warm. His coppery hair was studiously messy. He had designer stubble but it only made him look younger than twenty-nine. A terrible age to lose a mother.

Jake put his hands on Richard's hips and moved him aside like a piece of furniture. "I think I'm safe, Richard. I'm sure this was all a terrible misunderstanding." He turned to Helen and grinned. "We didn't know anyone was here."

Helen was still panting. She felt put upon and threatened. Though he quite evidently didn't know who she was, that changed nothing. He was a reminder of a really bad thing. She wished he'd go away. That the whole thing would just end.

She realized that all she had on was the top half of Harry's medical scrubs. She self-consciously pulled the hem down some to cover herself as the two men looked her way. There was barely enough material to cover her hips. What had been fun, sexy bedroom attire when she was married to Harry made her feel like a whore in that moment. She could feel herself blush. Yet the sudden realization that Harry's name was spelled out across its pocket made her eyes grow big with alarm. She moved one hand to cover the lettering. This was absolutely mortifying. As if things weren't awkward enough, she was wearing Dr. Harold Previn on her shirt. The man whom Jake wanted to sue for wrongful death.

Richard was still refereeing. "I got this, Jake."

Jake addressed Helen directly. "You're not going to run to *TMZ* saying I got into a chick fight, are you? Doesn't help my cred."

Richard's patience was wearing thin. "Jake!"

"Okay. Okay." Jake went meekly back into the house.

"What are you doing here?" Helen stammered.

"What are *you* doing here? I didn't, honest to God, expect to see you, Helen. You think I'd *want* to bring Jake Blackburn to kibitz with Harry Previn's wife?"

Helen could still feel herself shaking as her thoughts raced back to Richard telling Harry they needed to bury Jake Blackburn's mother in the desert to head off his ruining Harry's career. It was all very melodramatic and Hollywood. It was everything she hated about the business because there, in the person of Jake Blackburn, was someone who'd lost someone dear. A real person. Yet Richard was turning it all into a storyline for a film.

"I'm sorry about what happened to his mother but why were you threatening my husband?"

"I think it's going to be all right. Harry has been very helpful and perhaps we should consider the matter almost closed."

The thought that there was some sort of favor that'd mitigate the loss of Jake's mother mystified and unsettled her almost as much as running into Jake. It sounded sinister. "What could he do to make it right?"

He laughed. "Missionary work."

She became aware of his eyes looking her over. She gathered her shirt around her again, though by that point, her modesty paled beside the abject fear she'd felt when she thought Jake was going to discover she was Dr. Harry Previn's wife.

"You've got Harry's name on your shirt." He shook his head and grinned. "Nice touch!"

"Did he see it?"

"Just guessing, but he was probably more interested in your naked thighs. Actors! What can I say?"

"What are you doing here?" she asked again.

"Jake's art advisor wanted to show him the Daniel Richter. Jake wanted to see it."

"Why didn't you call?" she asked.

"We rang the bell."

The Ambien! She vaguely recalled hearing something but thought it was part of a dream. "I was asleep."

"At three in the afternoon?"

"Shouldn't he be grieving?" she demanded. "What's the matter with him? He's shopping for art!"

"His mother loved art."

She took a moment to reconsider this woman who, up until then, had seemed to be more a creature of Harry's world than her own. Jake's mom was suddenly no longer just a woman who wanted a facelift. She could feel a tear roll down her face.

"What's the matter?" Richard asked.

She wiped the tear away. This was manipulative. Her life had nothing more to do with Jake's mom than her death. Still, it was an awful thing. One life lost is too many. She took a deep breath and gathered herself. "What did you say Harry was doing to make amends for this woman's death?"

"I didn't."

"People just don't forgive the loss of their mother unless there's nothing to forgive," she countered. She was on to something. With this one statement, she felt she'd won the case.

"Maybe you should take this up with Harry."

"Harry and I are no longer." She'd succumbed to a sudden impulse to distance herself from Harry and his baggage. It felt wrong immediately. But there was no taking back what she'd said. And it was true.

"I'm sorry. He's a good man. It's none of my business, really, but I guess you and Guy Hennessy are…?"

"He's my art dealer," she said as curtly as she could.

He smiled. "Yes. Of course. I don't know Guy, except by reputation." He looked back at the house. "Nice home."

He was so transparent. He evidently felt he'd stumbled into some useful intelligence he could share with Harry. The idea that Harry might think that she'd run to Guy, that she'd more than likely left Harry for Guy, unsettled her. "I know what you're thinking, but Guy isn't even living here right now. So forget it, Richard. And another thing: I didn't walk out on Harry because Guy has a nicer home."

She was suddenly concerned about Harry, though she desperately didn't want to be. The thought that he had dealings with this man creeped her out.

"Excuse me," he said. "I just thought…"

She stopped him with a look that could kill.

15

WHEN BRICK STARTED WITH one of those Buddhist hands coming together at the heart gestures, Previn knew he was screwed.

"I have to apologize," Brick said.

"For what?"

They were still standing in the surgery alone wearing their green scrubs. Sara had left. Raj had only just wheeled the patient, some nose and neck work, into the recovery room.

Brick pulled off his latex gloves and tossed them into a bin for medical waste. "For not protecting you from yourself." He turned to Previn sharply. "Tell me you're not fucking that pop tart."

Previn looked uneasily toward the open door before closing it.

Brick continued. "I'd celebrate just about anything sexual if it meant getting one over on Helen, but you're better than this."

"There's nothing going on."

"Nothing? *Nothing?* Don't lie to me. Sara says you've been going to see Fay Wray almost every day for the last few weeks. You can bullshit Sara, maybe. But look at me. This is Brick. I've known you since med school."

They'd shared an apartment way back when. Whenever Previn had split a dorm and later an apartment, he'd found himself becoming best friends with whomever it was he was shacking up with, Brick in particular.

"You can't believe everything you hear," Previn said.

Brick looked over at him as if to say, *Who do you think you're kidding?*

Previn was annoyed Sara had said anything to Brick. It begged the question: Who else was she talking to? Although Brick was family.

Brick was not one to bite his tongue for long. "I fuckin' wet-nursed you through all sorts of shit like that psycho chick that wouldn't let go. It was me who told you how to put a restraining order on her, remember?"

Previn had unquestionably had his moments when he was younger, one of which involved a false pregnancy with a one-night stand who had taken to stalking him. However, there was no way that Previn's behavior in his early twenties matched up to what he was going through in the here and now.

"I'm looking in on her," Previn said, trying not to jump at Brick's accusation. "That's all. Making sure everything's cool."

"What surgeon makes house calls?"

"Me."

"Liar! You've never made a fuckin' house call in your life. What's going on?"

"It's not what you think. I go over there to change her bandage. Make sure she heals the way—"

"Every day?"

"I've been over there maybe six times in the last nine days, which is—"

"That's like watching paint dry! What surgeon does that? There's something going on."

Had his friend forgotten about Blackburn? He wasn't about to get back into it. Previn looked away impatiently.

"This is worse than I thought," Brick said. "I don't have the time to analyze the psychological shit that went on in your marriage that'd make it seem to you like this pop tart could fill the void. But you've got to let this girl go. Throw her back into the sea."

"She needs me."

"Do you think getting close to Fay Wray will help you get your wife back?"

Previn shook his head and smiled. "Interesting theory, Professor."

16

HELEN GROPED AROUND IN the dark with one hand for the ringing phone.

It was at least 1:00 a.m., though she wasn't sure. What jumped out at her was the caller ID. Guy Hennessy. *Shit.*

"Did you assault my client?" he began.

She sat up in bed. "You didn't tell me you were going to let some man into the house. I could have been raped."

"By Jake Blackburn? Are you fucking kidding me?"

She sighed.

Guy wasn't done. "When I invited him to *my* house, he had a reasonable expectation his life wasn't going to be put in danger."

Helen ran a hand across her face as she replayed the incident. "He rounded the corner. It was sudden. So sudden, I couldn't have known—"

"Don't tell me you didn't know who he was. He's only one of the most recognizable faces in the world."

Helen sat up in bed. From the tenor of his voice, she sensed he was about to ask her to pack up her things and leave his house. She couldn't blame him for doing so either. How could she have gone off like she did on Jake Blackburn? It wasn't at all like her. Maybe Dr. Perez was right and it was hormones. What made her wince was the realization that until now, when Guy raised it, she'd hardly considered how out of line she'd been.

"I'm a woman alone, Guy." She heard her voice become small like that of a little girl. "Do you have any idea what that's like? This is a big house."

"You're gonna play the woman card?"

She took one long deep breath, but didn't reply.

"You didn't call me," he continued. "Not a peep! Something like this happens, and nothing! It's exactly like your failing to tell me you didn't have anywhere near enough work for your own exhibit. I'm always the last to know. What am I, a bystander? I thought I was your friend. And representative. But what do I get? A frantic call from my sales gal, Phaedra, saying some woman sucker punched Jake Blackburn in my house!"

The wide-eyed little girl came out again. "I was scared."

"You know, I could get sued over this."

Yet another person Jake Blackburn was going to sue! She didn't like having put Guy in this difficult position. She felt like her back was against the wall. She was waiting for him to shoot her when she made what was a last-minute plea: "There's history."

"With Jake?"

"All of them."

"So you attack Jake Blackburn in my house?" he continued. "An international superstar! Cost me a sale. I don't want to sound like an asshole here, but you've got one hell of a way to show your gratitude."

"This is Harry's mess!" she shot back. Standing up and pacing. "I'm sick of it. I'm sick. Okay? We were splitting up when Jake's agent came over to the house to discuss the loss of a patient who just happened to be Jake's mother."

"Loss? What?"

"Jake thinks Harry killed his mother."

"No shit!"

She'd always been very careful not to discuss Harry's business with her friends and confidants. Something about the sanctity of patient-doctor confidentiality. Though in this circumstance, celebrity was also a big part of it. Not to mention Harry's standing. But Guy had put her in a corner and she felt like she had to explain herself. Yet in this case, the truth was unlikely to set her free.

"They were conspiring about how to keep Jake from suing him. It was awful, Guy." She took a breath then continued, her voice low as though she were afraid someone might hear. "What I couldn't have known was that on the very morning of the surgery, I told Harry I wanted to leave him. So it's not just his fault. I mean, I don't know if it is his fault at all. But it might have been mine. What if I put him in such a bad headspace he botched the surgery?"

"Jake's mother's dead? Harry's knife work! Wow!"

"You must never tell anyone I said this. Not Richard. Not Jake. Please. Oh, God. I didn't just tell you this. Don't say anything."

"I get it. You were defending your husband's honor."

"No."

"Then what then? Why punch Jake?"

"I told you. I was scared."

Helen waited for Guy to respond. He didn't right away.

"Can I give you a hug, Helen?" he said at last. "I know I'm on the other side of the world right now, but I think you really need one."

His quite unexpected reply choked her up.

"Did Jake know who you are?" he asked.

"No."

"This is batshit crazy!"

"If he knew, God! That'd make it all so much worse. If that were possible."

"I'll call Richard. Try to find out what's happening."

Her eyes grew big with fear. "You can't call him!" she shouted. "It'll get back to Harry. What will he think?"

"It's okay. I've known Barone for years."

"He told me he only knew you by reputation."

Guy snickered. "That's Richard. He knows people when it's useful to know them and only knows them 'by reputation' when he wants to play it fast and loose. Got to love it. Hollywood."

"I've asked Harry for a divorce. Thought you should know."

"What? But why?"

She climbed back into bed and pulled the covers over her. What was it about divorce he didn't understand? "Why tell you?"

"No. I mean, yes! Are you sure? He had it all. I want to say a man who gives of himself to help other people must be a good man, but then...if his patients are dying..."

"They don't die. He's a gifted surgeon. But what he does has never really been my thing, though I can see the art in what he does. It's the vanity of it that disgusts me. All these desperate, silly people." She swallowed hard. Her mouth had gone dry from the fright his call had given her. "I really shouldn't have said so much. I don't know what has gotten into me. If it gets out about what happened to Jake's mother..."

"You're a rare woman, Helen. I don't know how he could let you go. Every woman I've known has taken from me."

"All I ever wanted from him were children."

"You're going to make me cry."

"You're not the crying kind, Guy."

◆◆◆

"JUST AS I THINK I've pulled your nuts from the fire," Barone began.

Previn had just climbed from the shower when he heard his iPhone ring. He dashed into the bedroom dripping with water, a towel in his hand. He might have let the phone go to voicemail, but the Twilight Zone ringtone reserved for Tout and Barone told him that he better grab it. The one morning he didn't have surgery and all of a sudden, his stress level maxed.

"Huh?" Previn dabbed at the beads of water on his face and chest as a small pool of water formed beneath his feet on the hardwood floor.

"Your wife."

Of the five stages of loss, Previn was still stuck in denial over Helen leaving him, which was a pretty copacetic stage to be in. Yet as he waited for Barone to continue, he had a sense of foreboding that Barone was going to say something that would change that.

"I had to pull her off Jake Blackburn yesterday," Barone announced. "Is she on PCP or crack or something? Thought she'd kill him if I hadn't—"

"What? What are you talking about? Why would she do that?"

"That's what I wanted to ask you."

"Well, hell if I know!" Previn wrapped the towel around himself and sat down on the foot of his bed. "What did you say she did to him?"

"Tried to punch his lights out."

"What?" It was just as unsettling as the first time Barone said it. The thought of Helen trying to do this to Jake Blackburn was such a non sequitur. "She's been doing kickboxing class for years. Maybe twice a week. It's a great workout." He knew he was rambling, but he was actually at a loss for words. "Did she say anything?"

"At the moment, I'm trying my best to make sure Jake doesn't find out who she is," he replied. "He wants to know. He damn well has a right to know, if you ask me who his assailant is. But frankly, I don't have the heart to tell him. What would he think if I were to tell him she's the wife of the man who killed his mom?"

Previn suddenly had a memory of Fay Wray lying all bloody in the back of that limo as if there were some sort of symmetry between the two. "Is he hurt?"

"She's got a sledgehammer for a fist!"

Previn felt sick at heart. How could this be happening? "This isn't Helen."

He didn't know Jake Blackburn any better than any other average Joe who'd been to the movies. Yet it was hard not to feel for him. Sure, Barone had spoken endlessly of that wrongful death suit, but if a man loses his mother, he has a right to want to sue somebody. What he couldn't get was how on earth Helen could end up going off on the man.

"I want to say you don't know her like I do, but she's your wife and that sounds bad."

"Then why say it?"

Barone snickered for the first time.

"Where did you say this happened?" Previn asked.

"How long do you think I can reasonably keep lying to my client to protect you, Harry?"

Previn was becoming impatient. This was his wife. He'd had enough of hearing about all the ways Jake Blackburn was going to come at him. "I asked you a question."

Previn waited through a long pause.

"Harry, I'm your friend," Barone said.

"What is it?"

"You don't know she's living with Guy Hennessy, do you?"

"Of course I knew that!" he snapped. He didn't know how convincing he sounded. This was a hell of a time for pride. False pride. But damned if he was going to give Richard Barone the satisfaction of breaking his heart on top of everything else he'd done.

Although Helen had asked him for a divorce, Previn had actually felt they were in a simmering-off period where she might yet come round. Now he was realizing that perhaps he really was in the denial stage of loss when he more rightfully should have been in the anger phase. He'd known Guy Hennessy through Helen and he'd always felt him to be harmless enough. However, Previn was happily married then. How could Guy have possibly taken up with her so fast? Had this all been happening under his very nose and while they were trying to have a baby?

"My last wife had this soap actor from *Days of Our Lives* move in with her for a month, didn't mean a thing," Barone offered, evidently sensing Previn's unease.

"You trying to make me feel good?"

◆◆◆

HELEN CLUNG TO HARRY as tears streamed down her face. "I'm sorry. I've ruined everything."

"It's okay," he said again and again.

As she stared over his shoulder at the open front gate, she wondered how she'd gone from being so done with Harry to holding him for dear life. Only moments before, she was seated alone and despondent in the living room where she'd been pretty much since Guy's phone call, unable to sleep.

None of what had happened the day before made much sense to her. She could hardly believe she'd belted Jake. It was all too random and surreal. Though how could she not be angry with herself for what had happened? She didn't have to strike him. Nor did she have to create such turbulence in the lead-up to Harry's surgery on Jake's mother. There was so much to be angry at herself about, yet it was really about fate. Throw in the loss of her baby. That was most certainly fateful. Or maybe she should call it what it really was: bad luck.

As she continued to sit in the living room under the Bernard Richter, the unmistakable sound of the gardeners trimming the hedge shook her out of her reverie and prompted her to head back to her room. Had she not neared the foyer, she might not have heard Harry's car at the very moment it sped to a stop in front of the house.

She didn't have time to ask herself what he was doing at the house when he wasn't even supposed to know where she lived. She didn't consider that he might have even been angry with her. The fact that he had materialized at all, her go-to guy, was enough to prompt her to throw herself into his arms.

"I don't know what I was thinking to leave you before you were going into surgery," she said. "If I'd waited for another time...What was I thinking?"

"It wasn't that."

She broke away. "It was. Jake's mom would be alive today if I hadn't—"

"That assumes I fucked up."

"I didn't mean..."

"She couldn't handle surgery. It didn't show up in the tests we ran. So, what does that have to do with what you told me in the morning?

Nothing! Sometimes people simply die. Nobody ever wants to accept that. They always need to blame someone. I get it. Death is hard to accept. Don't you realize I've agonized over this almost every day? It's tough to lose a patient. I'm a healer. At least, I thought I was. I go back and forth. If she hadn't gone home…But what does any of that have to do with you, Helen? What?"

She threw her arms around him again. She could feel him pat her on the back. "I didn't mean to hit Jake Blackburn," she replied, breaking away again and looking at him steadily through her moist eyes. "He lost his mother. He didn't deserve to get attacked by some neurotic woman." As she considered what she'd said, she started to laugh. She tried to stop herself because it didn't seem right, but then he joined her. "It's ridiculous!" she said.

"You're crazy. You do know that, don't you?"

"It's all your fault, Dr. Previn!"

She looked down and regained her composure. Without question, losing the embryos had pushed her over the edge. She kept telling him she'd lost the baby and he didn't believe her. But when it became an established fact, he didn't take her in his arms and reassure her and tell her he felt her pain. Instead, he kept saying and doing all the wrong things. Packing the boxes to move was an act of sheer melodrama. If Harry had found the right words, it might have stopped the clocks and forced her to reconsider. What woman could have endured knowing that after such a loss, her husband was consulting with some actress about her nose? Or her breasts? If that weren't bad enough, conspiring with Richard about how to bury Jake's mom…

She caught him beaming at her. He seemed tired. Stressed. His face was gaunt as though he hadn't been eating as well. Or perhaps it was that he'd allowed his hair to get longer than normal. He needed to take better care of himself. She felt a pang of remorse that her actions had hurt him. But then he'd hurt her.

"You were defending me," he said.

The idea of him coming to her because he thought she was sticking up for him with Jake Blackburn made her smile again. "Harry."

He pursed his lips. "Did I get it wrong?"

"You can be so cute sometimes, Harry." It was hard not to love him in that moment. He was simply that silly boy she'd married.

The gardener neared with the hedge trimmer. They waited for him to pass. She looked at Harry. He wasn't looking at her. He was glancing around uneasily. Abruptly, the gardener shut off the trimmer and threw it into the back of his truck. The innocence of the moment had seemingly dissipated. "Something that's been bothering me," she said. "Richard told me you were making amends for Jake's mom, as if that were possible. It's a weird thing to say. She's dead. It's not like you can bring her back."

She'd known Harry long enough to note that the question put him on his back foot. He avoided her eyes. "I can't talk about it."

A red light came on. It was as if she'd overheard Richard telling Harry that they needed to bury Jake Blackburn's mother in the desert all over again. Her voice rose with alarm. "What has he asked you to do?"

He hesitated.

She raised her hands. "No. Don't tell me! I don't want to know." A few minutes before, he'd flat-out lied to her in saying there was nothing to Blackburn's death, which made her realize just how far apart they'd grown. He wasn't by nature someone who lied. He wasn't even particularly good at it.

"Does Jake have any idea you're my wife?" he asked.

"Do you think I'd have the effrontery to introduce myself to him? 'Hello, I'm Dr. Harold Previn's wife, Helen. Delighted to meet you!'"

"He might have asked."

"It was plenty uncomfortable already."

He looked past her at the house, darkening.

Her heart sank as she considered that Harry was in some sort of trouble that evidently involved Richard. "What is it?"

"What are you doing here?" he asked coldly.

She didn't have to turn to see he was referring to Guy's house. She knew what loomed behind her. She should have known the minute Harry rolled up the drive. He was battling his fears. Here she was thinking his coming to her was all about his better angels. "Is that why you came?"

She didn't need to hear another word from him. She knew Harry. She knew he was perfectly capable of being jealous, a perfectly human response.

"My wife leaves me and ends up at another man's house; it's safe to say there's something wrong with that picture. Is that why you left me? Was it him? Did you leave me for Guy Hennessey?"

She took a step back.

"I don't get it."

She felt her face become twisted with incredulity. "All you can think about is if I left you for Guy?"

"If? Guy was always hiding in plain sight. We used to laugh about his famous love life, if that's what you want to call it, and here you are. What was I laughing about?"

"What did you think, Harry? By coming here, you were going to rub my face in my infidelities? Yesterday I went to see Dr. Perez on my own about the baby. *That* baby. Yes. The one I was trying to have with you and which…" It was too painful to finish.

As he approached her, she raised her arm as if to strike him. She would have if he'd come any closer.

He stopped.

"Guy's in Europe, Harry. Been there the whole time. That's, like, fifty-five hundred miles away. He couldn't be further from my life, okay?"

His face registered surprise and confusion. As if it had never occurred to him that she might not be living there with Guy. Or that Guy might not be in residence. What Harry thought he might find by racing over there, she could hardly imagine, and she wondered if he even knew. She resented him doubting her. What right had he to do that?

Guy had certainly shown himself to be the bigger man.

17

Nick Valentine's body falling through space.

Previn stared at the giant movie poster for *Falling* that took up the whole wall behind the reception desk at Tout & Wilde. A yellow burst pasted on one corner read, "Countdown: 9 days!"

The offices of Tout & Wilde were in a low-rise building jammed between the Whisky a Go Go, The Roxy, and The Viper Room. That Tout would ask him to come to his office seemed meaningful. Though as Previn stood there waiting for Tout, he wondered why he hadn't asked Rox for a fuller explanation. It gnawed at him that he'd canceled several of his Wednesday consultations to meet with Johnny Tout as though he were some mucky-muck who mattered. He'd been to his house. He'd tended to his client. But who was he? He still had no idea.

Earlier, Previn had called one of his patients to whom he'd given back at least ten years. Ta-da! An entertainment lawyer, she must know of Johnny Tout, and she did. She described him as a former roadie who'd come over with the band INXS in the early nineties, soaring because he had a genuine ear for talent. She went on to describe three brutal, costly divorces, which had been his ruin. "Makes for one desperate, bitter man. He may be self-employed, but he works for them. The Exes. Let's not kid ourselves." She giggled girlishly. "Why didn't I become a divorce lawyer?"

Of course, she had to ask why he wanted to know. Without hesitation, Previn described Tout as a prospective facelift. Normally he'd never break faith in revealing the identity of patients, prospective or not, but since this couldn't be further from the truth, it seemed okay. He also got some amusement in planting the rumor with her that Tout was shopping around for facial work.

Previn was still staring at Valentine's falling body when Tout came forward, grasping his hand like an old friend before leading him down a hall lined with Grammy Awards and at least twenty gold and platinum records. Previn stopped to stare at one.

Tout gestured toward the wall. "Tombstones, mate!"

"What?"

"There are stars. And there are shooting stars. They come and go. This is one big happy cemetery."

Tout opened the door to the glass-enclosed conference room with four serious men seated around the table. A beauty shot of Fay's face commanded the entire wall. Previn recognized it from the cover of *Harpers Bazaar*. "The Face of Spring!"

When Previn came face-to-face with that poster of Fay Wray, he felt sad like a captain looking at a giant photo of the ship he'd lost at sea. But that was the wrong view. He'd been there for Fay. He'd helped her through most of her crisis. There was something unseemly about his attending to her all this time. Brick had raised legitimate questions for which he really didn't have good answers. He'd become too attached. And it wasn't like he was helping her at this point. He was a surgeon. There'd come a time when his skills could be drawn upon again, but this wasn't it.

"Gentlemen," Tout announced, "this is the very talented plastic surgeon I was telling you all about, Dr. Harold Previn."

Previn smiled. "Harry."

Tout turned back to Previn and started pointing at people. "Phil Stein, publicity for Fay. Attorneys Stanley Rosen and Harvey Bleeker. This handsome bloke here, my partner, Sid Wilde."

Previn eyed Sid Wilde suspiciously. Was he Fay's assailant? Was this the man she'd been raving about in the car that night?

"I brought you all together to get a status report about Fay. And as they say…" Tout turned back to Previn, who was still eyeing Wilde. "You da man."

"I'm not in the habit of talking about a patient's medical prognosis to a room full of strangers. Ethics!"

Even as Previn made this bold pronouncement, it occurred to him he hadn't even discussed Fay's condition with Fay herself. Only with Tout. Yet no matter how disingenuous his speech may have seemed to himself, there was a difference between discussing her status with her manager and briefing a small gathering that included not one but two attorneys.

"I've worked with this man for thirteen years," Tout said, pointing at his partner. "And I don't see how anyone can argue against bringing her publicist into the loop. Come on, Harry. This is the business of making music. That's why we're here."

"What about them?" Previn pointed at attorneys Bleeker and Rosen.

"All part of our happy family." Tout laughed. "Harry, Harry. Loosen up, mate."

They were waiting. Tout sat far back from the conference table, his ankle resting on a knee. He was wearing no socks with his dress shoes. Stein had a legal pad in front of him and a black pen sitting on top of it. He looked up at Previn through thick horn-rimmed glasses that were so nerdy they were cool. However, Sid Wilde just sipped hot green tea from a clear glass, seemingly indifferent to the whole business. His black shirt was immaculately pressed. His platinum-blond hair was short, dyed to the max, and gelled; his fingernails, manicured; his teeth, china white; his body, toned, as though he spent two hours a day at the gym. Previn would have been ready to bet money he'd had laser work done around his eyes.

The two attorneys wore expensive suits and one of them had a large briefcase that looked like it might contain his entire legal practice. Both were forty-ish and fit. This was the Capital of Good Looks, after all.

"I'm loose," Previn insisted.

"'Course you are, mate. My lawyers here tell me in her current state, Fay's record company is within its rights to tell us to fuck off. Though not if we can deliver her first video performance in three weeks, which is required by contract. So, Harry! What's it gonna take?"

Tout had eyes. Did he really think that somehow Fay would be ready or could be readied to film a music video in three weeks' time? Previn hesitated. He wondered if Tout wanted an honest answer. He'd gathered an audience. What were they expecting him to tell them? It occurred to Previn that Tout wanted Previn to deliver the bad news so he didn't have to.

"Best case. Year. Eighteen months."

Publicist Stein spoke up. "What's he talking about?"

Tout glared at Previn. "I...don't...know."

Stein shifted in his chair. Seemingly unable to sit still with this news. "You're going to fix her, right?"

Previn found himself on his back foot. It wasn't as if he hadn't done everything he could for Fay. If there were something, anything else he could have done, he surely would have.

"You just don't recapture..." Previn began. "I mean I'm going to do all I can do, but...How do I put this? She's going to be permanently, irreparably..."

Previn watched Wilde glance at Tout. The lawyers both busily began writing.

Tout barked at the attorneys, "Don't write that down! Forget he ever said that. It's not true. Harry, tell the truth."

"Why are you all looking at me like...?" Previn turned to Tout. He couldn't believe Tout had as much as called him a liar. "Johnny, you know. We've spoken about how she looks. I can only do so much. I told you about the lines of tension. The cuts run counter to—"

"You're blindsiding me, Harry. It's been two weeks! You never said—"

Attorney Harvey Bleeker spoke up. "Then that's definitive?"

Previn stared into Sid Wilde's blue eyes. Wilde was very quiet, but very present. Perhaps the most present. He seemed the most at peace with what Previn had said. He was either so disengaged it didn't matter or so on top of the situation nothing could surprise him. Tout, on the other hand, seemed to be grandstanding. For what purpose, Previn couldn't figure, though perhaps it was simply in his DNA to do so.

"You're a plastic surgeon, aren't you?" Stein asked. "You do this stuff, right?"

Wilde got up and quietly walked over to the coffee dispenser and refilled his mug with more hot water and dropped a new tea bag into it. He resumed his seat, watching everyone as he stirred his drink with a swivel stick. A painful silence followed until he'd stopped.

Tout addressed Previn. "How much time...how many hours have we spent together and not a word about you not being able to put this right?"

"Oh. I said it. Of course I—"

"Bullocks!" Tout thundered. "And you're not to tell her that."

"Why not?"

"She can't know."

"She has a right to know," Previn said.

Tout turned to Wilde. "Help me out here."

At that very moment, everyone looked up through the glass to see rock god Nick Valentine. Thirty-two and glam, wearing his trademark wide-brimmed hat over his long black stringy hair and open gray trench coat, he walked right up to the reception desk, as though he needed to be announced. Agatha Pike, who had become an instantly recognizable celebrity for nothing other than being his sexy, thirty-four-year-old blonde lover, hung on him as though she were part of his coat.

Although Previn knew he should try to change the subject, he couldn't let it go because Tout had questioned his credibility. "I never said she could be restored. The mere idea that I would suggest the impossible…Hers is a horrific injury. I can only do what I can do. And it's going to take time. A lot of time."

Tout lowered his voice so that it was almost hard to hear. "In about two minutes I'm going to start breaking furniture."

This meeting was sheer theater. Tout absolutely knew her condition. Not only had he heard about it, he'd seen it and lived with it. All Previn could think was that this performance, and it was a performance, was about creating some kind of public record that Tout had been as much in the dark about Fay's plight as anyone. Previn was beginning to think he was being set up somehow to take the fall for Fay. What else could it be?

The receptionist came in and whispered into Wilde's ear.

Wilde stood up. "Please excuse me. I'll be back."

They were all distracted by the arrival of rock royalty, even this crowd who Previn would have presumed to be jaded. Valentine was still visible through the glass. Previn stared out at him as Wilde greeted him.

Valentine started talking before Wilde was quite there, loudly enough in fact to be heard in the conference room.

"Why am I always coming to Tout & Wilde? We could be eating veal chop at Craig's."

"You don't eat," Wilde said at last. "I've never seen you eat. Anyway, you were supposed to be here two hours ago."

Agatha made a great show of braiding blond hair in front of her face.

"You know I don't get up that early."

Wilde tried to guide Valentine away from the public area before looking around, then said something in an undertone.

Valentine raised his voice. "Ah, man. I don't do bad news. I don't wanna know bad. Sort it. I'm a happy guy. I do happy. Don't do the bad drag thing. You know that. Sid Wilde, you know that."

"You're right. You're right. I don't know what I was thinking."

Valentine became all smiles. "Okay then. Let's grab breakfast."

"It's after two in the afternoon."

"Who sets your clock, Sid?"

Wilde came back into the room. "Sorry. This is gonna take a few…" But then he didn't leave.

With Wilde again seated at the table, Stein attempted to get away from the finger-pointing and back to the practical. "Can't you graft some new skin on her face or something?"

"In horror movies."

Stein pointed at the huge wall poster of Fay. "Look at her. She's… The Face. Her whole image is built around it. And I'm supposed to send her out on interviews and tour with looks that'd scare children." He slammed his fist on the table. "I'm sorry, but I can't accept she can't be made right."

"You don't have to." Previn noted the surprise in the faces of those around him when he said this. "I mean it. You can get a second opinion."

"That won't be necessary," Tout said.

Previn faced off with Tout. "I don't mind. Really."

Stein slammed the table yet again. "Damn! She's not Marilyn Manson."

"Fay Wray is a sex symbol," Tout said. "Let's get real. It's not about the music. Never was. Never."

The room went silent.

Wilde spoke up finally. "We're up a creek. Girl like her loses her looks, that's it. She's dead."

Previn shot back, "You can't say that!"

"Best thing ever happened to Elvis and Morrison," Wilde continued. "Sold more albums dead than alive. I'm a glass-half-full kind of guy."

"But she's *not* dead," Stein said.

"Tell that to Elvis," Wilde replied.

Tout jumped up. "That's it! What if they never died?"

"You're not going to sell me on the idea that Elvis is sitting on a beach somewhere, collecting royalties," Stein said.

"Why not?" Tout said. He had everyone's rapt attention. "Don't you see, if Fay Wray were dead, it'd solve everything. All our problems."

Wilde nodded several times thoughtfully as though he were actively considering it before going back to Valentine.

"We could play off the sympathy," Tout continued. "Release her records posthumously. There'd be the lost session tapes, her home recordings rerecorded and remastered."

"Tout, the chick is alive," Stein reminded him once again.

"A mere formality." Tout waved him off gracefully. "Sid's right. She's as good as dead. And that's dead. So we give her something. Keep her busy. And we market her as dead. Work it. Monroe is frozen at thirty-six. She'll always be thirty-six. That's the brilliance of this. We want the fans to remember Fay the way she was in her prime at…nineteen. You know, when she was The Face. We'll say she drowned…like that actress. Help me here."

"Natalie Wood?" Previn volunteered.

"Yeah. Tragic. It's got to be tragic."

Stein spoke up. "I'm old enough to remember that great *Rolling Stone* cover with Morrison, shirt off, big healthy brown bob of hair, looking like he'd come down from Olympus. Fuck! They'd put Jim Morrison back on the cover because The Doors actually got bigger fifteen, twenty years after his death. Oh, my God! That headline, 'He's hot. He's sexy. He's dead.' I could run with this. Never look back."

"You betcha!"

"You…you've gotta be kidding," Previn said.

Remarkably, judging by the way that they all turned to him with annoyance, what he'd said came across as the most controversial thing said.

◆◆◆

HELEN FELT WEIGHTLESS AS she floated on her back in Guy's pool. In the late-afternoon sun, the pool glistened like a disco ball.

Her hours had ceased to make sense. When she'd lived with Harry, her schedule had been regulated by his office and surgical sessions. After she'd left him, she felt like she'd become an artist again. No clock. No preconditions. She was all in her head. Finally, she had thought less about her loses and more about making art.

Then Jake and Richard walked into the house and she could hear the clock again. More like the tick of a bomb. Guy waking her. Harry showing up out of the blue. Though hadn't it all begun with Dr. Perez? She was trying to reckon if that really was the through-line. Had she not seen Perez, she certainly wouldn't have taken the Ambien, but would running into Jake have made her become any less unhinged? She felt as though she were vibrating with anxiety.

She heard a car come up the drive. Her head came out of the water as though a crocodile had suddenly come up beside her. Absolutely no one was expected, though a car definitely could be heard idling, and then voices. Unlike when Harry had showed up, the gate wasn't open.

It couldn't be Harry. Not again!

She jumped from the pool naked and ran to the hedge where she peered out onto the motor court. A driver lifted several pieces of luggage from the trunk of a black limousine and set them down near the front door.

Bobbing over to the driver in his white Converse sneakers, Guy handed him some cash with an ease that suggested there was nothing out of the ordinary about his return.

She ran for her towel. Was she supposed to welcome him home as if she'd just come from the shower? Her self-consciousness brought her back to the moment she'd seen her former self in the Jonathan Gold. She didn't want Guy to see her weight gain from the fertility treatments. It surprised her that she even cared, but she did.

He could have called. That was the customary thing. What was he doing back? It was all too weird. It'd been eighteen hours since they'd spoken, if that.

She came out from behind the hedge and met him just as the limo drove away. He stepped forward to embrace her and she stepped back. In spite of the towel, she already felt violated as if he'd come in on her naked. She'd spent her whole life being so free and easy with her body, but this felt different.

"What are you doing here?" she asked.

Guy smiled the most radiant, gracious smile, but she wasn't going to let him charm his way out of this.

"I live here," he said. "It's my house."

"You could have called."

"It was too early in the morning when I boarded the plane. I'd have woken you."

"There's e-mail. How 'bout after you landed?"

He had a boyish quality. Maybe it was the T-shirt he wore under his black sports coat. He always seemed to be well put together but ever so casual.

"I gave you a scare? I'm sorry."

He tried to reach for her cheek tenderly, but she stepped back again. This felt so awkward and wrong. Literally the day before they'd spoken, she'd told him about her filing for a divorce on Tuesday and presto, Wednesday afternoon he appears. He must have gotten on the plane a few hours later. Or about as fast as he could get a ticket and get to the airport.

She crossed her arms and held her towel closer. "I don't understand—we were only just talking about what had happened with Jake and now you're here."

He laughed.

She adjusted the towel just above her breasts. She couldn't believe she'd been put into this situation.

"I should leave," she said.

"Please. Go change."

"I mean, I should get out of your house. I thought staying here was going to be a kind of breather from what I've been going through."

"It is."

"I don't want to live with a man!"

That winning smile appeared again. A tan seemed to set off his hair as though it were a windswept wheat field. "Helen. This is a very big house; we'll hardly see each other."

"What are you doing here?" she heard herself shriek.

"I don't know. I spoke to you. And all of a sudden, I felt like I had to get home. You ever have one of those feelings? I've been away now for—"

"Stop. You simply decided?"

"That's right."

"But what about me?" She felt her voice become ever so small just then. Almost pleading. She was in near panic. "How is this going to work? I'll go. I'm not playing house with you."

"Helen, what are you talking about?"

"You know what I'm talking about!"

He grabbed one of his bags and set it down inside his front door. "You're not the only one in crisis, you know."

"Huh? Well, what—?"

"Don't want to talk about it."

With that, he disappeared into his house and shut the door behind him. She stood in the driveway in her towel feeling like a selfish imposition. This was supposed to be her crisis. Did he really just make this all about him?

◆◆◆

PREVIN HAD RUSHED BACK to his office following his meeting at Tout & Wilde, reeling from its crazy conclusion but hoping to get back on steady ground with a post-op and a new patient consultation.

"Ordinarily," post-op Jean May continued, "I wouldn't have bothered you like this. You must think I'm a silly woman."

"No. Not at all."

"I'm in a panic. Sunday night my husband returns."

Previn opened her file and closed it distractedly. He had only operated on her five days before. "I didn't think. I thought—"

"I know. I know. He wasn't supposed to come back so soon."

He'd only removed her stitches the day before. There was still considerable bruising, particularly around the eyes. The face was much fuller than it would be in a few months as it settled. This was normal, but not how Jean May, or any woman for that matter, would want to present herself to an estranged husband.

"Jean, you look terrific!" Previn knew she needed to hear this.

She lowered her chestnut eyes shyly. Set off from her blond hair, they gave her a gravity that was calming. She was very centered, even if she was in what could only be described as a delicate place.

"I wouldn't just say that, you know," he went on. "It takes many months for the face to get settled, to look, you know...lived in. I reckon you'll be about eight or nine days out when he sees you. You're healing very well. A little makeup."

"Oh my God. He's going to know!"

"When did you say you saw him last?"

"Six weeks."

"That's not yesterday. It won't be so clear to him what's changed, and inside of a few days, he'll think that this is you. Except maybe just a touch better than he remembered."

"My face is puffy. There's bruising around my eyes. He's going to think I've been slapped around."

Previn laughed. "So, tell him the truth. It shows you care."

She shook her head.

"But honestly, don't you love your new face? You do, don't you? Admit it."

"Harry, I never really thought I'd do this."

He was charmed by the innocence of her confession. Compare that with the cynicism Tout had shown and his indignation over Previn's not terribly surprising revelation that he couldn't restore

Fay. Tout knew better. How on earth could he suggest Fay's injuries would be anything but a simple fix?

Previn returned to his patient. "But are you happy with it?"

He watched Jean unclip her earring and roll it around between her fingers, deep in thought.

"The job? Yeah."

"Is it you?" he asked.

"Me?"

The question seemed almost too pointed for her. When it came to his patients dealing with their looks, they were capable of becoming exceedingly meek. He hadn't observed this in Jean May before. Until then, she'd exuded a quiet confidence and poise. After all, she was the wife of a big-time movie director. But she was also a woman at a delicate time in her life.

"I don't know. I guess it is." She hesitated. "I'd always wanted my grandmother's face. I thought if I could grow into her face…I wanted to know what God had intended for mine. But look at me. I succumbed. Now I'll never know."

Previn took a long, hard look at Jean May. At her face. He'd given her the face she'd wanted. No. He'd given her better. But to wonder what God had intended, to bring God into it!

What had God intended for Fay? Had he thought that for her sins she should have her face disfigured? Jean May was very fortunate, but he couldn't do the same for Fay, although he had been expected to do nothing less than restore her to however she looked before God had gotten hold of her.

"It's not really about your grandmother, though, is it? It's about you."

"Now I have my face from twelve years ago. Weird, isn't it? That we can turn back the clock?"

"I've met a few beautiful women. Same insecurities!"

Sara came into the office and handed him a file.

Jean May laughed. "Who are you fooling? I've heard all about you, Harry. You're the go-to guy for celebrity crackups."

"What?" he snapped. He didn't like the sound of this. Was she referring to Fay? Had people been talking about him? Had it gotten out? "Who said anything about celebrity crackups?" His mouth suddenly went dry.

"People."

He glared at her like he wanted answers. "What people?"

"People."

"Well, I'm cracking up listening to this!" Sara caught his eye, making him realize this was a vast overreaction on his part. If he wasn't careful, people would figure that something really was wrong.

"I'm saying this is my crackup. This is *the* crackup. My face. My marriage. What is he going to say to me when he sees this face?"

It suddenly became clear to him that this celebrity crackup line was just a line, something people say. Didn't mean a thing. Didn't mean people were talking around the water cooler about his doctoring up Fay. He was annoyed at himself for being so on edge. For allowing something so innocuous to give him a scare.

Sara shook her head and left the room.

He smiled. "You're not a crackup."

Previn got up from his chair and paced up and down as Jean sat there probably wondering what was up with him. But hadn't he just sat in on a discussion about Fay Wray dying? Of faking her death so that they could sell more records?

He felt like he was sitting on a pressure cooker. Something was going to explode. If it wasn't Fay, it'd be him. And if it wasn't him, it'd be Jean May because she'd never know what God had had in mind for her. Well, maybe God had put Previn together with her. Had she considered that?

This was a city where the stakes were just getting higher and higher. Where beauty was a life or death proposition. Jean had come to him not feeling alive in her marriage because her face had begun to sag, or rather that she was starting to look all too much like her grandmother. If she wondered about seeing her grandmother's face in her own, she should look again at her pre-op photos. He should show her those.

Nah. It wasn't Jean May. It was the whole damn rap. She was no less immune to feeling pressured to be young and beautiful for her husband. If she weren't, he'd leave her for the star of his picture, Aura McAdams, the flavor of the moment. And Aura would look beautiful on the screen, as actors do. She'd look immortal. That was it. On screen, there was immortality. It was the one place. On film. That was what he was competing against. That was what he was being asked to do: Lock in time. Lock in a look.

The idea of Fay Wray being locked into her prime like Marilyn Monroe was wild, but wasn't that what everyone wanted? Wasn't that what Jean May really wanted? Wasn't that what her husband wanted of her?

So, if Fay Wray had to die to be beautiful. If…

"I've turned myself inside out for my husband," Jean said.

Previn stopped pacing. "But he didn't ask you to do this."

"He didn't have to ask. A woman knows," she said with unshakeable conviction. "A woman knows when her time has come."

Jean was evidently quite delicate. The post-op consultation was either cause for celebration or led patients to take a hard look in the mirror.

"It's been a very difficult shoot," Jean said. "Working on a remote location in Nigeria, it's hard. He'd have been finished two weeks ago, but a storm tore through the set at the start of production. I know if things were okay with us, he would have asked me to come out."

"But you went over there," Previn insisted. It was a pressure cooker. He felt her desperation. "You went with him to Lagos and you visited the set. We spoke about this. Remember?"

"Look, he knows I like to have my nails done. I like to wear fine clothes. I'm a lady. I'm not someone who likes going out on location, particularly when it's some place where I have to use a porta potty. He didn't ask me to come back. This is the first time he didn't ask."

"Perhaps he knew it was no place for you."

"He didn't ask. A woman *wants* to be asked. A woman *needs* to be asked."

The rules of attraction are not always kind. They don't always take into account the twenty-five years this couple had been together or the two kids they'd had.

He didn't even get that chance with Helen. He'd never know what it would be like to grow old with her. He used to love coming home to her cooking. They had their own visual language. They could talk about various artists. It wasn't gossip. It was simply the joy of having someone around who shared his tastes. Evidently that wasn't enough.

If having two children and watching them grow up wasn't enough to cement a bond, then what was? He'd wanted children with Helen. They'd tried for them. God knows they'd tried.

Jean had fallen silent.

"And this weekend he returns," he said at last.

"Yes. Sunday."

"I think it'll be fine." He served up this statement with a generous smile. "You look terrific, Jean. I don't know if I've made that clear enough. He ought to be very pleased to be your husband."

"It is…a nice thing to hear from time to time," she said.

◆◆◆

AFTER HIS LAST PATIENT, Previn closed the door to his office.

In his desk, there was a folder containing the autopsy of Jake Blackburn's mother and several pictures from her post-op. He picked up one of them. She was actually smiling in the shot. Most people can't help smiling when they have their picture taken, but this particular smile belied the fact that hours later she'd be dead.

Her name was Simone. Simone Blackburn. She had sat in his office during her first consultation enthusing about her son, not the actor, but the man. "This is my birthday gift. My baby's giving me a new body for my birthday. Could I have a better son?"

"That's lovely."

"He would have given me anything, but he would have never thought to…He thinks I'm okay without surgery, but he's not a woman, is he? And I'm his mother. I had to ask. He wanted to send me on holiday, and I said, 'Give your mom…'" She started to cry.

Previn grabbed her a Kleenex. "Now, now."

"Thank you, Doctor."

"Harry. Call me Harry."

"We're close. I don't have anyone but my boy."

"You must be very proud of Jake's success."

She beamed. "He's my everything."

Simone was Versace through and through. All bright colors, which went with her blonde hair and tan in the most probable way. Very Northern Italian via Queens, New York. She'd written fifty-seven on the questionnaire he'd asked her to fill out, but he'd later learn she was actually sixty-three. Women often lied about their age, but not all of them went so far as to lie to their plastic surgeon. He'd thought her surprisingly healthy for all of her sixty-three years, not so for fifty-seven. It was because he felt she hadn't worn her age well that he wanted to do her some good.

"You have a long list of things you want done," Previn recalled.

"Don't all women?"

He laughed. "Surgery, even cosmetic surgery, can be hard on the body. We'll see what your history and physical—"

"What's that?"

"Want to make sure you're up to this."

"This is a birthday gift. I want it for my birthday. Jake arranged for me to take ten of my best friends to St. Martin for…it's my birthday, Harry. I have to be at my best. You do understand, don't you?"

"When is the happy day?"

"Five weeks."

He then offered up with the sweetest smile words that'd haunt him forever. "Happy birthday."

Six days later, she was dead.

◆◆◆

"I GOT MY WIFE asleep next to me. What's up? You in jail?"

Previn was calling the one man he felt might offer a way out of his predicament, his attorney, Ty Fanning. Previn stood across from a plastic-wrapped head on the pedestal in his studio.

"I'm sorry to bother you, but it's not going well," Previn said.

"Call me tomorrow morning."

"I've got surgery."

"You want to make an appointment? What time is it?" Ty pressed. He must have found a clock. "Fuck, Harry! It's almost one a.m."

"They're going to kill her off like they do on TV. You know like when an actor has a contract dispute, they kill the character off."

"What are you talking about? Who? What?"

Previn thought he could hear Ty get up from the bed and turn on the side lamp. Maybe he'd already moved to another room so as not to wake his wife.

"Fay Wray. They're talking about her demise."

"Like hit men or something?"

Why didn't he get it? Previn had been sitting in his art studio for an hour, wondering whom to call. He actually thought about calling Helen even though she wasn't right for this. However, Ty Fanning, attorney at law, seemed like the one man he knew he could speak to about justice. After all, this was about fair play. There were boundaries. There was some sense of propriety still and surely this man was in touch with that. "No," Previn continued. "Like in a story where they kill off the character, but the actor lives."

"Have you been drinking?"

"No! It has to do with this idea that if she's not pretty, she's dead."

"Well, if she's lost her looks, hard to see how she could have a career."

Ty Fanning wasn't supposed to agree with Tout.

"I'm up to my neck in this. It's awful. I don't want to be associated with anything like this. Beauty is not a life or death proposition. It may feel that way to some people, I get that, but not literally. I mean, come on!"

"You should try to see it from their perspective. Fay Wray is a brand. They're just protecting their brand."

"Is that all you think she is?"

"You said it yourself, like when they kill a part in a series."

Previn ripped the plastic off the sculpture and stared at it as anger and frustration got the better of him. "But Fay is alive. She's not a walk-on. She can't be cut. You don't cut someone like her."

"It's one a.m., Harry."

"God, Ty, don't you see how fucked up all this is?"

"You'd be surprised at some of the situations I'm dealing with on any given day. From what you've told me, this could be nothing more than talk."

"But don't you see? That's where it begins."

"You got it all wrong. Hollywood is *all* talk. People talk. But they don't walk the walk. You know what I'm saying?"

Previn sighed. Maybe Ty was right. Maybe this was why he'd called Ty Fanning, because he could cut through the emotion and see what Tout had said for what it was: talk.

"That's what I was thinking about with the wrongful death suit," Previn said. "That it was all talk."

"Don't jump to conclusions."

"But you're saying, talk is—"

"I'm saying, just do your job," Ty counseled. "Nothing's happened yet."

"Fay Wray's injuries."

"And you're tending to her."

"Trying."

Ty laughed pretentiously. "That's what I want to hear! Now get some rest. You sound stressed." Ty hung up.

Previn stared at the block of moist clay before feverishly digging into it with his bare hands. He felt desperate. Like he had to get into his work or do something reckless. He finally picked up the clay knife, working it until an eye emerged. He could only give so much. He was exhausted. He laid plastic over it.

18

FAY HAD PULLED HER bedsheet over her head. Her facial features were vaguely distinguishable underneath. As she breathed through her mouth, the white fabric went in and out like a suffocation mask.

Previn had stopped at the foot of her bed while Rox lingered inside the doorframe.

"Fay," Previn said at last.

Fay pulled the sheet down from over her head and peered out at him. Her bandage covered all but one side of her face.

"It's time to lose the bandage, Fay."

"Why?"

"Because you don't need it anymore."

Fay's hand went to her bandage possessively. "My face."

"It's about moving on. How long has it been, two weeks? More? That's a long time in the life of recovery."

Fay looked away sadly.

"I understand your wanting to cling to the bandage, but it's hiding."

"Look who's talking. You help people hide for a living."

Ouch.

Rox spoke up. "Listen to him, Fay. You want to be a one-hit wonder?"

"You so wanna be me, Raspberry." Fay eyed Rox's red hair and sneered. "And you never will be. That's the shame of it."

"If everyone had the production team you had."

"They overproduced my shit. Buried the vocals. I could be huge, if they'd just let me be me. And that's the truth."

"Yada yada yada. You go, girl."

Fay turned to Previn. "Johnny didn't come home last night. Rox's on the rag about it. But you were never going to be the only one, babe."

Rox smiled knowingly. "Oh, he came home."

Fay laughed and Rox actually joined her. It dawned on Previn that they so reveled in their dislike for one another that their insults doubled as endearments. Hard to tell when they were both so good at the cut and thrust. Fay at least seemed to take some joy in Rox delivering a good line. It told him she had an ear for a turn of phrase, but don't all lyricists?

This back and forth made him wonder about Fay having rivals. He thought about the simmering feud between Katy Perry and Taylor Swift. What if that had gone Tonya Harding? The idea that another female pop star might disfigure a beautiful rival like Fay or pay someone else to do it suddenly animated him. Was it so far fetched to imagine?

Probably!

From down the hall, a Lady Gaga "Bad Romance" ringtone erupted.

"Damn!" Rox said. "That's mine. Must have left it."

Finally! He watched her scurry off. Other than a few minutes just before surgery, he had never been allowed so much as a moment alone with Fay. Rox was forever there, hovering. Possessing. Imposing.

Maybe now he'd be able to get to the bottom of what was really going on. He sat down at the edge of Fay's bed. "Shall we take a look, Fay?"

Just as he leaned in to remove her bandage, Fay kissed him.

Her lips felt warm, buttery, and wrong.

He pushed her away. "No!"

He quickly shot a look at the door to make sure that Rox hadn't seen. He recalled the night he'd first encountered Fay in the car when she'd tried to kiss him. He was surprised at how flustered he was. Maybe it was that this was like tasting forbidden fruit. Or that the lines had already become so blurred between them. She'd become an increasing obsession. Although it was about the treatment and wanting answers, no?

She looked at him with her big green eyes and his mind raced back to countless moments they'd shared in what he thought was a patient-client thing, a kind of conspiracy all their own, but which she had certainly read to be smoldering desire.

"Isn't that what you want?" Fay asked.

"Fay. I…"

"You don't think I'm pretty enough."

That Fay felt this was the only way she could relate to men, that a man like Previn, her doctor no less, could only be attending to her because he wanted her sexually, spoke loudly to her issues. Maybe even the issues that had gotten her into her current predicament. She seemed to lean way too hard on the physical. That was her music. It was how she'd become famous. She put it out there. No doubt she'd had many takers.

This wasn't an altogether unique situation. Therapists had experienced transference where patients projected feelings onto them. The thinking was that it was a natural by-product of the sharing of intimacies. While he could certainly rationalize what had happened, it still felt a little icky. He was married. He was a married man. No. Actually, he was estranged from his wife and probably heading toward a divorce. It bothered him that, somehow, he might have contributed to making her think he'd be responsive. Could his caring be so misconstrued?

She actually thought there was something normal about his treating her and fucking around with her at the same time. That wasn't him. That was all Fay.

But then Tout was involved with Rox. The lines in her business were often blurred.

"It's not that. Fay, I'm your doctor."

He knew this was an evasion even as he heard himself deliver this explanation. If he could be honest with her, he would have told her he'd shared these little moments because he had so wanted to feel that they were on the same side. He had a yearning for her approval. To know that it was okay, even if he knew his attending to her wasn't quite on the level.

Mercifully, Rox reappeared at the door.

"Then when are you going to make me normal, huh, Doc? I'd like an answer. I want my life back. Give me my life!"

Previn looked to Rox for a lifeline.

She simply shrugged.

♦♦♦

PREVIN LED ROX FAR enough down the hall from Fay that she couldn't hear them speak. They'd often had little huddles in the hallway or in one of the adjourning rooms. They nonetheless spoke softly, as though they were conspiring against Fay.

"You see what it's like," Rox began. "She had her chance. She needs to get over herself."

"Hello. She's been through—"

"Yeah. Yeah."

"I didn't have an answer for her," he said. "I don't even know what I can or should be saying."

"Just bullshit with her."

"What?"

"You must have a million patients like her who just want to be told they're beautiful or going to be."

Previn prided himself on making his patients happy. That's what it was all about. Yet that wasn't the perception. Fay felt he helped women hide. Rox, that he simply lied to patients about their looks, as though what he did for them wasn't actually real.

"Is that what you think I do?" he asked.

"You've got to up her dose! I was only just telling Johnny she's getting to be too much. I know you work with stars, but not like we work with them. It can get hard to keep 'em in their cage without a little help, if you know what I—"

"She must be terrified."

"Fay? Terrified?"

He grabbed Rox's arm to get her attention. "You need to level with me about what's going on here. When this thing goes south, who do you think's going to be left holding the bag? You and me. That's who."

"Johnny's got our backs."

"Who's got Fay's?"

"When I get old and my boobs start to sag, I'm going to come visit you because you're good." Rox burst out laughing.

They stopped. As if on cue, two police detectives stood with Tout at the foot of the spiral stairs. One of them stared at Previn holding his medical bag. "Who are you?"

Previn was speechless. He knew who they were. They made these kinds of men in the same factory somewhere. The cut of their suits wasn't it. Maybe their build. Their haircuts. Something. But they were dicks.

"Dr. Previn was looking in on my daughter," Tout lied.

Previn hoped just then that their curiosity wouldn't lead them to want to look in on the little darling. They'd sure get a surprise. And Previn would have plenty of explaining to do.

Having an attorney like Ty Fanning at the ready didn't give Previn a lot of confidence. It wasn't like Ty saw the downside of risks like he did. If Fay were to be exposed, there was no way he was going to come out clean.

The detective opened the front door, took a hard look at Previn and then at Tout. "If you hear anything—"

"I'll let you know." After the detectives walked out, Tout took a long moment to gather himself.

"That was a lie," Previn said.

"Fay's mother asked them to check around," Tout replied.

"You gotta call her. What will she think?" Previn said.

"Keep Fay medicated. You know what medicated means, don'tcha, mate?" Tout made a gun gesture to his head as if to imply Previn needed to give her enough meds to blow her brains out. "And leave the mother to me."

Previn couldn't believe what he was hearing. "You can't hide this! What's the matter with you?"

"I'm protecting her, mate."

"I don't want any part of this."

"But you are."

"I'm not! I only treated her because she needed treatment. That's what I do. The rest...I don't know what that was."

Even as Previn made this speech, he knew better. He knew he'd crossed the line and now that line seemed all the more irrevocably drawn.

19

MALIBU FARM WAS ONE of Helen's favorite go-to places.

The restaurant sat at the end of an old wooden pier that looked out onto the historic Adamson House and a popular reef break, which at that moment had at least a dozen surfers. Sundays were always busy, but that day was overcast which made dining there at least manageable.

Helen had told Harry the night of their big fight she'd been driving all night because that was what she did when she felt sad. The truth was she'd sat in her car and cried. It was a good story that she'd been driving, but traffic being what it was even in the middle of the night, who drove in LA if they didn't have to? One exception was driving up the Pacific Coast Highway. The waves crashing on her left. This was one thing she could do to clear her head. She'd painted enough, and going home meant having to face Guy, and she couldn't.

"Don't punch me. I come in peace."

Richard wore dark, round Oliver People's sunglasses, a yellow Oxford, and loafers without socks. She was surprised he recognized her because she'd put her hair up, though she could have picked him out of a lineup. Her mouth opened when he set his *LA Times* and coffee mug down on her table, as if to claim it.

Her unease must have been apparent. "I can certainly sit somewhere else." He pointed back to the crowded table he'd been sitting at. "I was with some friends over there and it was either you join us or I join you, and I'd much rather join you because they're frankly tiring. You're probably the one person in this town who doesn't want to talk shop. It's a holy day for Christ's sake! Though I'll admit, I'm prone to be just as insufferable as the next in that respect. I suppose artists talk art. Is that true?"

"Sometimes."

"That's right. Harry's an artist too, isn't he?"

"He sculpts."

"But come on, you're the real artist. You can talk to me."

"He has a gift when it comes to figurative art."

"And here I was thinking it was just some sort of put-on to hustle facelifts."

"He takes sculpture very seriously."

He mulled the coffee in his mug before looking up. "Bet he was a surgeon long before he took to sculpture."

She didn't know why he kept probing about Harry. She was already impatient with the conversation. "What does it matter?"

He clapped his hands. "Just as I thought! What that man won't do to get ahead in the world."

"His art is his true passion. Really!"

He bobbed his head as if to a song as he delighted in his conclusion.

Helen wasn't having it. "Why are you asking all these questions about Harry? What do you want with him?

"He's a subject of some fascination to me. You know, I still haven't told Jake who you are. I pride myself on discretion, though by rights my allegiance should be with him, not you. Awkward."

"We don't have an allegiance."

Two seagulls landed on the rail across from their table. One of them tilted its head as if to contemplate what had been said.

"You and Harry should be more grateful," Richard replied.

"You include Harry? Thought you said he was doing some missionary work for you."

He smiled. "Did I say that?"

Her eyes were drawn to his hand as he fingered his coffee cup. His manicure was positively precious. She wondered why she hadn't noticed it the last time they'd met, though she was admittedly distracted then. It occurred to her that Richard might be gay. But perhaps he was more in the mold of a classic narcissist, which didn't quite make sense because his time wet-nursing stars was the stuff of legend. However, it took an ego to handle star egos. To be something more to them than a wet nurse, in fact.

"Have you seen Harry lately?" he asked.

"Thanks to you."

"Me?"

"Yeah! After you told him where I'm living."

"Did I really? That's so fucked up! I don't have boundaries. It's one of several faults I've become aware of, but only recently."

He held his smile for so long it became uncomfortable.

Why she kept up this pretense of politeness with this man, she did not know. She could only figure it was because Richard had some malevolent connection to Harry, which was hardly a good reason to feel obliged to humor him.

Her eyes narrowed as she stared at him. He was at the source of so much of what had gone wrong in her life. Guy wouldn't have come home early if it weren't for him. Harry wouldn't have thrown a jealous fit. She wouldn't have run into Jake and freaked out. Hell, Harry wouldn't have even operated on Jake's mom if it weren't for him! Yet it went deeper. Richard had somehow become a fixture in her life. Although she belonged to a different tribe, seeing him again reminded her that Harry had left hers for Richard's long ago. That whole star-fucker nonsense. Seeing Richard brought it all up again like nausea.

"What is Harry doing with you? What are you doing with him?"

"You try to help someone!" He raised his arms with the aside.

"You are all about Richard Barone."

"Where's the gratitude? Where? I've saved Harry from a public relations nightmare. Saved you from bringing the roof down on Harry. And all I get is grief. A woman's dead. Has life become so cheap?"

She winced. Had he actually implied that Jake Blackburn's mother's death hadn't carried with it a high enough price? "I'm starting to feel sorry for Harry. I wouldn't have thought anyone could make me do that."

He laughed.

This was her fault. In spite of Harry's protestations to the contrary, she knew better. She'd led Harry into Richard's arms when she'd erupted that morning before the surgery. It was that simple. She couldn't look at Richard and not feel the gravity of it all. It was about so much more than one woman's death. What? She did not know. But she had this sense of foreboding. She found herself crying uncontrollably.

Richard came around the table to comfort her. "What did I just say?"

"I feel for Harry."

Was that it? She'd blurted this and it sounded about right.

Richard pulled out his phone. "Why don't we call him and you can tell him that?"

"Put that away," she snapped. "I'm not speaking to him ever again!"

That she could have allowed Richard to comfort her caused her to sob even more loudly. Dr. Perez must have been right about the fertility drugs turning her into a hormonal mess. If this wasn't what that looked like, what was?

He stared at her. The phone still in hand. "One moment you're walloping Jake, next you're complaining about what was a perfectly sentimental gesture on my part."

"And what was that?"

"Trying to get you and Harry...love birds back together!"

"It's not helping! It doesn't...help."

He dabbed at his chest with her napkin. "You've gotten tears on my shirt, young lady."

She hadn't liked Harry finding out that she'd been living at Guy's house, though she knew she had nothing to apologize for. That Harry might think otherwise annoyed her to no end. She had every right to her own life. She was free of him. Yet for a moment, feeling Harry's arms around her again never felt so good.

Yes. She most certainly was hormonal. There was no other explanation for her inconsistency. She had always prided herself on having a level head.

Richard grabbed the rail and followed one of the surfers who had caught an epic right. He seemed to be on that very board until the surfer turned out of it and began to paddle back out in the channel. "I grew up surfing. I wonder if I'll ever get on a board again before I die." He turned back to Helen, who was musing about Jonathan Gold, the other surfer she knew. "I bought into Harry because I thought he could give people back years of their lives. I really expected more of him than I rightfully should have. But then, he engenders that kind of confidence—until, that is, he falls short."

She heard his accusation. It made her feel icky. If Harry had blood on his hands, so did she. But was it that? Or was it that Harry was still her husband? "Surgery is risky. People never think about that."

"It's a rare man who can heal a woman with a knife."

She narrowed her eyes, yet again. What he was implying about Harry sounded almost evil. "I wouldn't have put it that way."

"I would."

"You don't know Harry's heart. It may surprise you."

20

HER NAME WAS SUSAN, too.

Now that she'd called in the cops, Previn worried that Fay's mother might materialize at any moment. Then what? She was evidently out there somewhere eating herself up over the whereabouts and condition of her daughter. He was surprised she hadn't already gone to the media. He wondered why this thing hadn't blown up yet, but he could hear it ticking. He knew at some point it had to explode in his hands.

The sight of the damage to Fay's face would break her mother's heart, as it would any parent. Although Fay had rambled on about her mother off and on, she did nothing to reach out to her. She simply couldn't bring herself to open that door.

It was as though Fay secretly wanted to goad her mother into action.

Previn hadn't mentioned the visit from the detectives. Evidently, no one else had, either. It was as though it had never happened. Fay had no idea. Previn wondered if in some police report somewhere, one of the detectives might have written his name. At the moment, anyway, this was the only thread he could think of that led him back to Fay.

Previn feared this very thread might someday lead her mother to him, too. He rehearsed various scenarios in his mind. He saw himself walking around his desk, as he did in countless consultations, to sit in the chair across from Mrs. Susan Plouse. The idea was more than a little unnerving. He couldn't imagine how he could find the words

Fay hadn't. Yet he was always having consultations about a particular patient's prognosis. This one, though, felt different.

As if to make the statement that Fay still had access to the outside world, the next time Previn visited Fay's room, he spotted her silver bloodstained clutch lying on the bedside table. He hadn't seen it since the night she got hurt. With the drops of blood, it was anything but normal. It certainly brought him back to that terrible night she'd been injured—How could it not remind her, too?

Fay opened the clutch and pulled out her cell phone to play for them one of the dozens of messages her mother had left her. Her mother must have smoked because her voice sounded huskier than Fay's.

"The messages I leave you, they're all prayers you're alive and safe on an island somewhere. I'm crazy worried, Susie. Soon your voicemail will probably be full." She began to choke up at this point. "If you ever hear my messages, you'll know my heart bleeds for you. I pray to the Lord you'll call home so I know my little baby is still alive."

As the message played, Fay became hysterical. "What am I gonna do?"

"Call her," Previn insisted. "You've got to. It's cruel not to tell her what's going on. Fay, do it."

"She can't," Rox cut in. "Her mother doesn't know she drinks and does drugs and has premarital sex—and with more than one guy."

"Is that such a big deal today?" Previn asked.

"Is in the Bible Belt."

Previn turned to Fay. "So that's why you won't call your mother, Fay?"

"The woman's an evangelical," Rox said. "Would freak if she knew this child of gawd was up to her tits in sin and loving it."

"Shut up!" Fay snapped.

"Just saying."

"You don't have to tell her the truth, Fay."

Rox shot him a look.

Previn shrugged, then smiled. "Just saying."

21

Barone had asked Previn to join him and Tout at Craig's for lunch.

Previn found them ensconced in the corner booth. Craig's had become the stand-in for the Polo Lounge, the industry haunt where Barone had been an almost legendary fixture. When the Polo Lounge's owner, the Sultan of Brunei, decided that stoning gays and adulteress women back home in his kingdom was okay, Previn had seen Barone on the nightly news standing at former Tonight Show host Jay Leno's shoulder when Leno announced an industry boycott. Never let it be said that Barone didn't know how to get on the right side of Sharia Law. Previn finished giving the actress Stella Bonbright a hug.

"I can't tell you anything in this light," Previn said. "Come to the office and we'll take a proper look."

They embraced again, and then Previn sat down.

"That's the third celebrity in…Did you *do* everyone here?" Barone asked.

"You know I can't answer that."

In his dark suit and tie, Craig stopped at their table to shake Barone's hand. He seemed too young for such formality, but that was him. Craig knew everyone and everyone knew Craig. No joke.

Previn could see that Craig delighted in having Barone around. His restaurant catered to the Richard Barones of the world. Soho

House really wasn't right for someone like Barone, who wasn't looking for cool. That was more an actor and screenwriter hangout. Barone wanted to slide into a dark booth and do a deal. Chasen's had closed years ago. So had Le Dome. Even Morton's had shuttered. Now that the Polo Lounge was radioactive, what was left? The Four Seasons didn't have the vibe. The Peninsula? No. Not at all. Craig's felt like it'd been there for decades. It was a scene, but also refined and almost staid in a good way, like Craig himself.

"The best agents are never more happening than the stars," Barone volunteered as Craig finally walked off. "I struggle with it because I've been around now for some time. And I'm known. But there's a reason why I don't do rope lines. You're different, though, Harry. There's something very glam about a man who makes stars look younger and sexier than they are. Who gives them back their lost years. It's very Hollywood. Do you sail, Harry?"

"Been out a few times. But not really." Previn couldn't believe he'd been coaxed out of a busy Monday at his surgery for this. He smiled. What else could he do? "Why? You inviting me out on your yacht?"

"In a matter of speaking, yes."

Barone and Tout burst out laughing like two kids.

"That funny?" Previn asked.

"It's a renewed passion."

The waiter offered them all some bread from his basket, which Previn and Barone quickly declined. Tout grabbed two rolls. Previn watched Tout spread a thick layer of butter on the warm bread. Tout must have been one of the few people in this town that didn't have an issue with gluten or, for that matter, didn't worry about his waistline.

"We want to take Fay sailing," Tout said.

"I need to buy some new Topsiders," Previn said. "If I'm going."

Tout chuckled. "You're on shore duty, mate."

Previn wasn't sure if he should be offended.

Tout seemed to enjoy unsettling Previn. He continued, "Fay will get on the boat, only she won't really be on the boat, in which case she must have fallen overboard. You follow? The Mexican officials will sign Fay's death certificate because they'll do anything for money. And so begins Fay's new life."

Barone looked up from the menu. "The problem with death. The problem with it is, no one gets out alive."

Tout burst out laughing again. Barone joined him.

"Except Fay Wray, of course," Tout countered. "She's going to get out alive, all right. She's gonna be the first. Bloody gorgeous, mate!"

Previn looked around the restaurant uneasily. Stared at several patients seated at different tables. At the waitstaff. At the glittering scene that seemed to continue without the slightest knowledge that at their table they were ever so casually discussing the finer points of the crime of faking Fay's death.

What they were proposing reminded Previn of the criminal machinations spelled out in the film *Double Indemnity*. Fay didn't have to be on the boat, only appear to be. Someone else could fall off. Or perhaps the people on the boat could just claim she was there. With the Mexican officials willing to say almost anything for money...But there'd still be questions. A lot of questions. Could you pay anyone enough to keep such a fraud secret?

Previn knew that Hollywood had a history of covering up celebrity crime. One of the more notorious being Jean Harlow. After her husband was shot, studio dicks cased Harlow's house for the first eleven hours before calling the police. No one will ever know what they took. Or, for that matter, what really happened to her husband. How can anybody ever be sure it was suicide? Obviously, the husband shooting himself a few days after marrying this bombshell actress was a scandal in its own right, but how the studio behaved was perhaps even more of one.

That was LA. Had anything really changed?

There was so much people didn't know about what really went on in this town. Michael Jackson doing propofol, or "milk" as he liked to call it. Who knew? Had to be a lot of people who did.

Perhaps most of his handlers. But did anyone speak up? Then there was Anthony Pelicano, the legendary Hollywood private detective, who spent $35 million buying off the families of children Jackson may have molested. How could this have been happening in secret? Did they buy off the media, too? A cynic could have a field day in Hollywood where seemingly no storyline was too outlandish.

"It'll never fly," Previn said at last.

"I know you think it all a little improbable, but it'll work," Tout replied. "Smooth sailing."

"It's like what plastic surgery used to be, when you could give people another face," Barone offered with a smile. "But that's not so simple, is it? We were a little naive, Harry, thinking you or anyone could clean her up so thoroughly. Anybody want to go in with me on some oysters? Harry?"

Previn stared at Barone without replying.

"I'll do oysters." At least Tout had an appetite.

"What are you doing here, Richard? I get why Johnny's here, but you? The only thing I can think—Jake Blackburn hurt Fay. Yeah. He did it to her."

Previn had been fumbling around in the dark for weeks wondering whom the perp was and there it was right in front of him the whole time. It was almost too obvious. He'd looked everywhere but at Barone. It absolutely made no sense that Barone would be cavorting around with Johnny Tout if he didn't have some skin in the game, so to speak. Jake Blackburn was his big star, though it was Barone who was perpetually angling to keep Previn quiet.

"Fay doesn't know it, but she was contracted to be in Jake's next film," Barone said, strikingly unfazed by Previn's accusation. "Naturally I wanted to salvage her part when Johnny phoned me, so I called you in. Fay lost the part, needless to say, but I'm still here because I have a big heart. That's who I am. Always the agent. That's why I helped you, Harry."

Previn stood up to leave. "I want nothing to do with this!"

"Mate?" Tout stood up, putting an arm on Previn.

"Helen is with me on this," Barone announced quietly without looking up.

Previn stopped and stared at him.

"Sat with her Sunday," Barone continued. "She finds you as confusing as I do."

Previn clenched his fists. "Don't bring her into this!"

No sooner than he'd uttered those words did Previn realize he'd walked into a trap. Barone knew from their phone conversation that Helen was his weak spot and he was going to play it for all he could.

"Bring her in?" Barone asked. "Such petulant people, you and Helen. She belted my client. Practically disfigured his multimillion-dollar face. You should know a thing or two about that, Doctor. She couldn't be more *in*. Imagine if Jake knew she was your wife? I'm trying to help you, Harry, but you don't help me. What's with that? Huh?"

"Could you be any more subtle?"

"I'd be lying to you if I said Jake Blackburn isn't rightfully aggrieved. If he hasn't sued you for killing his mom, it's only because of me. So be nice."

There it was.

Tout coaxed Previn to sit back down.

"Harry will play nice. He just hasn't been house-trained, right, mate?"

"I had oysters yesterday," Barone mused.

Tout took charge. "You've got to talk to Fay, Harry. As a professional. As someone who knows faces."

"And beauty," Barone added.

"Help her see her way through. Tell her she can have a new life."

"She's got a life. What's wrong with the one she has?" Previn asked.

"Come on, mate. With her face, she's all but dead. Most women don't get a second chance."

"She'll listen to you," Barone said.

Previn stood up again. "You don't know that. You don't know that!"

"She will," Barone said, squeezing a lemon into his water. "Of course she will. They're all just dying to be beautiful."

◆◆◆

PREVIN'S CAR CAME TO a screeching halt in front of Tout's house.

Rox met him at the door. Her sky-blue dress was splattered with blood, a bloody steak knife in hand. "I can't be there every minute for her. I'm no Mother Teresa."

Previn focused on the knife. "Give me that."

She suddenly noticed the knife and dropped it to the floor.

"Fay?" he asked, grabbing her wrist. "What about Fay?"

Rox stared at Previn, her eyes enlarged, drawing breath frantically, as though she were having an asthma attack. She backed away from him and the bloody knife before charging up the staircase three steps at a time as if she were in mortal danger. Previn followed her to Fay's room, his mind racing almost as fast as his legs. Only hours before, he'd sat at Craig's discussing Fay's death. Was this it? Was this how it would be?

The bathroom door was broken and hung at an angle. Previn had to push it with some force to open it fully.

Fay lay on the bathroom floor naked, the good side of her face visible in profile, flushed, yet strikingly and incongruously alive in spite of the substantial bruising at the base of her nose, a sign that her recovery was still incomplete. There was blood smeared everywhere. All over the side of the drained bathtub and around the floor. Her two arms reached out, a yellow towel wrapped around them both. In the center of the towels, blood had soaked through. Fay was listless. In another place. She didn't look up at them as they arrived. Previn stared at the spot where the mirror was, then picked Fay up and carried her out.

Previn barked at Rox, "Grab the bedspread!"

◆◆◆

NO ONE WAS TALKING. Fay was seated on the examination table with bandages on her wrists. Previn was all business. He forcefully, almost violently wheeled an IV stand beside her. Went to a cabinet, took out a bag of fluid, inserted an intravenous infusion line into it, and hooked it to the IV stand.

Questions hung in the air, but Fay did not speak. Rox stood to one side, arms crossed.

Previn took Fay's arm, tied a tourniquet around it, and after dabbing it with disinfectant, jabbed her with a catheter. The two cuts to her wrists required six stitches each. As he applied them, he was painfully aware that he was back in his surgery center sewing her up yet again. This unblemished beauty had within a matter of days acquired multiple scars. Perfection spoiled. Canceled. Turned back.

Could he possibly hold her together with string and surgical tape alone? Here he was, sewing the same flesh, trying to hold blood in when the blood wanted out. Things had taken a sudden and dramatic turn, the impact of which was just beginning to dawn on him. The stupefying reality that while the first cuts had been inflicted upon her, this cut was self-inflicted. How could beauty be in rebellion against itself?

"Car accident victims have come to me," Previn said. "Shit, I had a TV star with burns. You're not the first person who's had...This makes me angry. This is so uncalled for. So...uncalled for! I'm here. I've been here. It's disrespectful, Fay. That's what it is."

"She didn't *even* leave a note," Rox said.

"Next time. A note just for you, Rox," Fay said softly. "Something like, thanks for fucking my manager."

Rox turned to Previn. "She can be such a snot. What am I going to tell Johnny now? How am I gonna explain this to him?"

"Don't say, 'next time,' Fay," Previn said.

"When I said I was going to do myself, Rox laughed. You laughed at me."

"She's always talking shit. But then I realized she just might. Found the door locked..."

Fay looked down at the floor.

Rox spoke up. "You washed your hair first, Fay. What's with that?"

Previn connected the IV to the catheter. He wondered if and to what degree he bore personal responsibility for what had happened. After all, she should have been treated in a proper full-service medical facility the first time. He knew very little about treating the resultant depression. Further, her relative isolation—which he'd also assisted in by agreeing to treat her at Tout's home and prescribing various benzos against his better judgment—had unquestionably contributed to her urge to do something extreme.

This act of hers had been a classic cry for help. And where had he been? Had he heard it? He'd thought he had. In his own way... in his own particular way, he *had* tried to be there. He'd stayed with the case. Stayed with her for several weeks. After treating her that first night, he could have walked away. Richard Barone and Jake Blackburn's wrongful death suit be damned. But what really struck him was the realization that he might have lost another patient.

"This party's fucked!" Fay said.

Rox could hardly conceal her disgust.

"That's it!" he raged. "Fay, what the fuck is going on? Who assaulted you? What happened? If you won't tell me—"

"Shut up, Harry! Fay, don't listen to him."

"It all started with what happened that night," he replied.

Fay looked down at the floor, silent.

"You don't know anything!" Rox said.

"Rox. This wouldn't have happened if—"

"If what? You were treating her?"

He'd never get anywhere with Rox standing there. She was Tout's eyes and ears and Fay knew it. He applied tape to hold Fay's IV in place as he tried to think how it'd come to this.

"Oh, good!" Fay said, finally. "Hook me up, Doc. What's in this? What's it gonna do?"

He recalled seeing her studying her reflection in the face of a steak knife. He hadn't thought that the same instrument she'd turned to for clarity could also be used to open her wrists. How could this have escaped him?

"Glucose. It's glucose, Fay."

"Will it make me beautiful?"

"Do you really think this is some sort of lark? Look!" Rox put her unsteady hands out. "I'm shaking! I'm still shaking. I can't do this. I can't. I hate you, Fay!"

"Rox!" Previn said. The last thing he wanted was a catfight.

Fay pulled the IV out of the catheter and tossed it onto the floor.

"Goddamn it, Fay!" he snapped. "What are you doing? You want to be physically restrained? That what you want?"

"Fun. Bondage."

Fay tried to get up.

"Fay!"

Previn attempted to stop her, but as he did so, she fell off the examination table onto the floor. He lifted her back up as she struggled against him. He held her tightly in his arms. Finally, she settled down. When Tout walked in, he was still holding Fay.

"If she's ready, I'll take her home," Tout announced.

Previn grabbed Tout's arm firmly, furious at his casual tone. "You told me about Kurt. You told me. Remember? You were standing right in the hall at my surgery. We can't let it happen again, Johnny. We can't."

"What?"

"Kurt. You know."

"My brother?"

"Kurt Cobain!"

"What the fuck are you talking about, Harry? Kurt's my youngest brother. Let go of the rock 'n' roll life after six lost years in LA. Lives in Brisbane now. Has three kids. I don't see 'em enough. Sweet guy."

What the hell?

Tout led Fay and Rox out the door like a father picking up his daughters from school and left Previn with the realization that Kurt could simply be someone's brother.

◆◆◆

GUY REACHED OVER THE table to pour Helen another glass of wine.

They'd been dining at the Hungry Cat in the Pacific Palisades. Helen could only avoid Guy for so long. She knew he hadn't done anything wrong by returning to his house, but his sudden, unexplained presence had unnerved her. Staying at Guy's was supposed to be like doing a detox from her marriage. But how was that to be if she were merely trading one man for another?

Guy had been nothing but kind throughout her predicament, which made her feel guilty about her intense reaction regarding his sudden reappearance. It was his home, after all. Wasn't he allowed to come home?

She closed her eyes as she drank whatever expensive red wine Guy had ordered. It warmed her insides and dulled her anxiety. Ever since she'd lost the embryos, she'd felt agitated, as though she was all abuzz. Leaving Harry hadn't helped. It seemed like nothing could make her anxiety go away.

"I've been working on a series of self-portraits," Helen announced as she held out her glass, as if she were toasting herself.

Guy waited.

"As you know, I'm not a self-portraitist."

He smiled and shook his head. "Then you've never really looked at your work. It's always seemed very personal."

"I don't paint myself. It's like a taboo with me. Am I uncomfortable with myself? Probably." She shrugged. "But I thought I'd give it a go."

"It must be a very liberating moment for you, Helen."

"As in a car that's lost control."

"When do I get to peel back the curtain on your new work?"

"Sorry, Guy. It's not the girl in the Jonathan Gold."

"You're really caught up with that painting."

She wouldn't have been studying herself at all had she not come face-to-face with the nude in his closet. The portraits all had her lying beneath a surgical lamp. After all, wasn't the extraction of her eggs where it all went so wrong? All of a sudden, she regretted mentioning that she'd made this study. How could she ever explain them to him? He'd see the surgical lamp and think she was longing for Harry. She couldn't tell him she was still mourning a lost baby. She'd already told him too much.

"They're not good enough," she said at last.

"I'll be the judge of that."

She looked down at what was left of her cornmeal crushed soft-shell crab. "I never said they were nudes, you know."

He smiled.

"If that's what you were expecting..."

She pulled at her wedding ring absently. She hadn't so much as considered removing it, which she knew was a glaring contradiction. How could she ask Harry for a divorce and not want to give up her ring? But hadn't she only just asked? She was allowed a little time to divest herself of something that had almost become a virtual part of her body.

She looked across the candlelight at him. His face was quite strong and manly in its golden glow. "Are we on a date?"

The question seemed naïve. She was embarrassed she'd asked. Only then did she start to realize why she resented Guy's return. It was that same thing as it had always been when men entered the equation. Sex was always there. She had had several weeks in which it had disappeared. But now...

"Isn't it enough for now, at least, to say we enjoy each other's company?" he replied without missing a beat.

She took another sip from her glass. They were on a date. What was it that made everything change? She'd had dinner with Guy before. She'd done it without Harry, even. But this felt different. The difference being she wasn't obligated to Harry in the same way. And at the end of the evening, Guy was going to take her home to his house, which seemed complicated if not impossible.

She'd dressed up three times since leaving Harry. She'd dressed for lunch with Guy, for dinner with Harry, and now tonight. She'd put on her diamond earrings, which she often wore and had been a gift from her father. She'd had her nails done. She'd tried on three different dresses before deciding on a green Chanel. She'd told herself she was doing this for herself. Pride. A woman had to take pride in herself. She'd applied pink lipstick before they'd left. And she'd reapplied it after they'd finished dinner. So she wanted to look good. What woman didn't? She reconsidered. It was about confidence. After the fertility treatments, she'd lost that. Dining with Guy was like a tonic. He was here to make her feel good about herself. The only problem was it didn't seem as simple as that. It just wasn't with men like Guy.

"You said something about a crisis the other day," she said.

He smiled faintly and looked at her. "You know all about the crisis."

"What?"

"A man travels because he's either looking for something or he's trying to get away. I thought I was looking. But I was needing to get away."

Helen sighed. Guy spoke so grandly about things. She was sure he had said more about the human condition in those few sentences than anything she'd ever heard. She couldn't travel. But she'd run. She'd run from her marriage. Traveling, though, seemed like something truly beyond her current abilities.

"Our conversations over the last few weeks made me feel very close to your...predicament. And I've wanted to help. But I've also felt so helpless to help you, Helen."

"I'm okay."

"No. You're not. When you told me you were leaving what's-his-name, I thought, she needs time. But when you told me you were asking for a divorce..." He broke into a grin. "I guess I couldn't accept the idea that you'd be out there on your own. I wanted to be here with you."

"What?"

He reached across the table for her hand. "Have I said too much?"

She didn't withdraw her hand. She was trying to think how long it'd been since anyone but Harry had made love to her. She should have known when she'd agreed to stay at Guy's that he'd inevitably make a pass at her. He was notorious for this. He'd had a lot of women. And now he wanted to add her to his list.

She was in a whirl of confusion. She'd forgotten about the embryos. She'd forgotten that she'd become fat from the fertility treatments. She felt like a little girl. She wanted to giggle. He hadn't really said this stuff, had he?

"I'm still married," she said.

"You're only as married as you want to be."

She had to think about that.

"Let's go, Helen. Let me take you home."

Her eyes widened as she tried to get her head around what he'd just proposed. It seemed so responsible. The only thing was her home was his. He was actually taking her back to his.

She watched him sign the credit card bill. His penmanship was perfect. So steady. He took one more sip from the Bordeaux he'd been drinking and stood. She could have remained, but she stood up because she was unclear about there being an alternative. There was something else. He had told her what they were doing and she responded to that. She was tired of thinking for herself.

She sat in his Baby Bentley and looked out the window at the wooded hillsides as he ferried her back to his. She was trying to figure how she'd tell him that she wasn't going to sleep with him. Could she actually walk to her room and expect that he'd walk to his? Were they to shake hands in the foyer and then go their separate ways?

She was full of anticipation and confusion. Guy was saying something about jet lag and how he was due for a second wind because it was going to be morning in Europe at any time.

It would have been normal on a first date to kiss at the end. But that'd be about the extent of it, unless of course she wanted to invite her date in and even then that might involve little more than a nightcap. This was something different. If she were to reject Guy, could she simply walk down the hall?

The car pulled up in front of the house. His house.

She walked in, setting her clutch down on the console table, as if she had lived there for years. She heard the front door shut behind her. He stepped in front of the yellow painting of the couple shown dancing from two angles. "Do you know anything about this Alex Katz?"

"Only that I like it."

"That's his son and his daughter-in-law. Can you believe it? The son is so fond of his wife, but she…not so much. She's somewhere else. Katz must have felt she wasn't into his son. But they're still married to this day and this was painted in the seventies. Go figure!" He laughed.

She stared at the couple and it gave her a sudden chill. All the paintings inevitably had their stories, including the Jonathan Gold.

"I knew the moment I saw the Jonathan Gold," she blurted, saying aloud what had been swirling round in her head. Not exactly a complete statement, but more the finish of a thought.

"Knew what?"

"You know."

He smiled. "No. Tell me."

She found herself staring back at him with only the soft picture lights illuminating the house. Guy must have liked having all the light on his paintings and the off spill on his guests.

"Guy. Don't make me spell it out for you."

"No. Please. Spell it out. I'd like to hear."

"Fuck you!" She fell back against the wall. She was drunk. "You knew that was me. It's just too weird to think you could have that nude hanging in your closet and not know. Don't tell me that!"

"There's a resemblance."

"There's more than a resemblance!"

He chuckled. "Yeah. I guess there is."

This was not the conversation she'd wanted to have. Clearly, finding herself naked at nineteen in his closet had gotten the better of her. She hadn't meant to flirt with him, but that was exactly what she'd done. How could she debate about how much she resembled a particular nude and not be perceived as flirtatious?

"Let's go take a look," he said at last.

She felt herself weaken. She couldn't do this. She'd only been away from Harry for a matter of a few weeks. She heard her voice; it was uncharacteristically faltering. "It's in your bedroom."

◆◆◆

AFTER TOUT TOOK FAY away, Previn went into a panic.

The image of a naked woman crouched on the lip of a Beverly Hills high-rise suddenly, vividly came to mind. The British socialite who'd plunged to her death had become a poster child for plastic surgery gone wrong.

"Beverly Hills Suicide Jumper Was Facelift Patient of Surgeon to the Stars." Some variation of this *Hollywood Reporter* headline written about the jumper would surely be written about Fay Wray, though her dying in a bathtub lacked the drama of a fifteen-story plunge smack onto the sidewalk in downtown Beverly Hills. The lurid details of that patient were difficult to forget. The socialite jumper waking in a fright. Her nurse unable to restrain her. The nurse being thrown to the ground by the patient, who then runs to the roof followed by a security guard. A four-hour deathwatch in which the police found the patient to be unresponsive as she walked the edge of the high-rise butt naked as hundreds of people looked on in horror.

It'd be described as a psychotic episode. Previn knew it as emergence delirium. In the days that followed, the incident had become a near obsession within the medical community. They all knew Brian Novack, the plastic surgeon. Previn had read that the deceased lived in Hong Kong and was a highly regarded jewelry designer, but nothing was written about what procedures were performed on her other than that she'd been given a facelift, which was shorthand for almost anything in the facial area. That the surgery had taken thirteen hours spoke volumes about the extent of the work and probable complications.

Given the marathon scope of the surgery, Previn wondered why she'd spent the night recuperating at the facility and not at a proper hospital. Obviously, Novack must have been set up for such post-op recuperation, though how she could have found her way to the roof suggested otherwise. That was the question. How does a post-op patient find her way onto a roof of the surgery? It was the stuff of medical nightmares.

The reason why there was such attention to post-op care stemmed from concern about how patients reacted to the medications they'd been given. First and foremost was the concern about the anesthesia, which was apparently what triggered the psychotic episode that led to this death. One didn't have to be a surgeon to know that thirteen hours is a long operation and a long time to be held under. Though Fay was still in recovery, the acute phase had passed and there had been no obvious reason to assume that she'd become suicidal. No obvious reason, that is, beyond the obvious. He'd been feeding her a steady dose of psychotropic drugs that had the potential to prompt a psychotic episode. Fay may not have felt like running onto a rooftop, but she certainly was feeling depressed.

The demise of the socialite jeweler was interesting, particularly to Previn, though it was also relatively textbook. These things happened. That was why patients were always placed under observation until they were ready to be released. What would be more notable and even more lurid about Fay, had she died, were the circumstances that got her to that point. Previn could not help but think his own fingerprints were everywhere, even on the bottles of prescription medication, as though it wasn't already enough that he'd written the prescriptions themselves. That he'd personally administered them suggested a level of culpability that made him wince as he considered it.

For this reason, he was relieved when Tout took Fay away, but this reaction was short-lived. What had he done to prompt Fay to attempt to take her life? How was this going to end? Was she going to be okay? He was reluctant to call anyone. After all, everyone was a potential witness. If this went south, anything he told them might come back at him. In the early hours of the morning, he succumbed to the very human need to share his burden with someone. Helen. After all, wives could not be made to testify against their husbands and technically, at least, they were still married. The phone rang six times before he was asked to leave a message. "Helen, I need you. I just need you. I don't know how else to put it. I need to hear your voice. To hold you. I feel like everything's crumbling around my feet and why aren't you there? Why aren't you picking up the phone? Helen. Please. Call me."

She was probably asleep.

He continued down the list. Drawing upon attorney-client privilege, he most certainly could try Ty Fanning, but he seemed like someone he'd want to call in later when he'd gotten more clarity in his own mind as to whether he was truly responsible for Fay's suicidal depression. Of course, Brick would only make him feel worse and give him the "I told you so." The only person left to call was Sara.

"Something terrible happened," he began as the sun was rising. Its first rays brightened the palm fronds outside his window.

"What?"

"Fay tried to kill herself."

Sara didn't reply.

"I said—"

"I heard you. I'm just trying to absorb it. That's all."

"Are you up?"

"Now?" Her question spoke to her unease with having to field such a crisis at that hour.

Previn arrived at her place about twenty minutes later. Sara lived alone in a one-bedroom condo in West Hollywood. Previn had been there once with Helen when Sara was celebrating her thirty-fifth birthday. But he'd never been there alone. It didn't feel strange until she opened the front door in her red robe. It was ridiculously early. It wasn't even 7:00 a.m., as it turned out. But he'd felt particularly small in his overlarge, scantily furnished home. After he sat down on her green velvet sofa, he felt too large for her place. It wasn't particularly tidy. But then, it wasn't like he'd given her much notice that he'd be coming by.

In the time he'd been married, he wouldn't have thought or imagined himself going to Sara's house so early in the morning, putting himself in such a compromising situation any more than he would have expected anything of the kind from Helen. He felt bad as he looked at Sara in her robe. What was he doing there? He had a sudden impulse to call Helen, to find her, wherever she was, and tell her that they needed to stop this madness right now. But he was a desperate man. Sara really was about the only person he thought he could call on who'd listen to him.

He described Fay's injuries as a doctor would to a nurse. The medical stuff was in their comfort zone. He even went so far as to describe the exact placement of the cuts, including into her ulnar artery.

"I still don't understand what happened," Sara said finally.

"I told you. She breached the artery but did not separate it."

"No. What *really* happened?"

"It's what people ask about suicide, isn't it? This is what I don't know. It's why I couldn't sleep. I don't know what happened. You deal with all the post-op stuff. You've helped patients get through recovery."

"It's why I said you shouldn't attend to her," Sara said as she stood in the center of her living room with her hands on her hips. "Where is she now?"

"Fay?"

"Yes. Fay!"

"I don't know. Johnny took her."

"You don't put a suicidal woman back into the very same—"

"Exactly."

"Harry. This is *exactly* what you did. You took her out of the frying pan, and then threw her right back into it."

"Don't think I'm not painfully aware of that."

"Well, what are you going to do about it?" Sara asked.

"I don't know. That's why I came here. It's not like I can go over there and demand that they give her back."

"Which is why you should have never let them take her back in the first place."

"You stand there and tell Johnny Tout not to do anything. The man is irrepressible and difficult, though…I know I should have held onto her. I know that. God! If she does anything else to herself…" He gripped his head in his hands like his head were ready to explode.

"If you had more of a personal relationship with your patients, you'd be more attuned to their needs," Sara said.

"I have a very personal relationship with all my patients. I fulfill their dreams. I make them into who they want to be. What could be more personal than helping them realize themselves?"

"Holding their hand as they heal," Sara replied. "Post-op is where feelings come out. The fear. Vulnerability. You had no business attending to Fay after the surgery. You were completely out of your depth."

"It's what they wanted."

"Do you do everything they want?" she asked.

He picked up a yellow glass butterfly off the coffee table. He had a good mind to smash it against the wall.

"What I'm saying is, if you were really doing your job as a postoperative nurse, you'd have picked up on her mood," she said. "You'd have maybe noticed she wasn't happy. I'm mystified. What was she telling you this whole time?"

He gritted his teeth as he thought back to Rox always looming at the door like a guard dog. "We were never alone."

Sara, who'd been pacing, stopped and stared at him.

Previn felt like he had to explain himself. "You know, prescribing drugs to patients is always trial and error. That's a lot of what happened."

She gathered some newspapers off one of the chairs and jammed them into the trash. Her failure to comment registered her disapproval quite loudly.

"This was far from textbook, okay?" he conceded.

This was always the problem with sitting down with a colleague, and particularly someone who had done a lot of post-op. Sara knew what was regular and what was irregular. Medicating Fay after several weeks was not standard protocol. He'd cut off giving her painkillers and anti-inflammatories after the first week. But what he had given her were barbiturates to take the edge off and he was quite right that it was difficult to know how a given patient would react to medication. All medication had side effects. Some patients simply didn't react well to particular pills, which is what he feared had led to Fay's depression and suicide attempt.

He shook his head to rid himself of that naked patient teetering on the edge of the high-rise. He was looking for similarities, but there weren't any. They simply weren't the same. The jumper wasn't even coherent when she stepped off that ledge. Fay was depressed, and for all he knew, she had a history of depression.

"I wonder about her overall mental health," he said. "Don't know a thing about it."

"Coffee?" Sara asked.

"Tea."

"I only have green tea. It's healthier."

"Of course."

Sara was a health fiend. She was gluten- and dairy-free and consumed only organic foods. It'd been an ongoing discussion with waiters whenever they'd gone out for a bite after work.

"The first hours after an attempt are the most critical," Sara said as she placed a teacup down in front of him. "But you know that."

"I don't know anything. I was thinking about Novack. You know the—"

"Plastic surgeon to the stars?"

Previn smiled and shook his head. "That's the one." They enjoyed mocking his competition and the monikers they'd planted in the press. Though Previn was painfully aware that this was one time when that label was unfortunate at best. Who wanted to be so high-profile that the whole world was watching after their patient jumped from the roof of their surgery? Or worse, so soon after they'd operated on her? "I don't know how he survived such a tragedy. I'm told he bought off the family, but who knows, really?"

"That's what I heard too. There's a lot of whispering."

"How could something like this happen to me?" Previn asked.

"How could something happen to Simone Blackburn?"

Previn set the glass butterfly back down on the coffee table. Why did Sara have to put it that way?

"Do you want me to go with you to look in on Fay?" Sara asked.

"They wouldn't want that."

"Then you better go over there yourself like right now. I know we have surgery this morning, but it can wait."

"I can't cancel surgery. That's not done." He let his words hang in the air before adding, "Though it's not like I've been doing much of anything by the book lately."

◆◆◆

PREVIN PAUSED IN FRONT of the image of Nick Valentine behind the Tout & Wilde reception desk. The film poster now screamed, "Countdown: 3 days!" He was about to address the receptionist when he caught sight through the glass wall of Tout meeting with Wilde and, of all people, Barone in the conference room. Previn didn't wait to be announced.

The receptionist leapt to her feet. "Excuse me. Hey! You can't!"

Tout could keep Fay secreted away from her fans, the press, and even the world at large. He could assign his personal assistant to become her nurse and keeper; he could even concoct crazy scenarios about the death of Fay Wray and an endless treasure trove of "lost" recordings. However, her suicide attempt had shown he could control and manipulate many things, but not her heart and mind. She'd still have to be reckoned with.

What Previn hadn't expected was to hear boisterous sounds. Could they have possibly been laughing? It sounded like there was a joyous meeting going on in there and the idea of it only quickened Previn's steps. But what he saw was Tout about to throw a punch at Wilde with Barone caught in the middle and none too happy about it.

Tout noticed Previn at the door. "Harry!"

They all turned to Previn.

"It's okay, Sally," Tout said, suddenly composed, as he ushered Previn into the conference room.

"I want Fay confined," Previn said. "Seventy-two hours is the norm. Should have done it last night."

They all stared at Previn. Finally, Barone tiredly lowered himself into a chair beside Wilde.

"What are you talking about?" Tout asked.

"I'm not a psychiatrist. Not even close! But we're so far off in the deep end here. We don't know what we're doing. She's got to be confined. We've got to do it. It's standard in these situations. Psychiatric evaluations—"

"I was just with her, mate. She's fine."

"She tried to kill herself."

"I've seen it before. Mariah? I mean, come on, mate. You remember all that shit with the ice cream wagon on MTV? I lived through that. I knew her people. I saw the footage of that. I saw the outtakes. The stuff nobody saw. And that was just the beginning, but it was cool. She turned a story in the tabs about her mental breakdown into the hit record, *Breakdown.*"

Barone nodded. "The artistic temperament."

"Of course, mate. Britney? Lohan? They all get a little strung out at some point. They just do. It's the thoroughbred horse. Spirited. They get wild in the gate. Can't function at that level without—"

"You didn't have to stitch Fay up," Previn said.

Tout chuckled. "They love their drama. That's all it comes down to."

"Don't tell me you're not pissing your pants. Why else are you all gathered here? I'm not stupid. Look at you. All of you."

"Mate, of course. Of course. But it's going to be okay." Tout tried to put an arm around Previn. "You'll keep an eye on her."

Previn brushed Tout's arm off him. "What am I to do, sit on her?" He gave it a moment. The gravity of it all weighed heavily on him. "Had she made a slightly different incision, we'd be making funeral arrangements."

Wilde became so agitated, he could no longer stay seated. "While you're measuring for her coffin, measure one for me, 'cause this business is killing me!"

Nobody said a word.

"I'll admit it. This ain't good for my health! Fay's your bit of paradise, Johnny." Wilde pointed at Previn. "And this is the best you can do. This man does boob jobs, for Christ's sake!"

"Sid."

Wilde shook his fist at Previn. "You're the one who said you couldn't make her look good. How's she to feel? How would that make any woman feel?"

Tout's patience was being tested. "Sid. Please."

"What kind of doctor are you?" Wilde said, kicking his chair over before marching out of the room.

"Sorry, Harry," Tout said with a smile. "My partner is not a patient man."

"As if you are!" Previn said. "You sat here and told me, told us all, she should play dead."

Tout didn't miss a beat. "Yeah. So?"

"Well, next thing we know she's cutting her wrists."

"You should have talked to her already. We wanted you to. If she knew, she could live on."

"You're crazy! This is insane! She's alive. She's a living, breathing, human being."

"Guys. Guys," Barone broke in. "No one wanted it like this." Then he turned to Previn. "I know you don't want to revisit the Blackburn mess, Harry, but it's not irrelevant now, is it?"

"Every time you don't get what you want, you come at me with Jake Blackburn."

"What a coincidence!"

Previn lunged at Barone. Tout met him forcefully, gripping him tightly in his arms like he was doing a rugby takedown.

"You're lying!" Previn yelled. "Lying, Richard. Jake isn't going to sue. There was no suit. You fuck!"

Barone chuckled as Tout held Previn in his powerful arms. Barone's reaction seemed to confirm Previn's suspicion that Jake Blackburn had no idea his deceased mother was being used in this way. It had become more than a little unseemly. For all Previn knew, a wrongful death suit had never crossed Jack Blackburn's mind.

As Previn stepped back, Tout let him go, but Previn wasn't done. He turned to Tout and pointed his finger. "You said if she were dead, it'd solve everything."

"We've been trying to help her. We all have. You wouldn't be here if we thought you couldn't make this go away."

"But it won't. Can't. Isn't. No way. No how. Haven't you figured that out yet?"

Barone sat down and wearily looked over at Previn. "You need to calm down."

◆◆◆

PREVIN COULDN'T REASON WITH those people. Why he'd even tried…

After the meeting at Tout & Wilde, having failed to change much of anything, Previn felt wasted. He just wanted to get back to his empty house and ride out the night. As his car pulled up to the front of the house, he was surprised to find Helen sitting on the front steps.

"Nice house," she said.

"You like?"

"Didn't seem right to let myself in." She stood up and looked back at the house. "It's sad. Sad coming back. Liked sitting out here, though. All those years, never sat on the doorstep."

Helen might as well have shown up with a ribbon wrapped around her waist. He could almost believe that he'd closed his eyes for a brief moment and his life had been restored to how it'd been before she walked out on him, the scant furniture in the living room the only hint that something was off.

They opened a bottle of wine.

"I hardly recognize it here," she said.

"No. It's the same," he lied. He hadn't wanted to mention her leaving. This was hard enough without getting into the obvious, that they were estranged. That she felt like a stranger. That he was going to talk about his work because, God forbid, he might bumble into talking about their failed marriage. "What about you?" he asked.

"You called me."

He looked around, and then at her. He'd finally had a designer furnish the room. She'd brought in a few quirky pop art pieces, which at least made the place happier.

"I did call you, didn't I?" he said, having in fact forgotten how she'd ended up in his living room. Though he wondered if it was merely his phone call. Surely, there was some other reason. Dare he hope she genuinely missed him?

He held back from asking if she was still staying at Guy's. The last thing he wanted was to sound possessive. Jealousy wasn't an outfit that looked good on him. That much he'd already established after rushing over to Guy's the last time. It'd been such a desperate act, but then hearing from Barone that she'd punched Jake while living with Guy...How could he have not blown a gasket?

He'd already apologized in countless voicemails after she'd failed to answer her phone...

She was curled up on the red lips-shaped sofa, but a few feet away from him. She'd gotten comfortable. Her shoes were off. That was a sure indication. A glass of red wine will do that. She was quick to pour herself a second.

"You ever finish your painting?" he said. "The one...I was going to say of this white piano, but it's a different room now."

"You asked me the same question not ten minutes ago."

"Did I?"

"You all right?"

"It's been a difficult day." He took a drag of air. "Richard asked me to help him with this pop star who suffered a horrible assault."

"I know."

"How do you know?"

"Stay away from that man."

"If only it were so easy. She tried to kill herself last night."

Helen sat up. "Harry, no!" She looked around as if she were looking for help, but then settled back into the sofa. "Haven't you figured out by now that Richard Barone will be your downfall?"

"I really do need to diversify." The absurdity of his reply made him smile for the first time since she'd appeared earlier that night.

"Diversify? Is that all? How many patients have to die before you get a clue? The minute you said pop star, I knew nothing's changed with you."

"You don't know that."

"Oh? She's a star, right? She's beautiful, check that box? Uh-huh! Who is she, Britney Spears? Katy Perry? Lady Gaga? Who has the ever-magnanimous Richard Barone brought you on his silver platter this time?"

"Just because she's a star —"

"She's never anything but a star. Who? Who is this STAR?"

"Fay Wray."

Helen laughed. "*Of course* she is. She was always going to be a *Fay* Wray, wasn't she?"

Previn washed down the remainder of the wine in his glass.

"Richard Barone is a monster," Helen continued. "Has he asked you to bury this one too?"

It would have reflected badly on him to admit that Barone had, more or less, asked him to do just that.

Until then, the similarity hadn't occurred to him.

He looked over at the white piano, then down at her foot, which was close enough to touch. Her toenails were painted lime. Something about the sight of her foot, the hint of veins, of life—he felt like he had to touch it. He took familiar comfort in the idea of feeling its warmth in his hand. He placed his hand gently on the base of her foot.

"I'm helping Fay. Trying."

"Because she's a star!"

"Don't be jealous."

Helen pulled her foot away, annoyed.

He went after it like he never wanted to lose it again, taking it firmly, only to get punched square in the jaw. He absorbed the blow. Took a moment to register what had just happened.

So that was how it was going to be.

He grabbed her. She struggled to get away from him before she fell into his arms and kissed him hungrily. He violently shoved everything off the jigsaw-shaped coffee table. She grabbed his belt and opened his trousers. They fell onto the coffee table...

He was on the coffee table, fucking her like it was one for the ages.

Afterward, he watched her crawl to the sofa, grabbing a throw pillow that she modestly used to cover herself. Previn edged off the coffee table onto the floor.

The room was fully lit. Up until about twenty minutes before, it had been all so very civilized. The wine glasses were still where they'd left them. But there were clothes scattered everywhere and magazines and…broken glass. They'd busted the bottle of pinot noir and there was a puddle of red wine on the wood floor. He'd scattered everything on the coffee table as he put her down on top of it and some of it simply wasn't meant to be shoved to the floor.

The pillow Helen clung to was very inadequate. Her red nipples sharply contrasted with her very pale skin. He'd loved her body, but his life or his own obsessiveness led him inevitably to look at her with the eyes of a plastic surgeon. Her large breasts were not at all symmetric. The left one was higher. Her nose, off-center. Her whole face, askew. And she was about fifteen to twenty pounds overweight.

She didn't look at all like she resided in the Capital of Good Looks. That had been one of the things that had attracted him to her in the beginning. He'd loved her for her flaws, but he could not keep himself from consciously taking inventory of them. It bothered him that he did so, as he knew it bothered her. This was a tendency that had gathered force through the course of their marriage, or perhaps it was his medical practice. He couldn't look at women all day long and then turn it off. He wondered if she was clinging to that pillow for this very reason. Now he was becoming self-conscious. She was a beautiful woman. A true individual. Surely, she knew that.

She lifted her head from the sofa to look at him with her green eyes. She had that bedhead look, her reddish hair ruffled, going this way and that. He'd had a clump of it in his hand only moments before. They were both sweaty, although he wasn't sure she didn't just shine with his sweat.

This wasn't supposed to happen. They were getting a divorce. He hadn't been with her in this way since she walked out of his life. He knew, or rather he feared, from the night she'd asked for the divorce that she'd made an irrevocable choice to end it with him once and for all.

She looked for her wine glass and found it on the side table. She put the red liquid to her lips and savored it for a moment. She was probably as surprised and as uncertain as he was with the moment.

He opened his mouth to speak only to feel a sharp pain in his jaw. He touched it and smiled as he recalled her punching him. He thought about saying something about her walloping Jake Blackburn but thought better of it. She'd never punched him until their big fight. Nor anyone else he knew.

It had been that kind of night. That kind of passion. A little crazy. Just as Fay's ongoing crisis had all but consumed him, like an answered prayer, he pulled into his drive to find Helen seated under the portico. There was no explaining it. How could she have even known that he was coming home? Though at no time was she more needed. More welcome.

He moved closer to her and put his hand on her leg tenderly.

Helen broke the silence. "Why do the lights always…Can't you turn them off?"

He turned off the lights and went back to her. He kissed her then suddenly she climbed to her feet.

"I can't do this," she said, grabbing her clothes, trying desperately to reassemble them around her body.

"What? Helen!"

Helen put her blouse on backward. She pulled it off and put it back on as he watched. She was otherwise naked.

Previn stood up to confront her. He was also naked. Confused. "Where are you going? Why are you leaving?"

His beeper went off.

"It was just getting good," he added.

"Good? I punched you."

He touched his chin as he savored the memory. "Yes, you did."

She looked back at him as though she didn't understand. Like she hadn't been there. Hadn't been a part of it.

"I enjoyed it," he said. "What can I say? It felt meaningful."

The beeper sounded again.

"Fuck!" he said.

"Answer your page."

"We made love."

"Love?"

The way she heaved that word back at him hurt.

He stared down at the coffee table. The room looked like a crime scene. On the surface of his jigsaw coffee table, the faint outline in perspiration from Helen's body. So vivid. So real. She could have been outlined in chalk. Even from a distance, he could make out the lipstick smudges along the edge of her glass beside the sofa.

His beeper went off again.

"You don't know," she said. "You haven't figured out, even by now, what it's like to be married to you. I married…What does it matter who I married? You're someone I hardly know anymore. Three miscarriages. Four if you count our marriage. Five if you count tonight."

"What the fuck! Why would you go there?"

"I'm sorry," she said at last. "We were in a rut. You wouldn't talk about our fertility problems. You had your patients and art. I hated you for that. Particularly because all those silly starlets don't need another beautician. But I needed a husband. And what's changed?"

"You think the miscarriages weren't hard on me too?"

"It felt like a sign."

"Hellie."

"Something had to give," she insisted.

Previn took her hand to look at her diamond ring. "You're still wearing my ring."

She yanked at it in an unconvincing demonstration. "Damn thing's stuck." She smiled in spite of herself.

He matched her with a smile before raising her with a chuckle. "Yeah. Of course it is."

The beeper sounded. Previn finally looked down at the screen.

"I've got to answer this page."

He found his phone on the floor by the coffee table. He must have looked every bit as gutted as he felt. He stared at Helen but didn't see her. Didn't see a thing.

♦♦♦

A NURSE BRISKLY LED Previn and Helen down an anonymous hallway to a waiting area in the emergency ward at the LA County Hospital, where they found Sara leaning against the counter of the nursing station. She broke from conversation with the nurse when she heard Previn's voice.

"What's taken you so long?" she snapped.

Helen stepped forward. "It's my fault."

"Helen!" Sara exclaimed. "It's been ages."

"It's not her fault," Previn said as he watched Sara and Helen embrace.

"They've already stitched her up," Sara said.

"Can I see her?" he asked.

"Do you really want to own this?" Sara asked.

He stared at Sara without answering. It was a provocative statement. "What's that supposed to mean?"

"Rosie Bottoms has been all over us for the last few weeks. But we didn't hear her. Neither of us, Harry. I'm not putting this on you. It's just that we were awfully slow to acknowledge her concerns."

"God," Helen said. "I thought she'd died or something. I haven't heard her name since that Vince Vaughn thing."

Previn was so engaged with Sara over his current predicament, he could hardly stop to consider what Helen had said.

"We tried to see her," he insisted.

"But we didn't, did we?"

It was charitable of Sara, at least, to use the word "we" instead of "you," because he felt her critique was directed at him. Perhaps it was inevitable he'd feel defensive about this. But was it really his job to anticipate such a thing?

Actually, it was.

Sara continued. "You know, when Rosie blew off her appointments, I was surprised because she seemed so keen to come in. They said she opened up her breasts with a hunting knife to get the implants out."

Helen gasped. "She's still alive?"

Sara shrugged. "Drove herself to the hospital, bleeding!"

"No!"

"When they get to a certain age, it gets delicate," Sara continued.

"She was in her mid-thirties!" Helen said.

"Exactly!"

A woman appeared before him, looking corporate with a hospital pass hanging over her green pantsuit. "I'm Dr. Lief. The attending psychiatrist."

"Dr. Previn."

"So I'm told. If you'd like to talk, we can go to my office."

Previn left Sara and Helen in the reception and followed Lief down the hall.

Somewhere north of fifty, Lief was very pale, as though she spent her life exclusively in that facility. She wore sneakers, probably because she was on her feet all day. He knew a thing or two about hospitals.

He took in the passing rooms, eyeing them uneasily. This ward was exactly what he might have expected, except it was run-down and in need of a fresh coat of paint and probably new floor tiles. The wing seemed dated, like it hadn't been upgraded since it had been built in the seventies.

"Did you know she had a boyfriend?" Previn asked. "Walked out on her right after the operation."

Lief stopped. Turned. Looked at him sharply. "This isn't about her boyfriend. You know that, Dr. Previn."

They finally arrived at her office. He took a seat in a rigid plastic chair that was, at best, functional. Psychiatrist Dr. Diana Lief's office at the County Hospital was cluttered, overbright, and small. Clearly not suitable for taking meetings. The only interesting thing in the office was a stuffed peacock standing on top of a tall file cabinet; its colorful plume swept five feet down to the floor.

"The patient needs psychiatric attention in the worst way," she said.

"I'm wondering how I can be of help."

"It isn't her body that needs fixing."

"I'd be insane to touch this woman again. I know that. But isn't there something…"

He recognized in this admission the same kind of reckless compulsion that had gotten him entangled with Fay. He should have backed out of that. But he hadn't. He was like a moth to flame.

"Let me put it another way." She pulled at the ID badge hanging from her neck as she gathered her thoughts. "Engaging with you again may be detrimental to her recovery."

"What?"

"I certainly don't want to offend you, Dr. Previn, but you're more the problem than the cure in this situation. I don't know how to be any more direct than that."

"You've got this all wrong. Her boyfriend walked out on her right after the operation. He disapproved of her implants. She was in a panic because she did it for him. Men can be so…If I'd known…"

"This is about fixation. If anything, she may have enlisted the boyfriend to support her idea for this body change. Did he like her new breasts? Didn't he think they were awful? Why not? Why so? Someone like her is capable of driving a boyfriend nuts with her relentless obsession."

"Thought they might help her career."

"Putting new breasts on her?" She made it sound preposterous, as though the mere idea of it was reckless doctoring on his part.

He realized she was obviously not Hollywood. "Putting 'em on the big screen. Most people don't know it, but even Marilyn had work done."

"So?" she replied.

"It's about self-esteem."

"Self-esteem is earned. It must be earned. You have a woman fixating on one part of her body more than one hour a day."

"Who isn't in this city? You could be talking about any of my patients."

"You don't think that's strange?" she said. "If you want to understand Rosie Bottoms, and I think you do, stop looking for answers in her breasts. Unless she feels better about who she is as a person, well, what good is any of it?"

Leif must have observed him staring at the giant stuffed peacock. "Husband's a taxidermist."

"Huh." What was he to say? The bird seemed out of place.

She touched her throat thoughtfully. "You wouldn't happen to…" She smiled bashfully.

"Yes?"

She waved it off.

"Go ahead. Please." He was surprised at this sudden awkwardness.

"It's not every day I have a plastic surgeon sitting in my office. Do…Do I have a double chin?" She broke out in a blush.

Previn laughed uneasily.

◆◆◆

OPERATING ON THE LIVING was a far cry from the disgust he'd felt using vile-smelling cadavers, his first subjects. The idea was if a surgeon could cut into a cadaver, he could cut into anything. Although the living really are different. Or they were. Previn had subsequently become so hardened that cutting into human flesh had become no different to him than cutting into any other meat. But someone cutting into their own flesh, that had to be something else. Had to be. How could she have done it?

He simply couldn't believe that Rosie and Fay had both cut into themselves within twenty-four hours of each other. He'd been pretty rocked over Fay, and now Rosie had taken a hunting knife to his work. Both acts were cries for help. Yet who was listening? Had he been listening?

On the drive home, he wanted to spill the whole thing to Helen, but he could see she was shaken by the Rosie Bottoms event. How would she take to hearing about Fay? And it wasn't like she'd shown such empathy toward him when Simone Blackburn died. It was a lot to ask a partner to take on. How many married men had this sort of carnage following them around? If Helen had found Blackburn and Rosie Bottoms a shock, then how could he explain his role in suppressing Fay's predicament? Not reporting the crime. Drugging her up. Not seeking help when she'd become suicidal. How could his estranged wife be expected to understand that, in his heart of hearts, he was actually trying to help and protect Fay?

As they approached his neighborhood, her old neighborhood, it occurred to Previn that it was very undecided as to what was about to happen. She followed him into the house. They stood silently in the dark, looking out at the pool that was still lit and shimmering. He felt her hand come to rest tenderly on his shoulder.

"I'm bruised," she said at last. "See." She extended her arm to show him but it was near impossible to see anything in the dark. "You've left your marks."

As she spoke, he stared out at the pool as though it were an abyss before finally trying to look at her. He wasn't quite sure how to respond. If this was supposed to be a love scene, he wasn't equipped at the moment to pull it off.

He finally said what had been on his mind: "You haven't said anything. You must think this is Simone Blackburn all over again."

"Oh, she has a first name now?" she asked.

"What I'd give to not have brought you into this tonight. I feel like I've all but gotten away with murder. There, I've said it. That morning we had that fight, remember? I don't know what I was doing in surgery. Though I went through with it. That was my choice. That was on me."

"Don't torture yourself."

"It's piling up all around me. You don't know what I'm—"

She tenderly put her fingers to his lips. "Shhh. It's not like it was intentional. I wouldn't have married you if I thought you were perfect. When we do our art, we look for distinguishing characteristics because perfect isn't interesting. Why can't you focus on that in your practice?"

"What?"

"You're an artist, Harry. Be artful. Rediscover imperfection. That's where the beauty is. That's where it always is."

"I want to talk about us, not my practice."

"I am talking about us! Where is the man I fell in love with? You're better than Cher's latest face."

He smiled because he couldn't resist delivering the punch line to what had become a running joke with them. "I don't *do* Cher. You know that."

"Fay Wray?"

He stopped smiling. It seemed unfair to throw that out there because she'd never understand the personal stakes of Fay's disfigurement. Helen only saw the pretty pictures of Fay that everyone else saw.

"Do something real! You wouldn't take pride in refining another artist's work. I don't see you in what you're doing anymore. I want a Harry Previn original."

"You want me to quit being a plastic surgeon?"

"Give up on all those years you put in? God, no! I'm not simple. Everybody must think this is where I tell you to give up your life's work for me. I knew who I married," she continued. "But where is that man? I can't have my husband leave me for Demi Moore's new face. Do an original. I want big things. Not small things."

He listened to Helen because he wanted to hear her out because he always had, but he did so against the background noise reverberating in his head. Rosie Bottoms and Fay Wray had both taken a knife to themselves inside of twenty-four hours. At such a moment, how could he not question everything he was about? And here Helen was saying that he'd suffered from a lack of originality, that he'd failed to think big enough. That he hadn't been enough of an artist.

He wasn't sure he appreciated the critique. It stung. Perhaps in part because she was right. "Anything else?"

"Yeah. You could give me a baby."

They stared at each other in the dark and he smiled. He knew she still loved him. Maybe it was all going to be okay.

22

THE CALIFORNIA SUN WAS therapy.

But Previn was in Fay's not-so-bright room replacing the bandages he'd put on her wrists two days before. The door to the bathroom still hadn't been repaired, as it still lay at an angle pretty much the way it was when Rox broke it down. Fay didn't seem to have anything to say. Previn wasn't surprised.

He handed her several pills.

"What are these?" she asked.

"Happy pills."

"Oh, goody!"

Lorazepam would help her not be so agitated, but he wasn't about to tell her that. The yellow pill. The blue pill. He wasn't sure he had found the perfect combination. He just knew she needed a lot of help.

After he'd finished with Fay, Rox led him outside. The Santa Ana winds had brought with them a heat wave, which met Previn smack in the face as if he'd opened the oven door. Tout was just climbing out from his pool. Dripping with water, he plopped down on the towel that was already spread across the chaise lounge and let the sun do the rest. He put on his bright mirrored shades.

Previn hadn't visited this side of the house in the more than three weeks since he'd started tending to Fay. The house opened up onto a flat expanse of lawn and an oval-shaped pool that sat in the middle of it. The wooden pool furniture was scattered around on the grass. To one side on top of a concrete rectangle was a bar and barbecue area. Oh, the parties Tout must have had.

Previn handed Rox a vial of pills.

"What are these?" she asked.

"Antidepressants."

"I could use some. Thanks!"

"For Fay." Rox's joke hadn't been lost on him, but he felt levity was in bad form, particularly in front of Tout. He didn't want to give him the wrong idea. He pointed to the vial. "Three times a day. I already gave her one. Didn't want to say what they were in front of her. If she asks, just say they're happy pills. I tell her that, she's always game."

"Yeah. That's Fay."

Tout got up and wandered over to the bar with his glass, seemingly oblivious that Previn and Rox were conferring only about twenty feet away. He grabbed some ice and topped off his lemonade with what looked like a heavy pour of vodka. Previn was pretty sure Tout didn't want to bother with him, but then why would Rox bring him out this way?

Previn watched Tout sit back down on his towel. Tout toyed with the music control, changing the tunes several times before shutting it off altogether. He took a long sip from his drink. He crunched on an ice cube thoughtfully, then without looking at Previn directly, he spoke up. "How is she, mate?"

"How do you expect?"

He looked up at Previn. "I asked you. You don't ask me. Where are your manners? I don't know what they teach in med school these days. In music school, we're all so polite and genteel. It's called bedside manners."

"I doubt you went to music school."

"I don't know how to take that," Tout replied with his first smile.

At that moment, Fay appeared. She wore her PJs, which she'd actually bummed from Rox, and her facial bandage. She also had a towel. "Think I'll sit by the pool. Be a reptile. Take in the sun."

"You've got the day for it," Previn replied.

"Could steal Raspberry's bikini, but I think I'll go bare ass."

He stared at Fay. He was surprised that this woman who'd wanted to end her life was finally showing some vibrancy.

Tout stood up. "Mate, got something to show you."

Previn followed Tout, who'd put on a shirt that he left open at the front, into his study, half expecting to continue the argument they'd been having about how to deal with Fay. Though seeing Fay in good spirits was encouraging. Depression could sometimes be matched with moments of elation, however her mood didn't seem extreme. This made him feel better and it must have made Tout feel better, too, though a few vodka lemonades didn't hurt, either.

"So what's the deal with this movie?" Previn asked, trying to make conversation.

"Movie?"

"*Falling.*"

"Any day now."

He *only* had his superstar making his Hollywood debut! Why such nonchalance? Previn just had to go there. "Nick Valentine know Fay?"

Tout paused to stare at Previn. "Intimately."

Previn stopped.

Tout burst out laughing. Then continued walking.

Previn immediately felt chastened. "Why are you laughing?"

"Because you're so bloody entertaining, mate."

Tout led him into his study. So distracted was Previn the last time he was there with the Doris Day flick, he hadn't noticed that the books that lined the walls were all related to Hollywood and pop culture. Tout had an exhaustive library of DVDs. Previn started to realize that Tout might be a closet film buff. There was a black leather sofa against the wall and a coffee table with a glass bowl filled with jellybeans. At the other end of the room was an eighty-five-inch flat-screen LED TV. Tout turned it on. "Check this out. Look."

Fay appeared on the screen in a music video. Previn was once again reminded of her beauty. Though it only brought home how profoundly damaging the assault had been on her career and person.

A full-production number. Over a wall of sound, Fay belted the lyrics with a rush of angst. It was very packaged. Commercial. The storyline was about her being jilted by a boyfriend who keeps bedding the woman in the apartment next to hers. Though she appeared only sporadically in the video, each time she did in a close-up, it was like a rose opening to the sun. As Previn stared at her face, he wondered if anything he might do surgically could ever begin to approach this living, organic, God-given standard.

"Like it? We're dropping it next week. It's called, 'I Was Yours, No?'"

"God. Is she a picture!"

Convulsing in wounded pride, but nevertheless holding back on the vocal, Fay sang,

I don't ask where you go

I was yours, no?

I don't have the balls to say

No no no no, no no, NOOOO!

The problem with Fay was she looked too beautiful to be abused like she was in the song. Looking at her sing, Previn wondered what man would want to bother with the woman next door when he had her.

Fay appeared in the doorway. She stood there for a long moment, never taking her eyes from the TV screen. Finally, she walked into the room. She seemed genuinely stunned by what she saw, as though she thought Tout had taken a great liberty in sharing the video with Previn.

"What's that?" she asked.

"What brilliant luck you had this in the can," Previn volunteered, more than a little taken aback by Fay's reaction. "It's so you, Fay."

"No, it isn't!" she shrieked.

"I'm sure Johnny didn't mean anything by sharing it," Previn countered. Could this erratic behavior be a side effect from the drugs he'd given her? Paranoia was not unusual. He stared at her carefully. The doctor looking for clues.

"That's not me!" she said, staring at the larger-than-life vision of herself.

Tout laughed as he downed a handful of jellybeans. "Fay. It's all right."

"Who is that?" she yelled, pointing at the giant image of her on the big screen. "Why are you both looking at me like that?" she asked. "I tell you, that's not me!"

Previn wasn't sure how to respond. Images don't lie. Could it be she feared having to compete with her prior beauty? That she didn't feel Tout and Previn's nostalgia for it? Didn't want this reminder? The contrast was dramatic. However, she'd have to learn to live with the before and after. Life was like that. It had stages. Moments. How many women did he see who desperately wanted to recapture their looks, though they were more often than not reaching back too many years?

"Fay, it's good you're seeing this," Tout began, upbeat, ever the salesman. He attempted to put his arm around her to steady her, but she brushed it off with a violence that reminded Previn of the night she'd cut herself. "I'm pleased Harry's here too. Note, the plastic surgeon can't tell the difference."

Previn turned to Tout. What was he getting at?

"Looks just like you, doesn't it? What can't be done on a computer! You're as good as new."

They all looked at the screen, at the larger than life image of Fay Wray. Her breathless vocals filled the room. Previn was stunned. Was it possible? Could that gorgeous image be fabricated from mere dots? Could Fay Wray be replaced that convincingly? Previn was aghast. Though not nearly as much as Fay, the flesh-and-blood version.

"This is me," she said banging her chest angrily with one hand. She pointed at the screen with the other. "That's *not* me!"

"Until your doctor here can put you right, this cyber Fay Wray can rule the world."

"I can only be me," she said in utter desperation, the futility of a woman vanquished by another woman. "Nobody can do me." With tears streaming down her face, her eyes jerked between Tout and the images still playing on the screen. Unquestionably, she felt betrayed. Violated. Unhinged. All of a sudden, she grabbed the bowl of jellybeans and hurled them at the monitor with a crazed scream. They exploded against the video screen, sending glass and jelly beans everywhere.

"Only me. Me!" She stormed out of the room and right past Rox, who had come running in at the sound of breaking glass.

"Fay! I thought this would make you feel better," Tout said as he ran after her. Previn could hear him in the hallway trying to console her. At one point, over her sobbing, he heard her say, "How could you do this to me?"

Tout appeared at the door a few minutes later. Deflated. "I know what you're thinking, mate. But I'm the bloke who told Prince he had to get out of Paisley Park. And years before they found him laid out in the elevator. Ever see that place? It didn't even have windows. No man should live in an industrial park. I think it's what killed him. And nobody talks about it. But it is. So don't say I don't care. I'm very intuitive and I vibe with people. What Fay doesn›t get is: I'm the only one keeping her alive. You've got to talk to her. Tell her about her new life. About the plan. Go up there. Talk to her now. The boat's waiting in the harbor…"

"You think that's what she wants?"

"Drawing it out like this, it's unkind. Go to her."

Previn turned to the broken monitor and stared at it, as if he were looking into a shattered mirror.

◆◆◆

PREVIN CAME HOME AND went directly to his studio where he encountered *her*, the statue he'd been working on. He stared into her face for the longest time. It had become almost an article of faith with him that being a plastic surgeon was about making people happy. And happiness was all about being beautiful—because aren't the beautiful happy?

Previn picked up the phone and called Ty Fanning. "I'm worried about Fay, Ty. This can't end well. Why are they holding her?"

"You always break into my days and nights to have philosophical conversations, Harry. Don't you know that attorneys bill by the hour?"

"This isn't philosophical. I feel like Fay's in danger."

Previn walked around the statue, studying it, measuring her every feature. Perfection. But Helen had said that beauty was in imperfection.

"If Fay agrees to a new life, then what's the problem?" Ty asked. "What's the danger in that?"

Previn stopped. "But she won't agree to it. If she did, the original crime would go away, wouldn't it? How can a dead person charge someone with assault? It's the ultimate cover-up, Ty."

"My next client is here. Don't do anything stupid, Harry."

Previn picked up his clay knife and drew a circle around the side of her face, then excavated until there was a large round hole going right through the side and out the back of her head.

He walked around her. Electrified by this reinvention, he stopped and spun the pedestal so it swirled and swirled.

23

PREVIN'S CAR TURNED INTO Tout's motor court, stopping near the front entrance.

It was to be a house call like all the others. Previn showed up with his medical bag in hand. He rang the doorbell and waited.

"Harry! Were we expecting you?" Rox asked.

He smiled gamely. "Thought you missed me."

After the suicide attempt, Previn couldn't be faulted for being extra attentive for wanting to take Fay's mental temperature, as it were, even if he'd been there only the day before. Fay met them in her room, as usual. She had on headphones and her bandage.

"What do you listen to?" Previn asked.

Fay took the headphones off. "Beyonce."

"I used to be more into music than I am these days." He stepped up to the window looking out onto the driveway as he continued to talk. "Now I just listen to National Public Radio when I drive."

"Figured."

"How are you feeling?" he asked.

"How am I supposed to feel?"

Rox stared at him, seemingly on guard.

"It gets better, Fay," he replied with an easy smile. He stepped into the bathroom and filled her glass with some water, and then reached into his medical bag for two pills. "Happy pills."

She took the glass and popped the pills. He was her doctor, after all. She'd taken so many pills over the last three weeks, she didn't even bother asking what they were anymore. Of course, Rox didn't, either. It was what doctors do, they medicate.

"Excuse me." Because the bathroom door in Fay's room had still not been repaired, Previn walked over to the bathroom down the hall, leaving Fay and Rox together. He stood with his back to the bathroom door and waited. And waited. When he heard Rox leave Fay to take a call downstairs, he went back into Fay's room.

"I feel kinda strange," Fay said, her hand on the side of her head.

"Drowsy?"

"Yeah."

He peeked into the hall for Rox who could not be more than a few seconds away before barring the door with a chair.

"What's going on?" Fay asked.

"Some people have bad reactions to the medication, Fay. It's going to be okay, though."

He reached into his medical bag for a syringe and ripped off the wrapper.

"Whoa!" Fay took a step back. "What's that?"

"Can you count to fifty backward?"

"Why?"

"You've got to try."

"God. What did you give me? Fifty, forty-nine, forty-eight, forty-seven…"

As she counted down, he put a tourniquet around her forearm and dabbed her vein with alcohol. He made a big show of filling the syringe, and then discharged a slight amount in the air.

Fay looked on, terrified.

Previn could hear Rox's shoes on the wood floor like gunshots. He had to hurry.

"Twenty-seven, twenty-five, twenty-four…I don't know why I'm doing this. Did I say twenty-five already?"

"Hold still."

Previn injected Fay, and then ripped the tourniquet off her arm and threw it and the syringe into his medical bag.

Rox tried the door. "Why's the door blocked?" The door shook but the chair held. "Fay! What are you doing in there?"

Fay fell backward. Previn caught her in his arms and tried to prop her up, though her legs were unsteady beneath her.

"Fay. Fay."

Rox pounded and kicked at the door. "Goddamn it! This isn't funny."

Previn slapped Fay's face hard. "Fay!"

Fay didn't respond.

He looked around the room once more. He spotted Fay's silver clutch by the nightstand. He tossed it in his medical bag.

"Open the fuckin' door, Harry. I hear you in there," Rox barked.

Previn whisked Fay up into his arms and, with the medical bag in hand, kicked the chair from the door, which Rox threw open. He walked with Fay's unconscious body in his arms right past Rox, just as he'd done after her suicide attempt only four days before.

As he carried her down the hall, Rox trailed after him. "What the—"

"Fay! What else?"

As he made his way down the staircase, Tout came running from the kitchen. "What about Fay?"

Previn had stopped at the front door. "Open the door. Damn it!"

Rox got there first.

Previn raced to his convertible. He laid Fay's limp body against the hood.

"What happened to her?" Tout asked.

"Hold her legs while I open the door. Hold her! Don't let her fall."

Tout and Rox braced her limp body as Previn opened the passenger door for Fay.

"You're scaring me. What's going on?" Tout asked.

Previn peeled Fay's eyelid back, showing that her eye had rolled back into her head.

Tout gasped. "Oh, my God! What has she done now?"

Previn hurriedly dumped Fay into the passenger seat without even bothering to put a seatbelt on her. He ran around to the other side and climbed into the Jag. Within seconds, he'd roared off, leaving Tout and Rox standing there in shock.

His car spun out of Tout's driveway and into the street, almost colliding with a station wagon. He gunned the accelerator to sixty miles an hour in what seemed like sheer desperation. Her body was inert. She lay slumped and unconscious beside him. Her face fell into his crotch. He had to shove her away from him at the first turn.

The moment was one vast adrenaline rush. As he passed several cars, he pounded his fist on the wheel, euphoric. He'd finally sprung Fay from jail.

"Yeaaah, motherfucker!"

◆◆◆

FAY STARED UP FROM the pillow, slow to register where and what she was looking at. Previn was in the chair across from the bed, a copy of *Angeleno Magazine* in his hand, although it was more a prop. His thoughts were very much in the last few crazy hours.

He'd succeeded in abducting Fay. Now what? Turned out carrying her off may have been the easy part, although under his direct care, she was invariably safer.

The bigger question, though, was how long she would stay with him? Would she want to? He didn't have the slightest idea as to what her future would look like. It would be a year before he could operate on her again; her face would have to settle first.

There was a crosscurrent of emotions. Concern for Fay's well-being, first. Although there was a lot of ego invested in his opposition to Barone and Tout. Call it being threatened with that wrongful death suit one too many times. Then there was a sense of justice done. Somewhere out there was the person who'd done this to her and he wanted to find the perp.

How innocent and almost naïve such ideas now seemed as she lay in the bed. Her mind would be cloudy with the powerful knockout drug he'd given her for a while yet.

Right now, Tout was probably on the phone to Barone. What were they saying? The one immediate advantage he had was that they must be uncertain as to what Fay's condition was. His phone vibrated. He looked at the screen. It was Tout. Already. He wasn't going to take his call. Let him sweat.

She stirred.

"Fay."

"What happened?"

Previn checked her pulse. He really didn't have to do that. It was more a nervous reaction on his part. He'd felt so victorious carrying her off. Suddenly he felt guilty for having done something decidedly illegal. He could lose his medical license. He could go to jail.

"Thought a little change of scenery would do you good."

She lifted herself up on her shoulders. Her clothes were still on, though he'd thrown a light blue comforter over her. "Where is this?"

"My place."

"What time is it? How long have I been asleep? How did I…?"

She wearily sunk her head back in the pillow and fell asleep before he could answer her.

Twenty minutes later, she tried to get on her feet but did so unsteadily. Previn reached to hold her elbow. She was evidently still groggy from the powerful sedative he'd given her. It wasn't quite the same as a patient coming to after surgery, but close.

"Did…Did you kidnap me?" she asked.

"Now, Fay."

"You did. You drugged me. You fuckin' drugged me. You prick!" She punched at him with a weak show of anger.

"I'm trying to help you!"

She was suddenly very awake. "This is so whacked. Wow! You broke me out of there. Who does that shit? What's your fucking deal? Why are you doing this for me?"

"Who says I'm doing it for you?"

"Well, who then? You're not one of those sick fucks who's going to hold me in the basement for ten years and make me have your children, are you?"

He of course knew she was joking, but he felt a little like that guy. He had certainly gone to great lengths to get her to his place and now he wasn't really sure about it. What was he going to do with her?

The phone rang.

"Hold on," he said to Fay, lifting the receiver and walking with the phone to his ear into the living room.

"Helen!"

Fay walked in as Previn talked to her.

"Missing me?" Helen asked.

"Every moment."

"Wow!" Fay spotted the lips sofa along with the red tongue chair.

"I have something I have to tell you," he conceded. "I've just done something which—"

"When's the party? Weee!" Fay plunged onto his sofa, delighting in it as if it were a bubble bath. "Oh, I love it. This is obscene. Obscene, man. Obscene!"

"I'm interrupting," Helen said.

"No, it's…a patient."

"Well, tend to your patient, then," she said curtly, and then hung up.

Previn mouthed her name into the dead phone. He needed a moment. This was just like her. He wanted to call her back to explain. But at the same time, he found himself feeling exhausted with her lack of trust. The life of a plastic surgeon naturally involved women. If she couldn't deal with it, then they didn't have a future. Though he knew damn well that this thing with Fay was something else entirely.

"What's the matter? I thought this was a party."

Previn looked away.

"Girl problems?" Fay asked.

"Fuck!"

"It is, isn't it? I knew it."

"There's no benefit of the doubt. No understanding. No trust. Nothing!"

"Tell her that," Fay said.

"Feels like we're past that now."

"I don't think you believe that. Call her. Go after her. Girls like to be pursued. It'll work. It will. I'll just make myself comfortable in these giant red lips and you can call her back and I can listen in and guide you."

"I didn't bring you here to..." He reached for Fay's wrists and slowly turned them to observe the healing.

"Do you have to do this? God!"

He let them go. "I'm not going to lose you."

"What is life if I no longer have my looks?" Fay asked.

"Don't say that."

"I don't have to say it. It's been said. It's written on the walls. I can't tour. Can't see anyone. Can't love. Who would love me?"

"Hold still." Previn reached for her bandage and pulled it off.

"What did you do?"

"It's time, Fay."

She walked over to the white grand piano, ran her hands over the top of it. Lifted the lid. Touched the keys without pressing down on them. Her fingers were tactile. They seemed to be making love.

He didn't recall Tout having a piano. This must have been the first time she was able to be musical since her injury.

"When I was a boy, there was a beautiful piano at school," he confided. "We used to sing all sorts of wonderful songs. And the teacher, this black guy who was like Louis Armstrong, he'd lead us. You know, I'm not musical. I can't sing worth a damn. I don't even play but I wanted a Steinway. Always thought I'd be with someone who played. Never happened."

Fay sat down on the bench. Put her hands in position. They were still for a moment. Then they commenced what was a grand dance across the keys.

Previn leaned across the piano, watching her play. He was so enjoying this moment, his annoyance with Helen fell away. This was the music he'd wanted in his home. As she started to sing, Previn was enraptured. She sang the same song, "I Was Yours, No?" as he'd heard in Tout's cyber-Fay video. However, this was real. This was Fay Wray. The song, stripped of all production value, had become entirely new. It'd become personal; poignant, even. Heartfelt in a way the other wasn't.

He pulled out his iPhone to film her performance. "You should see yourself."

Fay covered her face. "I don't want you filming me."

"Play."

He went to the side of her that was pristine, that hadn't been damaged so as not to make her too self-conscious all at once.

As she peeled off the first bars from "I Was Yours, No?" he slowly panned around her so that he was filming on her bad side in close-up. She looked straight into the camera as if in protest.

He continued filming, getting out from behind the camera so that she could engage him with his eyes. Their eyes were locked. She stopped playing the piano. Holding back tears, she belted out the line:

Look at me. Isn't this the girl you loved?

She resumed playing the piano. The performer in her. The show must go on. The dogged you-paid-your-money-and-I'm-going-to-give-you-a-show professional. He recorded it tight. Continued in close-up. She slammed her fingers down on the keyboard thirty seconds later. "I can't!"

Fay jumped up from the bench and grabbed her bandage. She defiantly put it back on.

Soon he was pulling it down from the cloud. The footage appeared on his desktop.

"It's bad, isn't it?" Fay said. "It's horrible."

Previn looked up with a smile.

"What?" she demanded.

"So many of my patients live and die by the camera, Fay."

Fay came around to look at the monitor. He stared at her as she watched herself perform. What he'd captured was a fascinating documentary, but the sight of her watching herself was truly the most interesting document. If her performance seemed utterly normal, Fay's reaction was anything but. She was like a specimen squirming under a magnifying glass. Her eyes, troubled. Her breath, quickening. "Stop it! Stop it!" She covered her eyes. "What does this prove?"

He stopped the video. "If you could see what I see."

"Why must you hold up a mirror to me? I don't want to look."

"You've got to start facing yourself."

"I don't want to face my face, okay?"

"You don't have a choice. Fay, this is my work. I know what you're going through. But you've got to start living with it. Let the whole world see. So what!"

She wasn't buying it.

"Okay," he said. He pulled out his phone again and put the camera on her as before. Fay automatically covered her face with her hands.

"No!"

"I'm going to film your good side," he said.

When she lowered her hands, he began to film.

"Why? What is the matter with you? Did you shoot me up with…whatever…to bring me here to make sick home movies?"

Previn lowered the phone. "That's good enough." He led her back to the monitor. "Look."

Fay stared at the footage. He'd shot her entirely in profile, a half person. There it was again, in the playback, her barking into his camera, *"Why? What is the matter with you? Did you shoot me up with…whatever…to bring me here to make sick home movies?"*

The video footage stopped.

"What am I going to do?" she asked.

"You know."

"Fuck off!"

"Thought this'd make it easier."

"For who?"

Her question hung in the air. He thought, for herself. But her implication was that he'd been cruel. Was his instinct to, show her doing what she loved; was that so far from right? Had he erred? Was this the height of insensitivity? Previn took her in his arms, trying to comfort her. After a moment, he let her go.

"I can feel the disappointment around me," she said at last. "Everyone's disappointed in me. *I'm* the problem."

Previn had been wrestling with this since that first night at the Chateau, but he'd had a hunch ever since he'd seen him on the wall and then in person at Tout & Wilde. "Nick Valentine did this to you, didn't he?"

Fay stared at him with evident disquiet.

"Why are you protecting him?" he pressed.

Fay traced her scars with her fingers. "I have a career, you know. He's like one of the biggest rock stars in the world and I'm…I'm just Susan Plouse."

He sat with Fay for more than a minute. Neither of them said a word. He didn't know where to go with it. She apparently didn't want to tell him what had happened that night. She walked over and turned on the television. He finally went toward his bedroom and closed the door. He pulled out his iPhone and looked at the screen.

Tout had called five times. Previn pressed the message replay tab. "What's happening with her, mate? You're scaring me. You've got to call me."

Previn sat down on the bed, taking a moment before placing a call. "Helen, speak to me. How many times do we have to do this? It isn't what you think…Why are we doing this to ourselves? You know me. You know me better than anyone. You know I'm not a fuck-around cheat. I love you. Come on!"

◆◆◆

FAY HAD HER BACK to him when he returned. The TV remote was in her hand. She'd already helped herself to a glass of red wine.

"What if Johnny comes for me?" She spoke to Previn without turning around, which had the effect of making her seem as distant as if she were in another room. "What are you going to do then?"

Previn moved deeper into the room so he could at least address her in profile. "He thinks you're dead."

Fay didn't know what to say.

"Your body was limp in my arms. He thinks he has blood on his hands."

"What did he say?" she asked.

"He held the car door. I put your body in the seat and drove off."

"And that's it?"

"Sorry."

"He hasn't called?" Fay pressed.

"No. Not a word."

She struggled to comprehend Previn's bold-faced lie.

"I don't know if he thinks I took your body to dump it somewhere. I don't know what he thinks." He couldn't believe what he'd said. But this was war. He wasn't about to jeopardize what he'd done just to make her feel better. Couldn't risk it. Not now.

Her eyes were drawn back to the television. "Oh, look. As if on cue." She turned up the volume.

Valentine appeared looking like a Versace model in a dark suit, wearing reflective shades. He lowered them to look down the aisle as his bride smashed her bouquet on the floor. "It didn't have to be this way," he said in the voiceover. Valentine's face turned to shock, as a red graphic bar splashed across the screen, "Now in Theaters Everywhere."

"Know what *Falling* means?" Fay asked. "Means falling in love. Puke!"

Another clip of Valentine without his shades on had him looking down at an empty, slept-in bed. Its sheets rumpled. The implication that someone had a very good time in it. Over the sheets with Valentine to the side of the frame, critics' favorable reviews ran down the screen. "You will fall for *Falling*." "Walk. No, run to *Falling*!" "Nick Valentine can fly!"

As he watched with Fay, it all suddenly made sense. "The film. That's it! The film."

"I can't watch," Fay said, blackening the screen with the remote.

Here was the matrix in which Tout and Barone's interests converged and it'd been staring him in the face. That damn movie poster that filled the reception area at Tout & Wilde. The film was the bridge between the different worlds of music and film. "So that's why Barone…*Falling* is his film!" Previn burst out. "That's why it was Barone who called me in. Now it makes sense!"

Fay turned to face him. "I was attracted to Nick Valentine, okay? I never thought he'd hurt me."

"Then why—?"

"He was kissing me, telling me all this crazy shit like guys do. He told me he wanted to you know, fuck. I was into it."

"Then how did this—"

"He couldn't get a hard-on, okay? I may have laughed, you know. A nervous laugh. I only saw the bottle out of the corner of my eye. But I felt it. All I was thinking after the blow, which stung like…was about the wine. That I had it all over me. That he'd gotten me wet. But it was blood. I had blood…"

Previn just stared at her. He'd always known it'd be something like this. A woman like her was more than likely to attract the wrong sort of energy from men. He'd seen it himself. If he'd been differently disposed, unprofessional, and more than a little creepy, he might have gotten together with her too. Still, whatever it was about her neediness, it didn't justify what had happened. Nothing could justify that. The same might have been said about actress Lana Clarkson being shot dead by the legendary music producer Phil Spector.

Victims meet victimizers.

"I didn't immediately think about my face, but he'd sliced it open," she was saying. "He'd sliced it! He should have killed me. Done me then and there. Finished me like when they put down a horse."

Previn picked up his cordless phone. Dialed 911.

"What are you doing?" she asked, alarmed.

He motioned for her to be quiet. "Hello. Hello. My name is Dr. Harold Previn. I'd like to report a crime."

◆◆◆

PREVIN WAS ANNOYED THEY had to go to the West Hollywood sheriff's station, as opposed to a detective coming out to see them at the house. But as this was a crime they'd waited almost a month to report, the sheriff's department didn't feel the urgency. He'd tried to make the case that she was a big star, however the dispatcher he'd spoken to had never heard of Fay Wray. He'd have pressed further, but Fay was sitting right there and he didn't want to give Fay reason to balk, much less have her be confronted with the limits of her stardom. He'd had enough famous clients to know how delicate they could be about such things.

She was surprisingly pliant after her initial shock at his 911 call. He'd come to realize she'd been hoping all along someone might do this very thing. The fact her own manager and the small retinue surrounding her were reluctant to come to her defense must have made her feel all the more vulnerable and small.

He would have driven directly to the station, but he had to stop at his surgery center to get her medical file and her blood-smeared dress. A treasure trove of evidence from the night of the assault. He slid it all into a large envelope, and then they drove to the station. She hadn't had much to say through much of the trip. She'd jammed a CD into his deck. An old Kate Bush record Helen had left behind from before she'd moved out.

Previn might have been wise to have consulted with Ty Fanning before taking this leap. Maybe Ty could have met them at the station. Seemed like celebrities always had legal counsel at these things. But Previn knew he was plotting a desperate course and stopping to consult an attorney seemed like it might derail everything. Every time he'd called Ty, he'd as much as told Previn to go along to get along.

No more.

Previn decided to make one last phone call just before they got to the station. "Talk to me. Helen, please. This isn't another Demi. I promise. Call—"

"Stop the car!" Fay yelled.

"Gotta go!" He hung up. They were literally in front of the station. "Fay, we're here."

"I can't," she said.

"What are you talking about? We're here. Let's go."

"I'm watching my whole career pass before my eyes."

At nineteen, she was still very much a child. He responded to that. He had all along. However, this was the moment to do something. She was in his car. In his control. They didn't have Tout to thunder on about damage to her career. If no one else would take her side, Previn would. It wasn't simply about putting this right. Now, more than ever, he needed to be needed. And Fay needed him in a way none of his other patients did.

"*We* agreed to do this," he said.

"*You* agreed to do this. Not me!"

She stared straight ahead as though she could see it all through the windshield.

Previn had the bit in his teeth. There was no letting up. If he had to carry her into the station, he would. He stared at her with impatience. He knew, though, that he had to convince her to come around. If she didn't seem to be making this charge willingly, then how could he expect the DA to run with it?

"Are you going to go the rest of your life pretending this didn't happen?" he asked, softly. "All we do is go in there, quietly make our statement. Go home. Eat ice cream. It's that simple."

Fay sat there, bolt upright.

"There's something you should know," he said, imbuing this declaration with all the cryptic drama he could. "Something I was supposed to get you to agree to. You were going to fall off a boat near Ensenada so that you'd forever be Fay Wray, the nineteen-year-old blonde beauty. They don't think there is a future for you anymore. They said you were as good as dead, given your injuries. They wanted me to tell you that you needed to do this, to die."

Fay's big green eyes glistened as she stared at him. Was she about to cry?

"You weren't really going to die," he continued, touching her hand. "They wanted me to tell you that you could keep making music, posthumously. I mean, it's crazy, but they said if you went along, you could always live on as the beauty you were in everyone's eyes. In photos. In that video Johnny made. It's nonsense. I'm embarrassed to even…This isn't what you want, is it?"

She didn't answer.

"Talk to me, Fay."

"That idea is rad," she said finally. "I love love love it. Why didn't you tell me?"

He'd fully expected her to scream hysterically. To pull her hair out. To want to kill herself again. To kill Johnny Tout. Anything is believable when you tell a woman that it's the considered opinion of those around her, those who care most about her, that she should end her life as she knows it because she's no longer pretty enough, but he hadn't weighed the fact that she was all about her career. That Fay Wray was a part she was playing. It wasn't her. Hers was a disposable life. All this flashed through his mind. He should have known this because whatever she was, she lived in the Capital of Good Looks, where beauty was everything.

All those weeks. Looking at her. Feeling like there was a connection between them. That he was there for her. Her savior. That she had come to trust in him. Suddenly, it was all bullshit.

Several sheriff's deputies walked right past the car.

She must have seen the look of incredulity on his face.

"What?" she asked.

◆◆◆

"IF YOU WON'T CALL it extortion…"

Previn left it at that. As they met with Detective Garcia at the sheriff's station, he found he wasn't having much success building a case against Barone for holding his feet to the fire using the wrongful death suit. But part of the problem was Previn's own murky rationale for wanting Barone charged. It was as if he secretly hoped it might assuage his own guilt at having lost Simone Blackburn through his recklessness.

"What happened to Fay is undoubtedly a crime," Detective Garcia relied. "But for this other, I need evidence. I need something real. You throw words around like conspiracy—"

"It *is* a conspiracy!"

Garcia tossed his pen down on his notepad. They'd been sitting in a conference room for more than an hour. The photos of Fay's injuries from the night of the assault, a plastic bag containing her bloodstained dress, her clutch, and the bottle fragments retrieved during the operation were all scattered across the table. Garcia seemed thorough and interested, which went a long way toward putting Fay at ease.

Previn couldn't keep himself from staring at the bridge of Garcia's Rocky Marciano nose, which had Garcia been in any other profession he'd have wanted to correct. But it gave him something. Detective Garcia. Tough guy. The nose made him look right for the part. Like he'd made a few arrests. Immaculately attired, he had on a powder-blue silk tie and gold cuff links. His starched white shirt showed off a chiseled physique. Garcia told them he handled the celebrity cases, of which they probably had more than a few. His being so presentable made him ideal. This being the Capital of Good Looks.

Much of the interview with Garcia had been consumed with his attempt to locate the room where the assault had occurred. Questions like if the room faced the hills or the city. He wanted to pin down the location so he could begin at a minimum to locate witnesses to link Valentine and Fay together at the hotel. This might explain his interest in the bottle itself. What were they drinking? Did she remember the bottle being ordered through room service? If in fact it had come from room service, he felt that there might be records. Garcia described it as a circumstantial case. Unless, of course, they could find her blood in the room Valentine had stayed. He wanted to find hard evidence. He was delighted to have her dress because forensics might find DNA on it linking Valentine to her person. He was all about the tangible.

Fay's recollection of the night was choppy. She described her panic as she woke naked on the bed, disoriented and in pain as Sid Wilde struggled to get her back into her dress. At first, she wasn't sure what he was trying to do and even thought he was trying to assault her. It was Wilde who had guided her down the hallway and into the stairwell. She vaguely recalled Rox trying to wipe Fay's blood from a wall, something that Garcia found of great interest. Her memory was clouded by drugs and alcohol, but trauma factored in heavily. Previn recalled that Tout had given her Valium at some point, which probably explained her being passed out when he first encountered her. It also explained how her recollection may have been as good as it was in the period just before they'd brought her to the limo.

The conversation finally settled into what Previn described as Barone's not-too-subtle attempt to keep him quiet.

Garcia was all about proof. It was very difficult to contest that Fay had been assaulted. That Previn had been pressed into covering up a crime was something the detective was struggling with. "That you've come to us now, whatever your reasons for not coming to us before—"

"But the reason I didn't come—"

"This isn't a confessional. That you came now or…you came. The timing—"

"I would have come before."

Previn watched Fay drag her fingers over her bandage thoughtfully as Garcia spoke. "The demons that you have, the reasons why you've come and what they may do to you, it's immaterial. You'll have to wait and see if they file the wrongful death suit against you. Doesn't mean it has anything to do with what happened to her or your coming here."

"My reputation. My credibility as a surgeon, it's all on the line."

"If you do deals with the devil, the devil will take his piece, or maybe not. Unless you've got proof, you don't have anything."

Previn lost it. "So I'm fucked whatever I do?"

"I didn't say that."

"You don't have to."

Garcia fingered the prints of Fay taken the night of her surgery, but he didn't dwell on them. He had something on his mind. "What's hanging me up here? Michael Jackson bought the silence of several dozen kids. Nick Valentine's worth gazillions. Why not go to you with his big checkbook?"

"I have anger issues," Fay conceded.

That statement seemed to stop traffic. Garcia studied her for the longest time. And Previn knew why. Up until then, she'd been the victim, but when she said that, a door seemed to open to a much more complex personality. Fay was a force to be reckoned with. She hadn't become a star playing a mouse. There was evidently so much more to her.

"Okay. Right. Charges could absolutely be brought against John Tout," Garcia announced at last. "Richard Barone's another matter. The connection is there, it just needs more excavation."

"You have me," Previn said.

"Not enough. But the DA will probably charge Tout with accessory. Conspiracy to fake her death is a much harder charge to prove because they never really did much with that other than try to enlist you. Wrongful imprisonment, perhaps."

These all sounded like pretty heavy charges. As they say, the best defense is a good offense. These charges would bury them and Jake Blackburn would probably fire Barone before he'd accept his counsel that he should file a wrongful death suit against Previn in lieu of the broader context of what was happening. It'd be so clear that Blackburn was pressing him to file suit because of Fay, not because he genuinely cared about his mother.

"Cool," Previn said.

Fay suddenly spoke up with what felt like finality. "No."

"What?" Garcia asked.

"Not Johnny. He's my manager. I can't—"

"But—"

"I said, no!"

◆◆◆

"I REMEMBER THE BIG gigs," Fay said, as they drove back to Previn's house. "There was always a letdown. It's why a lot of people do coke after a show. They want to hold the buzz."

"You feel buzzed?" Previn asked.

"Don't know how I feel."

"I'd give anything to see Johnny's face when they take his boy away in cuffs."

Previn looked over at Fay but she had her head turned away from him. She was staring out the window, deep in thought. After entertaining Tout's death plot earlier, who knew what she was thinking now.

"You need an attorney," he said. "I know some good lawyers. I do their wives. I'll have to call around. We'll find you a barracuda."

"I don't want to talk about this," she said.

"Why not?"

"Tired."

"Well, we've got to talk about it."

She got angry. "I hate this, okay!"

They drove the rest of the way in silence. Previn suddenly regretted being so out-front on the case, though it was difficult to see any way around it. She needed him. She really needed him.

◆◆◆

WITH A LARGE KITCHEN knife, Fay cut herself a piece of dark chocolate and popped it into her mouth just as the phone rang.

Previn answered and listened for a moment. He put his hand over the phone. "They've issued a warrant for Valentine!"

As Previn continued to press for more information, Fay rushed from the kitchen with the knife in one hand and a chunk of chocolate in the other.

"Oh...my...God!" she exclaimed. She ran over to the television and started surfing the channels for news. They watched a cable report showing the front gate of Valentine's estate.

A scene of bedlam. Beneath the glare of security lights, guards pushed reporters away so that three black SUVs could enter Valentine's compound.

There was a knock at Previn's front door. As Fay slinked into the kitchen to hide herself, Previn walked with his phone in hand to the door where a news crew and blinding camera lights confronted him. He closed the door, and as gracefully as he could, excused himself from speaking with the reporter on the phone, saying this really wasn't a good time.

When minutes later the phone rang again, Fay went into a panic. "Who told them we're here?"

There was yet another knock at the door. He stopped to look at himself in the mirror behind the bar. Rolling up one of his sleeves then unrolling it. After another knock at the door, he dashed through the house and returned wearing one of his funky, Paul Harnden "I'm-an-artist" handmade sports coats. Then went back to the mirror, straightening his collar and arranging his hair. The doorbell rang. He turned to the door, and then turned back to the mirror. Then back to the door.

"Jesus! What are you doing?" Fay asked.

"I'll deal with this."

"What have we done?"

"Don't worry." He steeled himself before opening the door to what looked like a large crowd. Several flashbulbs went off immediately, making him momentarily lose his composure. There were at least two television camera crews and twenty reporters and paparazzi standing in front of him. He stepped outside, gently closing the door behind him before being blinded by a salvo of flashing cameras.

Click. Click. Click.

"I'm sorry," Previn said to the crowd in front of him. "I know some of you have questions, and in due time they will all be answered." He heard his words as though he were having an out-of-body experience. He'd begun well. He could feel it. This man talking was in command. As soon as he finished this first sentence, the photographer's cameras flashed and flared like a cannonade. He couldn't help but bask in it. Were they really taking his picture? Were they going to use it? "But this is not the time…or the—"

"Is Fay Wray in there?" a male reporter asked.

"I can't get into—"

"Is this a publicity stunt?" a woman reporter asked.

This singular question upended him, bringing this vainglorious moment to a sudden halt. In one instant, the limelight had become an interrogation light, shining uncomfortably in his eyes.

"Of course not. This woman was brutally attacked."

"Then why is this only coming out now after Nick Valentine's film has just premiered? It's opening weekend!" the reporter persisted.

"Well…" This hadn't occurred to him.

The answer was greeted with deadly silence. He had to do better than that.

"Because I couldn't take it anymore. Damn it! I'm not a mob doc, okay?" he said, rallying, recognizing that his credibility—indeed, the credibility of their whole effort—was on the line. He searched the faces of the reporters standing in front of him, trying to gather his thoughts, conscious he had to speak in sound bites because that's what he knew the media expected. So he reached for the quotable.

"Ask Johnny Tout. Go to Artist's Unlimited. It's a conspiracy! They brought me in to…Richard Barone, write that name down…to surgically erase evidence of a brutal assault…They brought me in," he said, finding his rhythm. "If only it were so simple. Fix her face. Make her injuries go away. Make the crime vanish."

Click. Click. Click.

Previn winced at the onslaught of flashbulbs but held his ground. He hadn't intended any of this, much less to field questions, but there was no retreating. He had to face them.

A male reporter with a pad and pencil in hand coolly asked, "Was she raped?"

"Two people in a room. One came out bloody and battered."

"You're not saying he's a sexual predator then?"

"I'm a plastic surgeon. What do I know about that?"

"Will Fay Wray be at the arraignment?" one of the reporters shouted.

He hadn't considered this. His house was like a bubble. Outside the bubble, things seemed to be happening. The warrant for

Valentine's arrest. Where was he now? Where was Tout? Would he be making a statement? Surely, lawyers were being consulted. And now the press wanted to know what was happening, and he didn't know himself. What was the procedure? Why hadn't he consulted with his lawyer Ty already?

"What's your name?" someone else shouted.

"My name is Dr. Harold Previn. I'm an aesthetic surgeon. I'm Fay's surgeon."

"Is it bad?"

"Of course it's bad. Her face was repeatedly struck with a broken bottle."

"Is she going to be disfigured for life?"

Previn took a deep breath. While he was ever confident delivering prognoses, this one was never going to go down well. "It'll take time and there are no miracles. Her lacerations..." He faltered. The last thing he expected from himself was emotion, but talking about her injuries in this public way brought it out. He got choked up. "Fay...Fay Wray to this day...right now...doesn't matter what I can, can't do... is the most beautiful woman in the world." He couldn't talk anymore.

Previn went back into his house and closed the door behind him. Fay was watching Previn's press conference on the TV agog. Evidently, there was a twenty-second delay. He saw the flashing cameras across his own face, and then watched him say his last words, "That's all I have." A television reporter, microphone inches from his mouth, said, "That was Dr. Harold Previn..."

Everything had been happening so fast. He'd hardly had a chance to think about what he was doing. Events had been driving him instead of vice versa. He'd thought that going to the police was his taking charge, but then it'd all gone into warp speed and suddenly he found himself standing in front of the whole world unloading on Barone and Artists Unlimited. If there was a price to be paid, he had to be true to himself. If this was going to bring the whole house down around him, so be it. This confrontation with Fay brought it all into focus. Yes. He was a doctor. This was what doctors did. They saved people's lives. And if he had to put his own on the line…He hadn't felt so emancipated since doing fieldwork in Mozambique.

Fay muted the television set and turned sharply to Previn, upending everything. "Did you enjoy that? What am I going to do now?"

"Fay. What…What are you talking about?"

"I've got to call them," she said, looking hunted, suddenly breathing hard. "Got to tell Johnny it's all been an awful mistake. I didn't mean it. I'm not going to do anything. I'll go back to Johnny's house. I'll go—"

Fay moved toward the door, though it'd be insane for her to rush outside. She was in a panic.

He ran to the door to block her from leaving. "That makes zero sense."

"You got me into this. I didn't want to. You drugged me. I was there and then I was here. I didn't know what I was doing. I never would have…if it weren't for you."

"Please, Fay. You know that's not true."

"I'm a rat," Fay thundered, as she moved around the room. "A rat!"

Previn pursued her. "Fay."

Fay stepped up onto the sofa as though she were trying to address a big crowd. "Johnny Tout paid for me to record demos. He brought in A-list talent to support me and make me shine. To give me a look. Brought in stylists. Fashion stylists. They even taught me how to walk. How to walk!"

"So what?"

"He named me. Do you know what that means? He gave me my name."

Previn shook his head.

"I'm…an ungrateful bitch!"

"Stop it, Fay." He pulled her down from the sofa. "You're guilt-tripping. Tout had you sedated. He tried to cover Valentine's ass by scheming to fake your death."

"I know. I know what he did." She fell onto his red tongue chair that went with the lips sofa. "Outing him like this, it's still a rotten, back stabbing thing. You have no idea. I got, like, this far..." She indicated an inch with her fingers. "This far from taking a gig at a strip club. But Johnny saw something in me no other man did." She stopped and turned to the TV.

They were playing archival footage of Nick Valentine performing in an arena. He was wildly charismatic and hugely talented. And could he dance. A slug running across the bottom of the frame read, "Breaking News. Arrest Warrant Issued for Nick Valentine."

A reporter stood in front of Previn's front door. "Tonight, the music industry is all abuzz with allegations," she stated, "that rock star and now film actor, star of *Falling*, Nick Valentine brutally assaulted pop star Fay Wray three weeks ago at the Chateau Marmont hotel.

"Wray appeared today at the West Hollywood sheriff's station to file a complaint against Valentine. We are outside Beverly Hills plastic surgeon Dr. Harold Previn's..."

They broke into the reporter midsentence and cut back to Valentine's estate. Police cars were shown jamming the long driveway, some of which still had their colored lights flashing.

"We have breaking news. We've just been told the district attorney has agreed to allow Nick Valentine to voluntarily appear at the police station in his own car to avoid a public spectacle, though I might say we may be beyond that now."

At that very moment, the back door opened and a butt-naked Nick Valentine, but for his wide brimmed hat, ran from the house toward the media scrum behind the front gate.

The anchor was breathless with excitement. "We have to break in. Valentine has just been spotted running from the house. There he is!"

"Does he think he can get away? What is he doing?" the reporter asked.

Previn and Fay watched the TV as eight police chased Valentine across the lawn. A female officer took him down with a Super Bowl-worthy tackle.

Fay yelled at the screen, "Jerk! Loser!" Then turned to Previn. "I never wanted to see his sorry naked ass again." She turned to the screen again. "Put something on!"

Previn placed an arm around Fay to comfort her as they watched events unfold.

The police lifted Valentine to his feet and forcefully cuffed him. His naked midsection was blurred out.

"Hey, everybody," Valentine yelled to the reporters who must have been gathered quite close to where he'd been taken down. "Do I get points for style or what? For the real story, see my movie. *Falling.* In theaters now."

The female officer yanked on the cuffs.

"Easy. That hurts."

"So much for turning himself in of his own recognizance," the news anchor commented. "We have just witnessed a bizarre spectacle that's sure to go down in rock 'n' roll lore. If we didn't think we knew Nick Valentine, meet the new Nick—"

"His attorneys could not have known," the reporter replied. "This looks like pure improvisation. The equivalent of the obligatory celebrity porn video. If this doesn't go viral—"

"Where do you draw the line between fame and infamy?" the anchor asked. "I don't know that you do anymore in our culture."

Fay sat down on the sofa as though she'd had the wind knocked out of her. "Everybody loves a freak show. What do I have that can ever top that?"

Previn turned to Fay, not knowing what to make of her comment. This wasn't a competitive event. She'd won. Although to look at Valentine, it might have seemed like he'd managed to pull an ace out from under the deck.

The television report continued, "If anyone has just tuned in, we have been watching the sheer spectacle of rocker, and, dare I say film star, Nick Valentine's *nude* arrest. Yes. You've heard that right. Nick Valentine attempted to evade arrest on assault charges by running from his house naked. He stands accused of having violently assaulted pop star Fay Wray at the Chateau Marmont Hotel earlier this month, but they can throw in public indecency to—"

There was a thunderous crash against the door and a commotion. Previn rushed to the door, yanking it open.

To Previn's infinite surprise, he saw two reporters trying to restrain a woman...Helen. They were manhandling his wife! But before he could do or say anything, he witnessed her break free from the one and punch the other in the jaw. Obviously, they seemed to think she was trying to get some sort of advantage over the rest of them and would have none of it.

"Get out of my face," she screamed. "I'm the wife!"

Previn immediately went to her, taking her into his arms protectively, and led her into the house.

"I don't know what I'm doing here," Helen said, her voice still raised from all the excitement. "You kept calling. I didn't want to see you. Hear from you. Talk to you. Then I turn on the news and there you are saying the sweetest things about..." She turned to Fay who was just stepping away from his computer.

What Fay was doing there he did not know, but he soon forgot in the heat of the moment. Helen was back!

"You." Helen said, and then turned back to Previn. "I was so proud of you, Harry, and yet I don't know what you've gotten yourself into here. But wow! It feels...new. God, I should go."

She looked at Fay then turned to Previn.

"You've got plenty to deal with."

Previn grabbed her arm. "No, we don't."

"You're lying," she said, pulling away.

"Did you come over here to call me a liar?"

"Who are you arguing with? Introduce us," Fay said from across the room.

"I'm Helen Burke, Harry's wife."

"Oh, I didn't know you were married," Fay said archly. "I only live here, you know."

"You're a troublemaker, Fay." He turned back to Helen. "She's been here today. Just today."

"I should go," Helen said.

"You drive all the way over here, charge through that crowd, punch some guy in the face, all to get here to…to what? You're either going to stay or go, but I won't tolerate this nonsense anymore. I want you to stay."

"Are you asking me to stay?"

Previn put his hands to his head, exasperated.

"Thank God for a little excitement," Fay said, smiling. "You know, I was craving some drama tonight."

24

A FTER ALL THAT HAD happened the night before, it was ironic
Previn had to perform a blepharoplasty on Marvin Muckridge,
the NBC national news anchor, which meant removing the bags
under his eyes. Minutes before Brick was to put him under, Previn
visited Muckridge, who was lying on a gurney at 7:00 a.m. in the
hallway outside the surgery.

"I won't ask you any questions about Fay Wray if you promise
to make me look like a million bucks," Muckridge said with a smirk.

"You already look like a million."

"Save that schmaltzy bullshit for the ladies," he said gruffly. "You
need a publicist, bud. That's all I'll say. It'll make your life sane. This
thing doesn't look like it's going to blow over soon. You're news, bud.
I don't know if you've even thought about who you're going to give
your story to, but it's valuable. Take it from an old news guy."

Three images were circulating literally side by side everywhere
Previn looked when he reviewed the news on his iPhone: Previn
under the media glare, Fay looking beautiful, and an uncensored,
totally licentious image of Nick Valentine in all his naked glory
resisitng arrest.

What wasn't shown and what people could only imagine were
Fay's injuries. They were the only thing that could trump Nick
Valentine in the nude.

That Previn had become the third person in this affair still surprised him. Although he'd been living this for more than three weeks, he had no sense of his role being anything but behind the scenes. In fact, all his work had always been discreet. Now he'd always be known as Fay Wray's plastic surgeon. Whether that was a good thing or a bad thing, he really couldn't be sure. Though in his gut, he wasn't sure that this was the fifteen minutes he would have ever elected to have.

Previn laughed. "I knew it. You're using your operation as a ruse to get an exclusive."

Muckridge smiled for the first time. "Crossed my mind. Not going to lie to you."

He pulled at his smock uneasily. "But not today, Harry. It's about my eyes. Remember? My eyes."

"Piece of cake."

"Hope so."

This may have been a grizzled veteran of the newsroom, but the prospect of an operation had a way of making even war veterans uneasy. He'd seen it before in his male patients. Underneath the bluster, they were marshmallows. Previn clenched Muckridge's hand. "It's going to be fine, okay?"

"Okay."

◆◆◆

HELEN THOUGHT SHE WAS dreaming a woman's voice. She opened her eyes. Harry had already left. Yet she could still hear the voice.

Fay!

Helen looked for something to drape around herself. She'd been homeless since leaving Guy's house. One moment she thought she was coming home to Harry's, and then it turned out she wasn't, and now she was. She walked into the closet. Her whole side was just as empty as the day she left. She took one of Harry's shirts off a hanger and put it on.

She came upon Fay as she was leaving Harry's studio.

"Fay?"

Fay stopped and stared.

Helen smiled. "It's so early. What time is it?"

"I have to get out of here."

Helen didn't know what to make of what she was hearing. Fay was dressed. She seemed decided.

"Cat's out of the bag," Fay said.

"And?" Helen asked.

"Yesterday threw me off my game. I still don't get what's going on. I have to figure this out." She shook her head thoughtfully. "Have you looked in that room?" She gestured behind her with her thumb.

"Harry's studio?

"There's a head in there. Got a hole in it. The sun was passing through just now, it was like a sign from God."

Helen stepped into the doorway. On the pedestal sat a head unlike any she'd ever seen from Harry. Sure enough, he'd drilled a three-inch hole at an angle right through the side and there really was sunlight passing through it.

She turned back toward Fay.

Just as she thought, the hole was right at the place where Fay had her injury. Up until then, this kind of abstraction had been missing from Harry's work. Seeing it excited her. She walked into the studio and ran her hand over the face and along the edges of the hole, feeling it like she knew Harry did when he put hands to work. Hers was a visual medium. Harry's was also tactile. He often asked her to put her hands on his work, as though it couldn't be wholly explored or understood without feeling it.

She stepped back from it.

"It's Harry's, isn't it?" Fay asked.

"It's mysterious. Like coming upon some ancient totem or something." Helen put her hand on her chest as though to steady her heart as she continued to stare at the sculpture.

Fay nodded.

She'd been so consumed with her own artistic departure she was almost dumbstruck that Harry could have had one, too. Evidently, their estrangement had been good for Harry. As she stood beside Fay, she could see that she'd been something of a muse to him.

"They're still out there. Is there another way out of this place?" Fay asked.

Helen marched into the living room. She couldn't see the television vans from the window. "Are you sure?"

Fay looked away impatiently.

"Well, I guess they are. But where you going to go?" Helen said.

"I feel like I should talk to Johnny."

"But—"

"I know. I know what you're gonna say, 'Don't go there!' Kinda like when you have an ex who you keep wanting to call even though you know you shouldn't."

"We've all been there, honey."

"He was my first and only. That makes it different."

"I get it. My art dealer was my manager." Helen laughed bitterly. "Where would we be without managers?"

"I thought it was pretty cool he had Nick Valentine. You always want to be with someone who's got a starry list. Wasn't a problem until…"

Helen gave Fay's arm a supportive squeeze. "It's what's called a conflict of interest. I know a thing or two about that. I thought my manager was my biggest fan, and he was, but sometimes that's not such a good thing."

"He try to fuck you?"

Helen was at a loss for words. Waking up in her bed with Harry hadn't changed the particulars of what she'd been through. Larisa was only just saying to her, "You can't go home again." But this was home. She was home.

"He did, didn't he? No big. All men are like that."

Helen's heart sank. Fay must have noticed her unease with her last sentence specifically.

"Except Harry," Fay added.

"I'm learning a lot about my husband."

Fay seemed restless. She looked at Helen directly. "I gotta go."

"You're not really going to see Johnny, are you?"

Fay shrugged.

Helen had to respond. "You know that manager I mentioned? He'd love it if I broke down and called him, he'd probably make me feel like I'd done the right thing, even, but I wouldn't feel good about it after. And you won't, either."

Fay teared up. "I wasn't expecting this from you. I didn't expect it from Harry, particularly. He'll be, like, the perfect dad someday."

Helen took Fay into her arms and was still holding her when Fay's phone went off.

Fay took the call. "Okay," she said to her ride. "Meet you on the corner in three."

"You're going? Just like that? What am I going to tell Harry?"

◆◆◆

RIGHT AFTER THE SURGERY, Sara told Previn Helen had called him, urgently wanting him to call her back.

"What about?" he asked.

"She said it's important."

Still wearing his scrubs, Previn closed the door to his office before calling her. "Hi, Hellie," he began, his voice becoming almost syrupy.

"Thank God! I didn't know what to do."

"About what?"

"Fay."

He laughed uneasily. "What? What's happened now?"

"She's gone."

"What do you mean?" His smile evaporated. "You've been there all morning, right?"

"Has credit card and cell phone, will travel. Fay said she wanted to see Johnny."

"No. Not that." Previn recalled packing her clutch when he took her from Tout's home. He believed it might be useful evidence; he hadn't considered that it might provide her with the means to run away.

"She saw the statue," Helen said. "It had sunlight passing through the hole you'd put in it. She said it was a sign."

"To go back to those people?"

"She shows up at their door, they'll kill her."

Previn's heart sank. "This can't be happening."

◆◆◆

HE RACED OVER TO Tout's house. Tout probably wouldn't allow him to reason with her, but failing all else, he'd at least get a whack at Tout.

Previn breezed past Rox who had opened the front door. Barone stood in the foyer as he entered. No doubt Previn was the last person she expected to find at the door. "I'll get Johnny."

Previn watched her walk down the hall, her heels cracking like gunshots on the dark Mexican pavers. He turned to Barone. "What are you doing here?"

"I could ask you the same question."

"I came for Fay."

"Oh?"

Tout approached with his hand out. His purple shirt was open and his hair was wet as if he'd just come from the shower. He was in high spirits. "The man of the hour!"

"Let's skip the niceties." Previn walked right past him. "Where's Fay?"

"Oh, let it go, mate. It's good you came by. I want to thank you."

"For what?" Previn snapped.

"One of the most remarkable film and record debuts in history."

"That light romantic comedy of ours has got the mo," Barone proclaimed. "There are lines at all the theaters."

"They've got it projected to hit number one at the box office tonight."

Previn was incredulous. "What? You mean people are flocking to see that felon?"

Barone shook his head. "Only in America, huh?"

Tout was buoyant. Positively giddy. "Taking Fay to the police station to file charges, the press conference…Genius! You really have a knack."

Previn tuned away in disgust. These guys weren't the practical-joking kind. It had to be true.

"And of course, Valentine was not to be outdone. I mean, have you ever seen anything like his arrest?"

Previn wasn't ready to join the celebration. "Had I talked Fay into agreeing to the fake death, he'd be a free man today. She wouldn't have been able to charge him. You think I don't know that?"

Tout and Barone both laughed.

"Never thought of that," Barone said.

"Yes, you did," Previn countered.

"You're a cynic, Harry."

"He'll have to pay Fay a king's ransom. That's damages, mate, but he always was. Isn't that right, Richard?"

"Why would you cover for a guy like that?"

"I still think, had Fay fallen off that boat, she'd be viable today. Remembered for how she was, still able to record. That was the move. Feel it in me bones!"

"You cared more about Nick Valentine than Fay."

Barone broke in. "I've seen some real celebrity blood feuds in my day. We've had our share at Artists Unlimited, but never two of our own…I feel for Sid and Johnny, they were caught in the middle between…I want to say Rihanna and Chris Brown." Barone and Tout shook their heads at what was up until then the pinnacle of domestic violence between celebrity couples. "But this topped that by a mile. Not easy."

Tout acknowledged the compliment. "Thank you."

"Hey, I know. Talent is always a challenge."

Tout turned back to Previn. "I'm disappointed in you, Harry. That you'd suggest…You think I didn't have her back? He'll do time. He should. Be good for his soul. You never want an artist to seem uninteresting. After the bail hearing, he'll do at least three months of rehab. That usually does the trick."

"All I wanted was to buy ourselves a few weeks at the box office before this broke and killed the film's prospects," Barone added. "And that's the truth, so help me God!"

"But if I'd been able to repair her face, you'd have successfully covered up the crime."

"You watch too many movies."

But Tout couldn't let go of the grander idea. "If we'd have gotten her to die on that boat, she could have made the ultimate comeback. Fay Wray is alive! I could have brought her back from the dead with the new face you'd have given her. Would have been the most amazing star marketing ever."

"Not better than this, Johnny," Barone replied. "Give yourself some credit here. We're number one at the box office, goddamn it!"

Barone put a hand on Tout's back. Previn turned away. He actually felt ill. This was the ultimate triumph of cynicism. Could a perp like Valentine become instant box office gold? Could all this have actually helped sell the film?

Tout struck Previn with another knife blow. "That's all you, mate."

Previn turned to Tout. "You never answered my question."

"What?"

"Fay. Where is she?"

Tout simply stared at Previn as if he didn't quite know what to say. Rox came back in. "You have a phone call."

"I'm with me mates! Tell 'em I'll call back."

"It's important."

Tout looked at his guests, smiled, and said grandly, "Rome!"

Previn walked into Tout's living room followed by Barone. A portrait of a finely attired young woman caught his eye. Eighteenth-century English. What was Tout doing with what looked like a stuffy old master on his wall? Resembled a Gainsborough. But it was probably not such a noted painter, just a portrait reminiscent of that era. Oils such as this were how people were recorded. How they were remembered. The plastic surgeons of the day were the portrait painters. They knew how to enhance their subjects. They offered nothing less than immortality.

Evidently, Barone could feel Previn's disquiet. He spoke up. "You gotta understand something, Harry. We thought this was a sure thing. I know. I know. That's the oldest crock of shit, but when Johnny said he could bring Nick Valentine to the project on a plate... Nick Valentine? Come on! He wasn't even asking to be paid up front. He took points. Points! This seemed like the one deal in Hollywood where you put up your own money. I did. We both did. Sid too. But when this shit went down at the hotel, what wouldn't we do to save our asses? It's showbiz."

Previn didn't have a response. What was he to say? "I get it." Of course, money talks. Of course, it was about the money. How could it ever be about anything other than that? It was business. Show business. Call it what you may. Business is business. Previn got what he was saying. He just didn't agree. Moving decimal points one way or the other didn't make it smell better. At least Previn had gotten back in touch with something bigger. Doctoring had become as much about the money as any other profession, maybe more. Certainly plastic surgery. But there was more to it. There had to be. Otherwise, what was the point? Barone couldn't even find it in himself to say it was about the movie. That he really cared about the film they'd made. For Previn, it had to be about the patient. Life was too precious. He'd seen how tenuous it was when Blackburn died.

Tout came barreling across the foyer with Rox close behind. "In here."

Previn and Barone followed them into the study. Tout had replaced the flat-screen TV set Fay had smashed.

"Something someone saw on Twitter. Don't know what the fuck's going down."

Barone laughed, putting an arm round Tout. "Any more excitement and I'll have to check into rehab."

A female news anchor appeared with a photo of Fay Wray from better days, smiling and gorgeous. "This is a CNN exclusive. CNN has obtained a recording of the pop star Fay Wray shot yesterday. In it, the extent of her horrific facial injuries from the alleged assault on her by rocker Nick Valentine are revealed. A word of caution. What you are about to see is graphic and will disturb some viewers."

Previn's eyes widened. Fay was seated at his grand white piano. It was his iPhone video. He recalled seeing Fay mess with his computer the night before as Helen arrived. She must have sent herself the clip.

Uncut. Raw. Fay singing, "I Was Yours, No?"

"What…What is this?" Tout asked.

Previn's camera moved around from her good side to her bad. The close-up of Fay was remarkably crisp as she continued to sing.

Tout stepped in front of the screen. "This is bollocks! Bollocks!" He turned to the image of Fay. "Have you lost your fuckin' mind, girl?"

Barone almost choked as he saw the magnitude of her facial injuries. "Jesus!"

"What are you doing being filmed?" Tout barked to the screen.

Previn stared past Tout at the giant image of Fay. He heard his own voice: "You should see yourself."

Barone, Tout, and Rox all turned sharply to Previn. Stared at him suspiciously. Tout was livid but still processing what he'd just witnessed. Who was playing whom?

On the screen, Fay covered her face with her hands. "I don't want you filming me."

Previn was heard from behind his iPhone camera: "Play."

Fay resumed playing the pretty melody on the piano. They all turned back to the video, her performance too compelling to ignore. Fay's face filled the screen in close-up. The performer selling her song. Selling it to the viewer. Selling it to the world. Just as in the moment she'd sold it to Previn.

I don't know where you go
I was yours, no?
I don't have the balls to say
No no no no, no no, NOOOO!

Fay stopped playing. Through her tears, she sang that suddenly poignant, powerful line she'd pulled from the song and now reinterpreted as perhaps about as personal a line as anyone had ever sung:

Look at me. Isn't this the girl you loved?

That line sent shivers through everyone. Fay resumed playing the piano.

The anchor came back on at the end of the clip. "Remarkable. I want to cry." She turned to a reporter seated beside her. "To think only recently *Harper's Bazaar* labeled her 'The Face of Spring.'" She turned to the reporter. "Do we know where she is?"

"We've learned through sources close to Fay Wray…"

"Sources? What sources? Who?" Tout asked.

"I'm told she's gone to stay with her mother."

"If ever a situation called for Mom," the anchor said. "We wish her well. Have we—"

Tout muted the TV and then whipped around to face off with Previn. "You did this!"

"I didn't know. I can't believe—"

"What can't you believe? That that's Fay Wray? That she looks like shite? That you've wrecked the song?"

"It was a home recording."

"It looks like a home recording!"

Fay must have downloaded the clip from his computer virtually in front of his very eyes. He'd seen her doing it. That's all he could reckon. How else could this have ended up fronting a newscast? Never in his wildest dreams could he imagine her so boldly putting it out to the world. But that was what he told her she had to do. Wasn't that in part the whole purpose of his filming her—to make her come to peace with herself?

"You don't see her," Previn said to Tout.

"See her? I made her. All she had was that face. People will never forget this. And I'll never be able to release that song now without people seeing her this way."

They all continued to stare at the screen. Fay's performance on repeat. An almost perpetual loop. There was beauty there, a raw, naked beauty. As Previn realized this, he smiled victoriously. "I got her to sit at my piano. I pulled out my iPhone and filmed her because she had to see herself. It was one of those incredible moments that had to be captured. I had no idea she'd run with this, release this tape to the world."

Yes. He'd told her that she had to face herself.

Tout had a look of menace in his eyes. "I could put my fist through your face."

"She's owning it. Owning her truth."

"I own her," Tout thundered. "She can't do this to me! I would never release material like this!"

Rox spoke up. "It's so…Fay Wray. I'll bet she thought this'd trump everyone, make her *the* bigger star."

"What does she think, this is going to get her the Hollywood Bowl next month?"

"Yeah!" Rox said for all it was worth. "It's the *bigger* star play."

"Shut up," Tout snapped. "Shut the fuck up!"

Events had moved so fast it was difficult for Previn to process. Up until that very moment, the knowledge that Fay had sent the digital file to CNN seemed to flow out of her coming to terms with herself. It seemed like an act of liberation, an ultimate fuck you to the tyranny of the Capital of Good Looks. But what Rox was suggesting was something so much more calculated. Could Fay's competitive instincts have been such that she released the footage to trump Nick Valentine sensational nude arrest?

Previn had only known Fay as his patient, helping her through her convalescence—but not having any insight into Susan Plouse, that person who had the self-possession and raw ambition at fifteen years old to escape the cornfields for pop stardom. There was a different narrative in that.

He wanted to believe he'd helped to bust her out from the Capital of Good Looks and that all this other stuff didn't much matter. She probably didn't know her own motives in releasing the footage, other than it was the one way in which she could climb out from under this thing that was threatening to define her. He understood that. He understood as a plastic surgeon that it was all about defining one's image. And if that's what he'd helped her do, then he'd done good work.

"She's given you the bird, mate!" Barone said to Tout with the hint of a smile.

"She's under contract."

"Oh, really? That looks like a contractual problem to me. You have to believe she's gonna walk. Be foolish not to read it that way. I don't know who's advising her, but..."

Barone continued to stare at the full screen-sized image of Fay while Tout glared directly at Previn as if in response to Barone's question.

Previn laughed. "What can I say? She's a Harry Previn original."

Acknowledgments

To MY LATE MOTHER, Karen Strausser, a sculptress, whose spirit haunts this book.

Special thanks to the medical professionals who advised on background: Jan R. Adams, MD; Jason Taylor, MD; Leslie Howard Stevens, MD; FACS; Julia T. Hunter, MD; Gabriel Chiu, MD; Thomas Matimore, MD; Dorrie Emrick, RN.

Additional thanks:

Kate Woods
Doug Miro
Bird York
Max Sharam
Steve Stevens
Barbara Ligeti
Danny Nathanson
Holly Baxter
Francisca Viudes
Noah Wyle
Christine Chiu
Sean Day Michael
Chloe King
Philippa Leach
Will Emrick
Federico Lapenda
Tamsin Lonsdale
Grainger Hines
Tony Callie
Rob Brownstein

David Henry Sterry
Julia & Jared Drake
Anastasia Belotskaya
Lana Clarkson
Rigo Saenz
Jillian Kogan Dunn
Teresa Emrick
Frank Strausser, Sr.
Anna Granucci
Brian Wolf
Ali Gunn
Chateau Marmont Hotel
Chris Manby
Erin Brown
Soho House/WH
Caitlin Alexander
Tyson Cornell
And everyone at
Rare Bird Books